MY NOT-SO-
Fairy~Tale
Life

D0062029

MY NOT-SO-
Fairy~Tale
Life

A Novel

Julie Wright

DESERET
BOOK

Salt Lake City, Utah

To my mom and dad—
Thanks for everything you do
and for always doing everything.
I love you!

Library of Congress Cataloging-in-Publication Data
Wright, Julie, 1972–
  My not-so-fairy-tale life / Julie Wright.
     p. cm.
  Summary: Having been cruelly abused by her mother until the age of sixteen, a young woman numbs the pain with drugs and loses herself until she finds God through the Mormon Church.
  ISBN 1-59038-476-8 (pbk.)
  [1. Child abuse—Fiction. 2. Alcoholism—Fiction. 3. Unmarried mothers—Fiction. 4. Christian life—Fiction. 5. Mormons—Fiction.]
  I. Title.
  PZ7.W9552Myan 2005
  [Fic]—dc22   2005013975

Printed in the United States of America   72076
Publisher's Printing, Salt Lake City, UT

10   9   8   7   6   5   4   3   2   1

Acknowledgments

First I'd like to thank my Aunt Jan Herold for thinking Suzie was worth loving, but mostly for talking my dad out of buying my prom dress at Kmart. Thanks to Scott for your love, support, and patience with me. Thanks also to Josi Kilpack, Valerie Holladay, and Pearl Wright for polishing the manuscript into something worthy of Deseret Book and to Annette Wright for your fabulous typing skills. I will be eternally grateful to my friends at LDStorymakers for letting me lament to them over the saga of my writing and for letting me be *me* without fear of judgment or censure. Thank you, Chris Schoebinger, for believing in Suzie's story enough to never give up and carry this novel through to the end. Thanks also to my editor, Richard Peterson, for his work. When he e-mailed me to say he had shed his first tear over the story, I knew we were going to have a great author/editor relationship. Thank you, Laurie Cook, for your typesetting skills and Sheryl Smith for the fabulous design. I know they say not to judge a book by its cover, but I think they could on this one. The book is beautiful! I love the dandelions!

Thanks as well to my kids for forgiving their frantic Mommy author for saying "in a minute" when she really means "in a few hours" or maybe even "wait 'til tomorrow" . . . or better yet, "go ask Daddy to do it." I love you guys!

And last but not least, thanks, Walt Disney, not because you had anything to do with this book, but because I'm taking my first royalty check and going to Disneyland!

Julie Wright
www.juliewright.com

Prologue

SHE WAS ON THE PHONE AGAIN.

"Mo-ommm . . ." My voice sounded whiney, even to my five-year-old ears. She had been on the phone for almost an hour, and I'd been waiting for at least an hour before that, for her to get me a drink. I would have gotten my own, but that wasn't allowed. "Suzanna!" she said sharply, "can't you see I'm busy?" She turned away from me. "Oh, it's nothing. Just my daughter." She was twirling the phone cord around a perfectly manicured finger and laughing. "Oh, Evelyn, I can't believe you did that!" She was sitting with her back to me on the arm of the leather chair she had made Dad buy only a few months previously. It was part of a set that was meant to match the hardwood floors. The couches were cream colored; the floor was a golden brown. I didn't see how that matched, but Mom said it did, so it must have.

I could feel my lip quivering, but I couldn't cry. If she were to see me crying . . .

"Woozie Suzie!" Sam called from the kitchen. I followed his voice and snickered when I saw him, my tears quickly forgotten. He'd climbed on a chair dragged over from the table and had gotten the Ovaltine can down from the cupboard.

"Mom's gonna be mad at you." I looked over my shoulder to the living room, where I could still hear her talking on the phone.

"She won't be mad. I'm helping her." He grinned, revealing a hole in front where a loose tooth had fallen out the day before.

Sam was older than me but not much. In fact, at Thanksgiving and Christmas every year, we were the same age. Dad said it would be like that our whole lives.

"Did she say you could help?" I asked. Sometimes Mom didn't like it when we helped. There was still a yellowed bruise on my hip from the last time I got caught helping.

As Sam was climbing off the counter, he accidentally bumped the can of Ovaltine. It landed on the floor, popping the plastic lid off and spilling the chocolate powder everywhere. I held my breath. Sam froze halfway off the counter, his legs dangling over the edge. We waited.

Mom was still laughing on the phone and hadn't heard the can crash to the floor. Sam and I moved quickly. I opened the bottom drawer where Mom kept all the kitchen towels and tried to reach the tap to the kitchen sink to get the towel wet. Sam took it from me and tried to jump up to turn it on, but terror made him clumsy. He couldn't reach it either.

"I'll g-g-g-get it d-downs-s-s-stairs," he stuttered. He only stuttered when he was really scared. Dad said he'd grow out of it, but Mom said it was because he was stupid and that people don't grow out of being stupid. Sam ran to the back stairs. While he was gone, I started scooping the pile of powder with my hands and putting it back in the can as fast as I could. That was when I heard her high heels clicking on the tile floor behind me. I froze.

"What are you doing?!" she roared. "I thought I told you to *wait!*"

I shrunk back into the counter at the same time Sam reached the top of the stairs. He dropped the wet towel. His eyes went wide as mine squeezed closed. She was hurting me again.

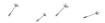

It was almost an hour later when Sam crept into my room. His eyes were still red from crying, even though it wasn't *him* she'd been hitting. I remembered hearing him whimpering over my own cries.

"Are you hurt bad?" he asked, sitting on my bed and looking at me to check for visual damage.

I shrugged, setting my jaw. "Not much," I lied. I was almost six, and I needed to learn how to be brave.

"I'm sorry, Suzie."

I shrugged again. "It's okay."

"But it was my fault."

I had no response to that. It wasn't really his fault. He was just trying to get me a drink of chocolate milk. True, she might not have known we were into stuff if he hadn't kicked the can over. But I wasn't dumb enough to be mad at him; it was "just one of those things," as my dad liked to say.

"It's not fair," he said. "If I hit you, I get in trouble, but she doesn't get in trouble when *she* hits you."

"Moms don't get in trouble for anything," I said.

"Maybe if we told Dad . . ." We both knew that was a dumb idea. We'd seen her throw things at him, too. And, anyway, he already knew what she was doing to us when he was gone. He just couldn't stop her. Sam put an arm around my shoulder, and I snuggled into him, feeling his chin rest on top of my head.

"We should run away," Sam said.

"Where would we go?"

"Where do you want to go?"

"Disneyland," I said.

"I don't think people can live there." Sam looked doubtful.

"How would you know? You've never been there."

"Neither have you."

He was thoughtful for a minute and then finally sighed. "Maybe we shouldn't run away." We both fell silent until we heard Dad's car in the driveway. Sam smiled. "It'll be better now." He sounded hopeful. Sometimes things were better when Dad was home.

By the time we scrambled off the bed and down the hall, Dad was already in the kitchen. "Doris!" he called out cheerily as he stared into the fridge. "I'm home!" He heard the floorboard I was standing on creak and turned to see Sam and me. "Well, there are my two monsters!" he said, shutting the fridge and beckoning us over. I winced when he wrapped his arms around me to hug me.

"What's wrong, honey?" He lifted the sleeve of my shirt up to reveal the red marks that were already turning into bruises.

"Not again." His voice shook. I tried to step away, but he stripped the shirt over my head entirely to see all the other bruises. "No! Not again!" He kept repeating it over and over.

"Doris!" he called again, though not cheery at all anymore. I whimpered and backed up into Sam, turning into him so I could hide my face in his shoulder.

"I didn't mean to let him see," I said into Sam's shirt. Sam patted my bare shoulder softly and edged me toward the stairs, away from where Mom would soon be coming in. When she did come in, she glared at us, her red lipstick lips turned down, and her eyebrows bunched together in the center.

"What have you done to her?" Dad yelled.

"You should have seen the mess she made!" Mom said without flinching at all.

"You're going to kill them if you can't get hold of yourself." He was really mad, but it didn't matter. He'd been really mad before—when Sam got a black eye. They didn't let him go to school for a couple of weeks. They told the teachers that Sam had chicken pox. Sam had never had the chicken pox.

Mom and Dad glared at each other, no longer seeing us, as Sam pulled me down the stairs with him. When we got to Sam's door, I looked at him. "Can I sleep in your room tonight?" The thought of having to go upstairs and around my parents to get to my room made me want to start bawling right then and there.

He nodded, and we went into his room together. I pulled out the sleeping bag Sam kept under his bed while Sam shut the door to try to muffle their yelling. But we could still hear them through the heat vents.

We listened to them quarreling upstairs for a long time into the night. I knew it was over when Mom started crying and telling Dad that he just didn't understand. He agreed to get a nanny to help her out. He agreed she needed to get out of the house and away from the children more. He agreed she should go back to school and develop herself better. He agreed . . . he agreed . . . he agreed.

chapter
1

My EYES SNAPPED OPEN, and I sat up fast to look at the room around me. It had only been a dream. No. A nightmare. My heart was still racing, and the sound of Sam crying still rang in my ears.

Of course it was just a dream. I was twenty-two years old, and my mother hadn't hit me since I was sixteen, though the memory was like a fresh welt in my mind. I hugged the blankets to me and took a few deep breaths. The familiar trappings of my own room surrounded me, although there was no memory of how I got there. Trembling fingers rubbed at my temples to try to bring back the events of the previous night. The last thing I could remember was being at Gina's, helping to host party night. I vaguely remembered having a drink-off with a new guy in our group, but no recollection of even a minute beyond that.

I shook my head, trying to remember. Shaking my head was a mistake in my hung-over condition. The morning after regrets had already begun. Gingerly, I pulled myself out of bed and wandered through the house. No one was home. Typical.

I went back into my room and kicked the door closed behind me. When Sam moved out to go to college in Utah, my parents had let me take the basement bedroom. It was bigger and more private than my room on the main floor, and after some whining and begging, I even got Dad to knock a hole in the wall to the bathroom, my own personal Shangri-La. My parents hadn't agreed to the change of rooms to make me happy. It was their way of retaliating against Sam for joining the Mormon church. It made it so that he couldn't come back home, even if he wanted to. But it didn't matter. Sam wasn't coming back. Why should he?

After pulling my black dyed hair into a ponytail and getting dressed, I went upstairs to forage for something to eat. As usual, there was nothing in the fridge. That was one of the things I hated about my brother being gone. When he lived at home, he would spend his own money on groceries, and there was always stuff to eat. But since he moved out, no one bought groceries.

Rummaging through an assortment of beer cans, wine bottles, and a couple of old take-home containers of Chinese food, I spied a jar of jam and turned to scan the counter for bread, grinning when I saw there was part of a loaf still there.

The bread wasn't really fresh. It was at least two weeks old. It crumbled a little when I pulled two slices out, but at least it hadn't turned moldy. I ate the sandwich quickly and had almost made it out the door when my mom walked into the kitchen.

"Suzanna?" Her voice grated on my headache, like fingernails on a chalkboard.

"What do you want, Doris?" She didn't blink at my calling her by her name and not the traditional title of mom. It had been a long time since I had afforded her that courtesy, but she didn't care. We had left behind any mutual respect long ago.

"Where have you been all week?" she demanded. Her brightly painted, sticky-looking lips turned down into a frown.

"What do you care?"

She didn't answer. She didn't care. The question was a formality, nothing more. She finally said, "Sam's coming home next week."

My mouth twitched involuntarily. "So?" I said, shrugging as though I were unconcerned, but the thought melted me. *Sam.* He was exactly ten months and seven days older than I was. My mother had never made a secret of it—my conception had been an accident on top of an accident for her. That knowledge had been one of the bonds between Sam and me while growing up.

"It's his wedding, remember? He wants you there and sober."

"Oh, please! It's not like I can even go to his wedding anyway. He's getting married in that big church, and they only let cult members in."

"But there's the brunch and the reception afterwards. Suzanna, you *will* be there and you *will* be sober!"

"Don't talk to me like I'm some kind of drunk, Doris. I'm sober most of the time."

"Like last night?" she shot back.

I narrowed my eyes at her. "Were *you* sober last night?" She stiffened. Apparently she hadn't been. She and my dad had gone to a party in Marlboro. "Anyway, he's marrying that freak I used to work with. I don't want anything to do with it."

"Well, that will look nice if the groom's own sister doesn't show up, won't it?" she said sarcastically.

"You're not worried about anything except how it will make you look. Don't pretend it's about Sam. It's always about you!"

"You watch it, young lady, or I'll—"

"Or you'll what? Put me in time-out? Club me with a rolling pin? It's too late to play mommy now, Doris. And I'm not going to Sam's wedding. Ciao."

I walked by her and went outside where I took a deep breath. She still had the ability to push my buttons, and it was all I could do to keep from screaming at her. I hadn't really meant it when I said I wasn't going. But anything I could do to annoy or upset Doris felt good. The truth was I wouldn't miss Sam's wedding for the world. He was happy, and I was happy for him, even though it really annoyed me that I wouldn't be allowed to go to the actual ceremony, to be there at the moment when he lifted her veil and kissed his bride. It did my heart good to know that Doris wasn't going, either. She didn't deserve to witness the beginning of Sam's good life. A day was coming that I would get away from her, too, and I wouldn't be looking back. A day was coming soon.

Hey, Suzie Cue. Pick up a stick and we'll play," Chris said. I'd just finished my shift at work and dropped into the club.

"Hold on. Let me get a drink first. I'll be right back." I hurried to the bar.

"Hey, Bruce."

"Cue! Good to see you, babe." He was a cute guy who wore a goatee and kept his bleached hair cropped short and spiked on top. But he wasn't my type, even though I sometimes played him along.

"I'll buy your drink if you'll go out with me tomorrow." He tilted his head to view me better.

"You know I don't date guys from the club."

"Like I said before, I'll quit right now if you'll make me a guarantee."

"Aw, Bruce, you know I love you, but I can buy my own liquid."

He sighed. "Doesn't hurt to try . . . same as always?"

"Yep, and don't forget the lime this time."

"Your wish is my command," he said, giving me a little bow and turning to get my drink.

As he set the bottle on the bar, he looked me over and grinned. "You know, Cue, you shouldn't advertise if you're not willing to sell."

"What are you saying?" I flipped my dyed black hair over my shoulder and tried to glare.

He put an innocent look on his face and held his hands out in a gesture of helplessness. "All I'm saying is that little outfit doesn't leave much to the imagination."

I glowered at him. "You can stop drooling, Brucey. You aren't a high enough bidder." I turned away from him and walked to where Chris, Kevin, and Gina were waiting at our favorite table. They were laughing, and Kevin pointed his stick at the bar.

"Teasing the bar boys, again, Cue?"

"Always!" I grinned. "So are we gonna play pool or just talk about it?"

The Hideaway was dark and smokey. The regulars there always said that the only thing more ripped than the Hideaway patrons was the felt on the pool tables. The music was loud, and the crowd was louder. What I liked most about it was that it was away from my parents' house and Doris's crippling criticism. It was a place for me to hide.

"I'll break," Kevin said, lining up his shot. There was a loud cra-ack as the white ball smacked into the others, splaying them from one end of the table to the other. Kevin was skinny—we all kidded him that his growth had been stunted by years of smoking that began in his preteen years. Chris had filled out better, but was still fairly thin. He always wore a beanie cap pulled down to his ears. I had already downed my drink and was looking at the bar again.

"I'll be back in a minute," I said.

"But it's your turn, Cue," Chris complained.

"I know. I just need . . . hang on." I hurried over to the bar. "Give me another," I said, setting my empty bottle on the bar. Bruce leered at me, showing off the fangs to his wolfish grin. I rewarded him with a wink.

I knew that I drank too much, but why drink if you're not going to get wasted? My second drink was almost gone by the time I got back to the pool table. I set the glass down, wiped my mouth with the back of my hand, and took up a stick . The white ball rebounded off the curb at the diamond mark I had estimated and hit the solid yellow ball with a crack, slamming it neatly into the corner pocket. Chris grinned triumphantly and kissed my forehead. "That's why you're my partner, Cue. You could be stoned, drunk, and have a cold and still make every shot."

"I don't get stoned anymore," I said.

"Yeah," Gina interjected. "She's reformed. Clean as a school girl at communion." I glared at her. Her curly hair was pulled up on her head in a sloppy pile, and fell down her back in a tumbling cascade of red lava.

I had been clean from drugs for over four years, ever since I got out of rehab. My parents had sent me after I got out of jail for stealing DVDs to sell for money to buy drugs. I guess they figured if I got clean, I'd stay out of jail, too.

Gina bent over the table to take her shot and missed; the red stripe swirling as the ball thudded softly against the worn felt curb on the table. Kevin cursed as she frowned at the table. "I need a new partner," he complained.

"It isn't my fault," she insisted. "The table isn't level."

"The table hasn't ever been level," I said. "You just gotta learn to play when you're not tweaked."

Gina glared at me this time. I snorted at her. She could be mad all she wanted, but the fact remained that she wasn't too sharp even when she was sober.

We played a few more games, and Chris and I won all of them. Gina had finally had enough. She got mad, grabbed her jacket and Kevin, and stormed out without saying anything.

"Buy you another?" Chris offered.

"Sure," I said, following him to the bar.

Bruce rolled his eyes and laughed. "I don't know why you waste your time on her, Chris. She's a tease. All you're ever gonna get out of her is a swift kick in the ego while she laughs at you."

"Don't listen to him; he's just jealous," I said.

Bruce snorted. "Whatever."

"I'm not lookin' for anything," Chris declared.

Bruce shook his head. "Lucky thing," he said, turning to help someone else.

"So are we going to hang out tomorrow?" I asked Chris.

"Can't. Got a job interview."

"A job interview?" I said in disbelief.

"Yeah, you know, I dress up and tell some guy how great I am so I can work my butt off eight hours a day for them until they fire me. A job."

"But, why? You have that job at the plant."

"That's a nothing job, Cue. It's a place where guys with no education go to get money. I may not be a college boy, but I have enough smarts to do better than that." He bit his lip and looked away from me, off into the dance floor filled with gyrating bodies.

"So is Bruce entirely right?" he asked. The music was so loud we almost had to shout.

"Right about what?"

"Are you ever going to stop looking at me as just Chris, or am I just one more guy you can toss your head and walk away from?" He kept his focus on the dance floor, purposely avoiding my eyes.

"What? What are you talking about?"

"Hey, we've been friends since high school, and not once have you ever looked at me as anything more than just Chris."

I tried to laugh. "So what? Is your name really Joe?"

"Suzie . . ."

"What? Where did this come from? I don't even know what you're talking about. Besides, you just told Bruce you weren't looking for anything." I looked away from him. The very idea that Chris had feelings for me was as offbeat as a heart murmur. I had seen him with the ladies. He worked a party better than I did when it came to flirting. Sure there were times when I thought there *might* be an attraction to Chris, but when it came right down to it, there was nothing really there. He was exactly like me, and truth be told . . . I didn't really like me.

Chris looked at me and said, "I'm not looking for anything like what he has in mind. It's not like that. It'd be real. I care about you, Cue. I mean, you flirt with every guy in the world, but never me. I thought if I cleaned up a little, got a decent job, maybe you'd look at me like I was somebody and not just a buddy you grew up with." He looked down at his hands. "I figured if I had some better money . . . a better car, maybe, you'd see me as somebody."

I rolled my eyes. "This is crazy. You *are* somebody."

"Yeah, but not good enough. It's like Bruce said, I'm not a high enough bidder."

I threw my hands up over my head. "Stop saying that!"

"I'm just saying what you're thinking."

I stared at him. "I gotta go," I drained the last of my drink and got off my stool.

Chris beat me to the door. "So you don't care at all, do you?"

"Of course I do. We're friends."

"Fine. Just Chris it is!" He held the door open for me and slammed it shut after I went through it.

I wanted to cry, though I wasn't sure if it was over Chris's bizarre outburst or if it was because I'd had too much to drink. I *didn't* see him as anything more than "just Chris." In the back of my mind, where I still allowed dreams, I pictured being in a real relationship. But not with someone like Chris. Chris was a part of the nightmare life I was living. He was too fused with it for him to be anyone I could ever want to dream about. I dreamt of a relationship where I was cherished and *normal*. Where the guy, whoever he was, thought I was smart, where he looked at me as more than just another one-nighter. The dream was there, but it was never going to happen. I was *not* the kind of girl who had relationships. I had tried to be loved before by someone . . . and if my own mother couldn't love me . . . what was the point?

Doris was still sleeping when I awoke the next morning but was up by the time I had showered and gotten dressed.

"When did you finally get home?" she asked.

"Morning to you, too, Doris, sleep well?"

"Don't be smart with me."

"Considering my genetics, you should be glad I have the ability to be smart at all."

Doris scowled at me. "I mean it, Suzanna."

"Is there a point to this conversation or can I go now?"

"Your father wants you at his office after work. He has some work for you."

"I won't have time today."

"You'll make time."

"Are you deaf? I said, not today."

"Suzanna!"

"Later, Doris!"

I walked out of the house before she could say anything more. But after work, I went straight to my father's office, not because of Doris, but because I enjoyed being with him when she wasn't around, and I needed the money he paid me. I got to see snatches of the man he really was, not the man Doris strong-armed him to be. Besides, I wasn't ready to face Chris again, if I were to run into him at the club. There wasn't anything I could say to him without feeling dumb about it.

So, I went to Dad's office. I pushed through the double glass doors, almost running right smack into my father. "Suzie," he said in earnest surprise. "Your mother said you weren't coming."

"Yeah, well, when was the last time Doris had her facts straight on anything?"

He ran a hand through his hair and closed his eyes. "Please, don't talk about your mother like that."

"Then let's not talk about her at all." I walked toward his office. "So, who's delinquent?" I asked, dropping my bag to the floor by the desk.

My dad was a good accountant but a poor businessman. He had a foolish practice of letting people pay him out of their tax refunds after they came. Unfortunately, by the time some of those people got their refunds, they often conveniently forgot who had prepared their returns. Though I harassed him for letting people get away with it, I actually respected that he let some clients never pay him at all, especially if he knew they were financially strapped. It was another glimpse of the man he wanted to be. Of course, Doris didn't know he did anything pro bono. If she had any clue, she would freak out, and he would never hear the end of it.

Dad handed me a list of delinquent accounts. I snapped my gum at him and turned on the computer. "Why don't you make your secretary do this?"

"Because she doesn't get results. For some reason, when you make a threat, the world is ready to believe you."

I grinned at that. "I don't make threats so much as get commitments."

He shook his head. "Well, whatever you do, it gets results."

I smiled at him fondly. He was pathetic, really—a man so blinded by love for a woman who was incapable of returning that affection that he had become nothing more than a shell. It was sad. It had taken me years to understand why he never helped Sam or me when she hurt us. Years to see why, even though he was the adult, he was as helpless as we were. Like Sam and me, he was afraid of her—afraid of losing her. I hadn't realized that until I worked it through while in rehab. When I finally figured it out, I was able to say, "I forgive my father." I was able to love him after that, but it made me hate Doris all the more.

Dad gave me a slight, one-armed hug and left to go home. He didn't dare be late and incur the wrath of Doris.

I went straight to work. There were eleven delinquent accounts, owing a total of more than $13,000.00.

I grimaced at the amount of money. I was going to need to let dear old Dad know that I wanted my commission kicked up. I typed up a letter of demand to each of the accounts and signed them under the title of "Collections Manager" and got them ready to go into the mail.

It took me an hour or so, and after I finished I wandered around the deserted office before locking up. There was an old family portrait on Dad's desk, from well before Sam left for college. Our smiles were forever frozen into the paper behind the glass. Sam's hand was on my shoulder, and I looked like a little girl. I remembered the big fight I'd had with Doris over going to have the picture taken. It was the last time she was able to convince me to participate in a family photo.

I scowled at the image and turned it face down.

Sam is coming home. The thought made me both happy and sad. I was happy for Sam's happiness, but I was sorry we no longer had the close relationship we had once shared. It bugged me that he was perfect and I was still me. As I locked up Dad's office, I wondered how coming home might be for Sam. When I thought about how close we had been and the hard things we had shared because of Doris, I decided it would probably be hard for him.

chapter
4

I STAYED AWAY FROM THE CLUB FOR THE next few days. I was afraid of seeing Chris and was reduced to raiding my parents' liquor stash to keep from going crazy.

But Friday the battle of the bands was playing at the Hideaway. I had been looking forward to hearing Fuzzy Ball of String for weeks, and even the thought of running into Chris wasn't enough to keep me away.

When I arrived, the place was already packed. Bodies were tightly mashed together, and the nauseatingly sweet odors of booze, sweat, perfume, cigarette smoke, and fog machines oozed from the front door. I pushed my way to the bar, where I caught Bruce's eye. He greeted me without a smile and quickly placed my regular drink on the counter in front of me. I waded through the crowd of gyrating dancers to get closer to the stage. My stomach felt like it was holding in every butterfly ever born as I scanned the room for Chris. When I spotted him, he was standing next to some girl. I wasn't sure what her name was, but my jaw dropped to see him whispering in her ear. Not like anyone could really whisper with music blaring all around them.

I glared at them. *Wants to be more than "just Chris," huh?* It looked as though he wanted to be more than "just Chris" to more than "just me."

Someone touched my shoulder, and I turned to see Gina, holding onto the arm of some guy who was totally wasted. He was unsteady on his feet, and his bloodshot eyes were glazed-over, but the way his leather jacket hung on his broad shoulders was reason enough for someone like Gina to let him hang all over her.

"The lead singer's hot, huh?" Gina shouted over the music. I nodded, laughing to myself that the guy she was with was too trashed to notice her scamming on other guys.

The dance floor was filled with bouncing, swaying, bodies, all pulsing in time to the beat and lights. Some guy dressed in slacks and an untucked button-up moved eerily in the flash of lights, moving his body as though he had no bones in it to hinder him. If he had a dance partner, I couldn't make out who it was. He was totally into himself, and the way he danced creeped me out.

While watching Mr. Creepy, I heard someone gag and turned in time to watch Gina's "flavor of the hour" throw up. I quickly moved away, trying to distance myself from the stink, and bumped straight into Chris. Flushing deeply, I mumbled something incoherent and exited the club as fast as I could push through the crowd.

My head was pounding. I hadn't eaten much during the day, and the stress and smell and the noise and the alcohol and watching someone else retch was more than a sick stomach could take. I tried to hold it in, but I ended up losing it into the hedge next to where my car was parked. The taste was awful, and I stood there for several minutes, spitting into the shrubbery, trying to clear the nasty taste from my mouth. After I got home, I brushed my teeth three times before going to sleep.

I awoke in the night, my stomach rumbling and a feeling of nausea in my throat. I knew there were only seconds before I would be throwing up, and I bolted for the bathroom, where the floor was tiled, not carpeted. I just made it. After I finished retching, I continued kneeling next to the toilet and rested my face on my arms, waiting for the strength to stand and go back to bed.

I remembered I had been dreaming about Sam. We were fighting, and he was leaving me alone in a bog of sticky mud. He wouldn't help me because I wouldn't say the magic word, but I didn't know what the magic word was, and he refused to tell me.

I cursed him, spit into the bowl, and got to my feet. I didn't know why his coming home to get married was causing me so much stress, but it was horrible. I couldn't stand it.

Tired from being sick all night and all the stress of Chris, the club, and Sam, I fell sound asleep until morning. When I finally awoke, it was because I thought I heard Sam's voice.

chapter
5

S LEEP WELL, SIS?"

I bolted upright and stared. Sam was sitting at the desk in front of my computer. I cursed. "What are you doing in my room?" I demanded.

"Mom said you had a computer. I needed to check my email." He didn't really look at me, too engrossed in whatever he was doing to care about me. My stomach rumbled again, and I jumped out of the blankets and made another dash to the bathroom.

"Well, now I really feel like I'm home," he quipped as I came out of the bathroom, holding a wet washcloth to my head. "Must've been some party last night."

"I wasn't partying!" I said. "The sight of you first thing in the morning is enough to make anyone sick."

"Aw, c'mon, Suzie. Let's not fight."

"I'm not fighting. I'm explaining. I should warn April that you have no respect for privacy. I can't *believe* you barged in here! What if I'd been naked?"

"You always sleep in sweats."

"Yeah, well, people change."

He cocked his head and studied me, smirking at my sweatpants. "When did you dye your hair?"

I shrugged. "It isn't all black," I said, pulling out the braided strand tucked behind my ear. It was a pale blue color. He turned briefly to look and then went back to his computer, shaking his head.

"What?" I demanded.

"I swear your hair is going to fall out the way you treat it. Why don't you go say hi to April? She's upstairs with Mom."

I snorted. "I feel sick enough without having to talk to Doris. Besides, I need to get ready."

He didn't respond as I pulled clothes from the closet and dresser then went into the bathroom, slamming the door behind me. I locked it and dropped the heap of clothes onto the floor.

I didn't bother to shower. I wasn't going to work, and I sincerely didn't feel well enough to go anywhere or do anything. Sam's unexpected appearance had added to my rotten mood. I had known he was coming but figured he'd be staying in a hotel or something. His new life and marriage were a reminder of how much my life sucked, and thinking about his happiness was irritating.

As I got dressed, I studied my reflection in the mirror. My eyes were brown, like Sam's. When we were kids, our hair was blond and because of how close we were to the same age, people used to think we were twins. But we didn't look much alike now. I looked at my hair. The black dye job didn't look bad on me. My dark eyes and coloring made it look almost natural. Thinking about Sam's comment, I was miffed that he would question my choice to dye my hair. What business was it of his? I wondered what he would say if he knew about my belly button ring.

The thought of April being upstairs was irritating. The last time we were together, I'd been drunk and apparently said something vulgar to her; at least, that's what Sam later told me. He had said he was "disappointed" in me. I hated it when he treated me like that—like I was a bad little girl. Besides, April was such a Miss Perfect, she made me sick. She needed to hear something vulgar. The thought of seeing her and having her for a sister-in-law was almost more than I could bear. I was just glad they would be moving away and that I wouldn't have to be around them. With all its self-righteousness, this "Mormon thing" Sam had discovered was really disturbing. It was enough to make you puke.

"Your room smells like an ashtray, Satan," Sam said when I came out of the bathroom.

"So?"

"You better be careful or you'll end up hooked and dying of cancer."

"Yeah, I bet you'd just weep for me."

He finally turned to really look at me. "I would, Suzie. I really would." I couldn't mask my surprise at his sincerity and just stood there looking at him. He stood up from the desk and came over to me and put an arm around me, leading me to the door. "C'mon, let's go say hi to April. You two need to go out today to make sure the dress sizes Mom gave to the seamstress are right."

I squirmed out from under his arm. "I don't need a dress."

"You can't go to a wedding without a dress," he said.

"Right! And since I won't actually *be* at the wedding, I don't need a dress."

"But you can be to the brunch and the reception. Please come. After all, you're the only sibling April and I have. You're going to be the only aunt our kids have."

I rolled my eyes. "Tell me you really want your kids hanging out with someone like me."

He didn't respond, making me wonder if he hadn't already thought about that.

I followed him upstairs, where April and Doris were sitting together on the couch. They had a large binder spread across both of their laps. They looked cozy, like a normal mom and daughter planning an important event. The twinge of jealously I felt was immediately stamped out by resentment.

Doris looked up. "Finally pulled your backside out of bed?"

My eyes narrowed. "Not exactly. He woke me up." I jabbed a thumb at Sam.

"Well it's about time. We have a lot to do today."

"Hi, Suzie," April patted the spot next to her. "Want to come see your dress?"

She was smiling at me, and I looked away, unwilling to look her in the eye. "I guess so." My head felt like it had been clamped in a vice all night. The queasiness was still there, too.

I didn't sit down but stood next to her and looked down at the book. The dress she pointed out was a black formal. It looked like an evening gown, not a bridesmaid's dress at all.

"Aren't bridesmaids required to wear pastels?" I couldn't keep the sarcasm out of my voice.

April shrugged. "I don't like pastels. A black and white wedding is what my mom calls elegant and my dad calls intelligent. Besides, I thought you can always wear a dress like this to other things."

"I like it," I conceded. "It's classy . . . but you know the old saying. You can dress 'em up, but you can't take 'em anywhere. I don't really think that dress is me."

"Exactly," Doris cut in. "Won't that be a nice change?"

I could see April tense up, waiting for me to respond. For some reason, I decided not to say anything.

Sam was the one who spoke up. "Hey, lay off, Mom. If you guys are going to argue, do it on your time, not mine."

April looked up at Sam, probably shocked that he'd talk to Doris like that. But Sam and I had learned long ago that you had to speak up and talk back with Doris. It was the only way she knew how to communicate.

They'd already made their plans; we would all be meeting April's mom at the seamstress's and getting shoes afterward. "I can't go," I finally said.

Silence. Doris hissed between her teeth and drummed her red acrylic nails on the plastic pages of the wedding binder.

"Suzanna, now is not the time for one of your performances. You're going."

"No, I'm not."

"Why not?" Sam interrupted, doing his best to keep Doris and me from fighting.

I faltered. "I . . . I just don't want to." I shrugged.

Sam's eyes narrowed. Being with Doris had apparently made him grumpy. "C'mon, Satan, we've paid for the dress already, and it'll give you the chance to be a creep to everyone all at one time." He winked at me to show he wasn't trying to be bossy, even though he was.

"And . . ." Doris piped in, "your father will not pay you for the work at the office if you don't, Suzanna."

My jaw dropped, indignation flashing hot though my mind. "Dad won't let you take away what I've already earned!"

"Yes he will." Doris said placidly.

She was right about that. Dad was a good enough guy, but he crumpled like a house of cards whenever Doris wanted something.

"That's extortion," I sputtered.

"Whatever works," Doris said with a shrug.

April hesitated, folding the enormous planner closed. "If she really doesn't want to go . . ." she began. She looked so uncomfortable; I felt a pang of remorse at being difficult when she was trying so hard to be nice. "Fine," I broke in. "I'll go. But I'm only going to make certain the dress fits right. I don't wanna go out in public in a tent."

The entire trip with them bored me to tears. We tried on shoes, and April scowled at the slim stiletto heels I picked out, though she was too nice to say anything. We went to lunch where both Sam and April stared at me when I ordered a beer and then spent the entire time trying to ignore it sitting on the table. April had stopped drinking years before, and I half wondered if she resented me being a reminder of her not-so-perfect past.

We went to the dress shop, and April's mom smiled uncomfortably when I asked if the dress could be altered into a sleeveless. I was glad she had her own car and left to go home after we finished with the seamstress. April's mom was so arrogant. A "hoity-toity" type, as Chris liked to call them. And Sam thought *I* was Satan.

Sam had left us after lunch to meet his old buddy, Eric, and there were only April, Doris, and me in Doris's car as we headed back to our house.

"So, where you guys staying?" I asked April.

"I'm staying at my house, and Sam is staying at yours."

"What? You're not staying together?"

"Nope."

"Why not?"

"Suzanna, it isn't any of your business."

"I wasn't asking you, Doris." I swiveled to look at April in the backseat. "So why not?"

"We've agreed that it's just better we don't stay together until after the wedding," she said.

I pursed my lips and winked at her. "Ohhh, I get it. No nooky before the big night, huh? That's crazy. What difference does it make? One day versus another day. What's the difference? What makes it such a huge sin today and perfectly acceptable tomorrow?"

"It makes every bit of difference," April said defensively. She looked out the window, tight-lipped, with her hand gripping the seat.

I really didn't understand. They were getting married anyway, and it made no sense to me for them to wait. I wondered at the idea of going through your life having had only one partner. I was tempted to ask April her feelings on it, but I was certain she would think I was just being sarcastic.

April all but leapt from the car when we got back to my house, and as fast as she politely could, she was in her rental car and backing out of the driveway. I was actually a little disappointed to see her go. Doris was better behaved with April around.

I telephoned the seamstress after I went inside. Sam walked in as I was hanging up. "Where's April?"

"She left. Told me to tell you she's running away with an old boyfriend. Sorry, man. Love bites."

"Oh, really? Is that what she said?" He gave me a crooked half smile.

"She did. Told me she's decided true love is bunk."

"Still the same old Satan." He knuckled the top of my head.

"You're still the same Sam-Halo." I said, swatting his hand away. I called him that to bug him . . . but the endearment was there, too.

"I better go get cleaned up. I'm meeting her and her parents for dinner." Sam slugged my shoulder softly as he passed me.

"Stay out of my bathroom. I need to get ready, too."

"Where you going?"

"To the club to get drunk and play pool. Want to come?"

"I'll pass this time, thanks."

"Maybe next time."

"Whatever." He turned his back on me and headed down the stairs.

"Where are you going?"

"To get ready," he said without stopping.

"Didn't you hear me say, 'stay out of my bathroom'?"

"Sorry, Satan, can't hear you. You'll have to speak up." He disappeared around the wall at the bottom of the stairs.

I swore and bailed down the stairs after him. By the time I'd made it to the bathroom, he was already in there. Door locked. I could hear him laughing.

I thumped my fist against the door and swore at him to open up. He started to whistle. "I hate you, Sam!" I shouted and went back upstairs.

"Get Sam out of my bathroom," I demanded when I saw Doris.

"He has to use yours. The guest bathroom doesn't have a shower."

"Yeah, Doris. I live here too and I know that. Why can't he use your bathroom?"

"I don't see the problem. You used to share that bathroom before he moved out."

"Yeah, when I was like ten. I'm an adult now and I need my privacy."

"He's only staying two days." She said absently.

"What about me?"

"If you don't like it . . . go stay with Gina."

I gaped at her. She was always telling me to go elsewhere, to be anywhere other than where she was, but each time she did it, the feelings of abandonment flooded me. "Fine. I will."

"Fine."

Tears were threatening to fall. My eyes were burning. I stalked out of the room so she wouldn't have the satisfaction of knowing she'd upset me. It made no sense why I was upset exactly. It wasn't like Doris had ever cared about me. What difference did it make that she didn't care today?

Sam came out of the bathroom as I was stuffing things into my green army duffel bag. He stopped when he saw me. "Are you crying?" "No!"

He snorted. "Peeling onions then?"

"You're so funny." I jerked the zipper closed on the bag.

"Where are you going?"

"Gina's. Doris thinks it's more important that you're here than me. So . . . I'm leaving."

He stepped in front of me, blocking the door to my bedroom. "Suzie, if this is about the bathroom—"

"It's about everything, okay, Sam? Tell me something . . . Does it feel good to be the golden child? Is it nice to finally have her acceptance?"

"I don't think I have her acceptance," he said slowly. "I don't think anyone—"

"Well, it sure looks like it from where I'm standing. Would you please get out of my way?"

"No! You can't leave me alone with them."

"You're not alone. You're going to dinner with your shiny new parents. But don't worry; the old ones are finally worshipping you, too. Now move!" I swiped a tear from my cheek.

"C'mon, don't cry." Sam reached out to touch me, but I slapped his hand away.

"I'm not crying and don't worry, I'll show up to your precious wedding so you don't need to keep me a hostage until then!" He didn't budge, so I balled up my fist and slammed him in the gut. As I skirted past him, he lunged for me but missed, and I ran up the stairs two at a time. *Please start,* I thought, turning the key in my ignition a few moments later.

Gratefully it did, and I sped off to spend the next forty-eight hours with Gina.

chapter

6

"ARE YOU REALLY GOING TO THIS WEDDING?" Gina said. She was wearing a tight black patent leather belly shirt that was so shiny I could see my reflection in it.

"I have to go, it's my brother's wedding." My muffled voice carried through the folds of black as I pulled the dress over my head.

"Come with us instead. We're your friends and he's just a brother you never see. I promise this party is gonna be so wicked good, way better than a night with your hoity-toity sister-in-law and her family. Or even your family, for that matter."

"Would you mind not criticizing my family in front of me?"

She pursed her lips and smoothed her belly shirt. "Fine, whatever. You're the one always saying how much you hate them."

Instead of responding, I did the velvet black buttons up and turned so Gina could see. "Wow," she said. "You don't look like any bridesmaid I've ever seen. You look like you're going to dinner at Cisero's or something."

"It is a wicked dress, isn't it?" I slipped on my black stilettos and turned to the mirror. I couldn't help grinning. It wasn't something I would normally wear, but the low-cut, sleeveless look was pretty slinky.

I rubbed a little body oil into my ivy anklet tattoo so it didn't look

33

scaly and sprayed some Victoria's Secret "Pink" at my neck, and I was ready.

The dread of going to the wedding brunch and the reception had left a knot in my stomach. The only good thing was that it would be only a few more hours until Sam and April would go away and my life would be back to normal. With any luck, I'd never have to see them again.

I was late to the brunch and tried to sit at a table in the back, but my father spotted me and waved me over to a seat up front. When they saw me, April's jaw fell and Sam rubbed his temples like he had a headache.

"What have you done to that dress?" Doris hissed.

"Altered it," I said, turning so she could get the full effect. "Don't you like it?"

"That dress was not yours to alter," she said, icicles dripping from her tongue. "And where were you after the ceremony? You were supposed to meet us at the church."

"I was at Gina's. C'mon, Doris, you know that. After all, you were the one that kicked me out and told me to go there."

"Don't you get smart with me."

"Yeah. It's lots easier for you to be around dumb people, then that way you don't feel left out."

The people at the next table were looking at us, and that's what kept Doris from slapping me. Even so, her hand flinched.

"Nice control, Doris. Those anger management classes must be paying off." I moved further down the table to distance myself from her and seated myself next to Sam's best man, John. I remembered him from visits he'd made to the house when we were in high school. I trailed an eye over him appreciatively. He sure had filled out nicely.

I was about to flash him my best smile and say something witty when a hand fell heavily on my bare shoulder. I swiveled to see who was there and found myself nose to nose with Sam who was kneeling next to my chair.

"Hey, Satan. We need to talk."

"But I haven't eaten yet," I argued.

He stood and pulled me up by the elbow. "There's plenty of time for that."

He quickly made his way through the tables, dragging me after him. Stumbling along in my high heels, I practically had to run to keep from tripping as he pulled me out of the dining area and into a little room off the hallway.

"What is your problem?" I demanded as I straightened to glare at him.

"Do you want a summary or the long version?"

"I'm not really interested in either, but I know you're going to insist. So how about the summary?"

"What happened to your dress?" His eyes flashed angrily.

"What about it?"

"You're missing half of it!"

"Oh, that. It was suffocating me. I had it altered."

"Do you have any idea what that gown cost April?"

"Twenty bucks?" I sneered.

"Try three hundred!"

"Well, that's her problem. Remember, I didn't ask to be involved. Besides, I'll bet the other guys here won't mind looking at it."

"Oh, stop it, Suzie. You don't have any idea how ridiculous you look, do you?"

"Excuse me?"

"Forget it. Where were you earlier?"

"At Gina's."

"You missed the family portraits we had done!" he said angrily, trying to keep his voice down but not succeeding.

I'd forgotten all about the portraits. "I was busy!" I yelled back. "And don't pretend to care Sam-Halo; it isn't like I'm a real part of the family anyway. Just another broken branch from an otherwise perfect tree!"

A man walking by shot a quick, curious glance into the room where we were arguing. Sam shut the door firmly to give us privacy.

"Would you knock it off?" he said.

"Knock what off?"

"Your stupid, 'poor-little-me' routine. I'm tired of hearing it. This is an important day for me, and you missed most of it and ruined your dress." He sniffed at me. "And you've been drinking, too!"

"But I'm not drunk," I said defensively.

"Does it make any difference?"

"It does to me, because I wish I were drunk!"

Sam inhaled deeply, his nostrils flaring. "Look, I'm sorry. I just really wanted today to be perfect. Your little no-show made us all late since we waited for an hour before starting; hoping you were just running late."

It made me cringe to think of everyone waiting on me, but I held his glare levelly. How dare he just show up in my life after not having spoken to me more than twice in the last year and try to make me feel guilty for not being a better member of the family? He knew where we came from. Could he really think it was possible to care about making my parents wait for a little while when I had spent my whole life waiting on them to treat me like I had any value? "That's your fault for waiting." I said finally.

He shut his eyes tight and without opening them said, "I swear, you have to pour vinegar on anything that might be good in your life, just so you can see it curdle."

"See, Halo, that's where you're wrong," I blurted. "My life *is* vinegar. It was curdled before I got here!"

"What in the world is wrong with you?" he demanded.

"Do you want the long version or the summary?"

Exasperated, he shook his head and muttered, "Oh, forget it. Let's just go back inside and get this over with."

"The sooner the better."

It was tough to follow him back to the table with the food when what I really wanted to do was to ditch out the side door and head to the Hideaway.

There were four other girls with dresses like mine . . . well, like mine *had been* anyway. I didn't know them and decided I had no desire to get to know them. They were all younger than me and all giggly. Just watching them made me want to gag.

I pushed my food around on the plate absently. It all looked terrible to me and smelled even worse, turning my stomach and making my mouth water like I was on the verge of throwing up. I decided that Sam's presence was giving me an ulcer.

The reception started immediately after the late brunch, in another part of the building. The evening was horrible. There was no formal reception line. The bride and groom and their parents just mingled with the guests. I don't know what the other bridesmaids and I were supposed to do. We looked absurd, all standing together, so I avoided them as they tittered behind their hands, their eyes darting toward and away from me. As they greeted the guests, April and Sam ignored me.

"It's just a stupid dress," I muttered.

"Oh, it's way more than a stupid dress," a voice to my left commented.

I turned. "Chris!" I was so glad to see him I couldn't stop myself from throwing my arms around his neck.

"What are you doing here?" I asked.

"I just wanted to see if you're okay. When I asked Gina where you were, she said you weren't happy about having to do this little gig, and I thought I'd give you some company."

The truth was, I was so glad to see someone from my world, I couldn't help giving him another hug, even though I didn't want to give him the wrong idea about the two of us.

When I let him go, he asked, "Can we talk for a minute?"

I was scared about what was coming next and gave him a skeptical look.

"Don't worry. Everything's cool. It's just that I've been thinking about what you said to me—you know, about there not being a chance for me to be anything more than 'just Chris.' I just don't want things to be weird between us. It's okay if I'm 'just Chris,' as long as we're still friends. I just need to know we're still friends."

"Of course we're still friends, you freak."

He smiled, the tightness around his eyes easing up. I was glad he'd come by. There was no way I would've made the first move toward normalcy. If he hadn't, we probably would never have spoken again, and I would have lost a very good friend.

"So . . . having fun?" he asked.

I snorted. "Everyone here thinks I look like the very devil."

He grinned as his eyes followed the curves of my body and back to my face. Then he shrugged. "Naw, I seriously doubt the devil looks that good."

I smiled gratefully. "You're lookin' fine, yourself."

"You think?" He stepped back and held his arms open. "I stole this suit from my brother when I had the job interview."

"So you gonna give it back?"

"Probably not."

I laughed at him. His face in this crowd of unfriendlies had calmed my tumbling stomach. He leaned back against a wall and surveyed the crowd. There was a group surrounding Sam and April, waiting their turn to speak to them. Chris gestured toward the cluster of people. "So that's the brother, huh?"

"That's him all right," I said.

Chris shrugged. "He looks okay to me."

"Only because you don't know him. He's self-righteous, judgmental, and he was mean to me just a while ago."

"His female's kinda pretty, so he's got good taste. He can't be all bad."

"His female is pretty," I agreed. "But *her* taste isn't very good. Look at who she's marrying."

Chris arched a brow; his goatee twitched with a smirk. "C'mon, Cue. She looks nice. He looks nice. Quit being the evil sister and let your brother have a nice day."

I glared at him. "I thought you came here to be moral support for me."

He popped an éclair into his mouth. "Nope," he said around the chunk of pastry. "I came for the food."

We walked outside and around the building. I pulled a pack of cigarettes from my purse, tapped one out, and lit it. Inhaling deeply, I felt sicker.

"I thought you quit," Chris said.

"I did." I exhaled, blowing purposely in his face.

He didn't flinch in the new halo of smoke around his head. "You kind of have to wonder about someone who says they've quit but still carries a pack of cigarettes in their purse."

"Oh, fine." I stamped the cigarette out and wandered back inside with him in time to hear a small chorus of laughter rise up from the crowd. Sam and April were cutting the cake. I glared at the back of them. "Have you ever been happy like that?" I asked Chris.

"Happy? Hey, I'm always happy."

"Oh, yeah, you're a real ball of joy," I said and then thought to myself: *like all the times you sliced the top of your arms just to see them bleed. Or maybe you're meaning the time when you rolled your car on purpose in a suicide attempt that failed and landed you in ICU for two days.*

"Well, have you ever been happy like that?" he countered.

"No. I haven't. That's exactly my point. We don't belong here. Look at us. We're like dogs someone dressed up and brought to a wedding. We have on the right attire, but under the clothes, we're still dogs."

Doris laughed raucously off to my right. I didn't have to turn to see her to know that she was being crude. Doris was a dog in a dress, too. I closed my eyes as if I could drown out her voice and laugh with the sheltered darkness behind my lids.

Her voice got louder. She sounded like she was drunk, but if so, she would have had to furnish her own booze because there was no alcohol present at this reception. She was surrounded by a group of her friends, and she was becoming more boisterous by the minute. Wherever she had gotten it, it was clear to me that she had been drinking.

"Can you believe these Mormons?" she was saying. "A huge event like this and not one drop of alcohol! Hard to believe my boy turned out to be such a prude. Next thing you know they are going to call us all to repent for wanting to drink a toast to the occasion."

Her friends laughed with her, and grimacing, I turned to see if Sam had noticed. He had, and the look in his eyes reflected more than just sadness. I could see shame and disgust and disappointment as he turned away, trying to ignore her.

I couldn't take it anymore. Maybe I never would be happy like he was. Maybe *I* would never feel so completely loved by another person that I would want to spend my life with them, but there was no way on earth I was going to stand by and let Doris mess up Sam's happiness too.

In the same way Sam had grabbed my elbow earlier, I took hold of hers and dragged her out of the place entirely. She was too shocked to protest. I had no idea where my father was, but he deserved to be slapped for leaving her to her own devices at an event as big as this.

"You're disgusting!" I hissed as soon as we had cleared the building.

I released her with a shove, and she straightened herself, smoothing down the folds of her gown, and scowled at me. "You have no right—"

"Right?" I cut her off. "You have some nerve to lecture me about right, when it was just last week that you were hacking on me to make certain I came to this affair sober, and here you are, drunk, and acting so rude that even I'm embarrassed by it!"

"I was chatting with some of my friends. I don't see how that could be something that would have any relevance to you at all," she sniffed, a little unsteady on her feet.

"You were making fun of Mormons in front of an entire room full of them! Are you that stupid?"

"Who are you to tell me I'm behaving badly? You show up here, dressed like some tart, after having ruined that beautiful gown and missing family portraits and fighting with Sam on his wedding day! I'm embarrassed to claim you as part of the family."

"I don't know why you *would* claim me. I certainly don't claim you!"

She pulled her hand back and slapped me so hard in the face that I saw stars. I staggered back, the sting of her handprint burned my mind more than my face. *How many years had it been since she struck me last?*

"Get out of here!" she hissed, pure hatred in her eyes. I could only gape at her. "Get out of here!" she yelled. "You don't belong in decent society."

"Fine," I said. "I didn't want to be here anyway!"

"That's perfect since no one wants you here!"

"Fine!" I yelled and spun on my heel and stomped to my car. I would have run if the skirt to the dress hadn't been so tight. Tears had already started to fall, and my stomach had tightened so much it felt like the worst cramp I'd ever had.

I could hear feet pounding the pavement behind me. I turned, expecting to see Sam, expecting to hear him fix things and tell me everything was okay like he always did. I expected him to hold me and cry with me and tell me that it wasn't my fault and that she was wrong to hit me.

Chris panted as he caught up to me. "Aw, Cue, don't cry," he said, taking my arm and turning me to peer into my face. "Who needs 'em, huh? Hey, since we're already dressed up, why don't we just go to the party with Gina over at the Hideaway?"

"I don't want to go anywhere!" I said angrily.

"Okay, okay, no problem. We can just go back to my place and chill. Okay?"

"No! Look, Chris, I know we're tight and all, but we are never going to be more than friends. You just need to get that into your head, okay?"

His face fell. I didn't care. I got into my car and turned the key. Nothing happened. I cursed and tried again. It started, and I backed out of the parking space and peeled out, leaving Chris standing there.

chapter
7

I WAS ABSOLUTELY BAWLING, SPEEDING DOWN Route 9, wiping at tears
with my hand, squinting against the glare of headlights, swerving in and
out of traffic, cursing anyone who got in my way, and leaning on the
horn. All the horrible events of the day played through my mind, culmi-
nating in Doris smacking me in the face. I was furious. I hated everything and everybody.

When the traffic light ahead of me changed from green to yellow, I
was in no mood to stop, and instead punched the accelerator. But as the
light changed, a car that had been waiting to make a left turn, turned
in front of me. Instinctively, I hit the brakes, but it was too late. I heard
the screech of brakes and the sudden crunch of metal as the front seat
was filled with shattered glass. The impact threw me forward into the
steering wheel and then the airbag deployed, slamming me in the face
and chest and pinning me against the seat. Then, except for the sound
of my breathing, everything went quiet. I sat there, stunned.

Someone jerked my car door open.

"Are you okay?" a man's voice shouted.

I stared into a stranger's face.

"No," I whispered as the face blurred out and everything went
black.

I slid in and out of consciousness, only vaguely aware of people shouting, flashing red and blue lights, the sound of a saw cutting through metal, and hands pulling on me. There was no pain, but I could feel something warm and wet on my face, blurring my vision. Then I was laid on a stretcher and something large, stiff, and uncomfortable was wrapped around my neck.

After the stretcher was lifted into the back of an ambulance, a woman's warm smile filled my eyes. She was holding a cloth to my head. "You're going to be fine," she assured me. Someone else was manipulating my arm, and I felt something prick me. I closed my eyes, content to settle into the darkness. I was as tired as I ever remembered being, completely unable to will myself awake and without any desire to do so. The entire moment felt like an eternity.

I awoke with a start. A nurse was looking down at me, with a furrowed brow. She was taking my blood pressure.

"Where am I?" I asked. I had a hard time mouthing the words.

"Fairfax General, in the emergency room. How're you feeling?"

I tried to sit up, but she put her hand on my shoulder and held me down.

"Lie still. You need to rest," she said sternly.

"How . . . how long have I been here?" I asked.

"Only about half an hour."

"That's all?"

"That's all. You took quite a banging. How do you feel?" she asked. Though it didn't sound as though she really cared.

"Like I've been hit by a car," I said dryly.

She grunted. "The doctor will want to get some X rays—to make sure nothing's fractured or broken. Is there any chance you're pregnant?"

I scowled. "Pregnant?"

"Yeah, you know . . . baby, nine months . . . pregnant."

The suggestion made me mad. "No. Well . . . I guess there's always the chance, but I doubt it."

"Well, we've already drawn some blood. We can just run a test from that."

"How efficient of you," I said, reaching to touch a bandage above my left eye.

"You sustained a cut on your forehead," she explained, without any apparent sympathy. "You'll need stitches."

She adjusted the drip on my IV, then said curtly, "I'll be back in a while. The doctor should be in anytime."

I was glad to see her go. Someone needed to talk to her about her bedside manner.

About fifteen minutes later a middle-aged man with a paunchy, middle-aged belly came into the room. He pushed his glasses up with a thick finger and pulled his stool on wheels over to sit down by me.

"Suzanna Quincy," he said, reading the top of the chart in his hands. "Looks like you've had quite an eventful evening."

"Without a doubt," I answered. This man made me nervous, though I couldn't say why.

He took my wrist in his hand and studied his watch. Then he peered at me through his lenses thoughtfully. His eyes softened with . . . what? Was that pity? Why would he pity me? I felt bruised but certainly not broken. There was no reason to pity me, other than I had no idea where my car was.

He cleared his throat. "I'm Doctor Borne." He reached to push his glasses up again, although they were as high on his nose as they were going to get. "We've run some tests, Suzanna, and have found," he cleared his throat again. "We've found that we won't be able to take any X rays because you're pregnant."

It was like someone had shot liquid ice into my heart, and it was now being pumped rhythmically through my veins to my extremities. "What?" I blinked.

"You're going to have a baby," he said.

"There must be . . . I can't have a baby . . . There must be some mistake."

"Blood tests are almost always accurate. Are you late?"

"Late for what? Oh! That. I don't really know." My voice was a dry whisper. He was wrong. He just had to be wrong. "I'm always irregular," I heard myself say, realizing there was no way to erase the uncomfortable ache settling over me. It wasn't pain from the accident, but more the ache of realization.

"Well, we need to check you over to make sure you're okay from the accident. Aside from some bruising where your seatbelt was and that goose egg on your head, you should be okay, but it's better to make sure."

He stood and lifted my arm. "Does that hurt?"

I shook my head slowly and looked up at him. "What do I do now?"

His face mirrored the ache I felt as he sat back down on the stool. "Are you married?"

I swallowed hard and shook my head.

"Boyfriend?"

"No," I rasped.

"You'll want to let the father know."

"That's not possible," I blurted out. He didn't pry as to why it wasn't possible.

"Do you have family around here?"

"I live with my parents."

"Well, you're going to want to let them know so you have a support group. Then if you decide to have the baby, you'll want to get a good doctor—an OB-GYN, and start taking care of yourself. I'll give you some literature on prenatal care."

I lay there, stunned. It had never occurred to me that I might be pregnant, but it made sense. Maybe that was what had been causing the nausea I had been experiencing. This was a disaster! I didn't want to be pregnant! It was the last thing on earth I wanted to be.

"Suzanna?" the doctor said. "Are you all right?"

I shook my head but said nothing.

"You didn't suspect that you might be pregnant?"

Again, I shook my head.

"Well, it's a tough thing, but you're not the first young woman to find herself in this situation."

I finally found my voice. "I can't honestly think of anything worse," I said, and I meant it. Even dying in that car wreck would not have been worse.

An intern came in to see me after a while and stitched up my cut. He was a nice guy and apologized for hurting me, but I didn't care about the pain. The real hurt was too big.

He put a bandage over the stitches and helped me sit up on the edge of the gurney for a few minutes. Then the ornery nurse came in. She gave me a bottle with a few pain pills in it and said I was free to leave. I'd lost my shoes and realized how odd I must look—barefoot, with a bandage on my head, and wearing a bloodstained, sleeveless, evening gown. But I didn't care. There was only one thing I could think about now.

No one answered the phone at my parents' house, at Gina's, or at Chris's, forcing me to call a cab to get home. Luckily, someone had put my purse in the ambulance with me, so I had some money to pay for the taxi.

I didn't bother to turn on any lights after the cab had dropped me off on my doorstep. I made my way through the dark to my room and fell onto my bed fully clothed, hugging a pillow to my chest. No wonder I felt sick all the time. No wonder I felt like my emotions were at the brink of collapse and tears all the time. *Pregnant.*

I tried to imagine who the father was, but then decided it didn't really matter. No one I had been with over the last three months was anyone I even remembered, let alone knew. I was on the pill, but was really relaxed about taking it. I usually used protection, but that was from fear of social diseases more than worry over pregnancy. Though I hated to admit it, I was as relaxed about that as I was about taking the pill.

Stupid! How stupid I was to not think about this possibility. What had I been thinking? Did I really believe I was the exception? That it could never happen to me? I shut my eyes to the darkness around me. The truth was . . . I *had* thought I was the exception. I was a goddess on a pedestal, making my own rules, looking down at the world, but now, someone had reached out to kick the pedestal from under me.

A sob was muffled by the pillow. What was I going to do now?

8

"Mom, I need to talk to you."

She was rapidly flipping through the phone book.

"Suzanna, I simply don't have time to deal with you right now. You're lucky I'm even talking to you, after the scene you made at Sam's wedding."

"Fine, forget it."

As I turned away from her, she said, "Did you just call me 'Mom'?"

"I guess I did," I responded without turning again to face her. "My mistake." I left the house and stared at the empty spot where my car should have been. I had forgotten that I didn't have a car. My body was heavy from sleep. Without the energy to go back into the house, I sat on the porch and pulled out a cigarette. I lit it, but after the first drag just held it in my hand.

When Doris came out, she nearly tripped over me. "You're still here?" she said testily.

"I guess I am." I flinched as she passed me, an involuntary reaction to the smack she had dealt me the night before. I let out a breath I hadn't realized I was holding when she made it by without striking out at me. It made me sick to realize the power she still held over me.

"Where's your car?"

"Totaled. I was in a wreck last night." I flicked ashes from the cigarette onto the grass.

She cursed. "You were drunk, weren't you?"

"Oh, you are so wicked stupid, Doris. If I'd been drunk, I'd be in jail right now."

She ignored my sarcasm. "So what happened?"

I shrugged. "Someone ran into me."

"You could sue him."

"Please, Doris. I'm no snake."

"Well, I've got to go. I called the salon, and they said they could do my nails today if I come right in."

"Well then hurry off . . . wouldn't want you to be late. Oh, by the way," I called out as she clicked down the walk. "You're gonna be a grandma."

It felt good to see her stumble on the wake of my words. She slowly turned around, her face a mask of disbelief.

"You're joking."

"Sorry. I'm not twisted enough to joke about something like that."

"How?"

I snorted. "Hmm, lemme think. It wasn't a stork. Come to think of it, I don't remember any birds or bees involved, either."

She had her hands on her hips. "Who's the guy?"

"I have no idea."

She sighed in relief. "Well, that's one thing in your favor. You still have a chance to avoid ending up like me."

I held up my hands. "Oh, please. Not another lecture about you being robbed of your youth by a shotgun wedding with Sam nestled in your belly. I simply don't care."

She ignored my monologue. "You need to make an appointment."

"Mmm. I don't see how getting my nails done is going to help me here," I said, contemplating my belly ring and wondering what it would look like when I got big.

"Don't be ridiculous, at the abortion clinic. You don't want to keep it."

"The abortion clinic?" It amazed me that I hadn't thought of that on my own.

"Of course; you can't keep it. It would ruin your life."

"Did Sam ruin your life?" I asked. The answer was apparent in the way her mouth tightened in a sticky red line. And of course, she lumped *me* into the sum of things that had ruined her life as well.

"That was a long time ago. You have options I didn't have. And not having a father involved makes it easier. We'll make the appointment when I get back," she said decidedly and left to get her nails done.

I just sat there watching my cigarette burn. I found that I couldn't smoke it no matter how much I wanted to—the taste and odor turned my stomach.

I hated to admit it, but Doris's solution seemed to be the smartest thing to do. After all, I wasn't capable of raising a kid, and I just couldn't bear the thought of watching my body go berserk without being able to do anything about it. I flicked the butt into the grass and went back inside to use the phone.

"Women's Health Services, how can I help you?"

"I . . ." I faltered. What could I say? "I'm pregnant," I finally sputtered.

The woman's voice was calm and businesslike. "What is your name?"

"Suzanna Quincy."

"Middle name?"

"None, just that."

"When was the first day of your last menstrual cycle?"

"I don't know. Two, maybe three months ago."

"It's okay, it's no big deal to know it exactly," she said. "How old are you?"

"I'm twenty-two." I could feel tears, but there was no way I was going to cry.

"Do you have medical insurance?"

"Yeah."

"What kind?"

I gave her my social security and group number for the insurance I had decided at the last minute to sign up for through my work. At least I had made one intelligent decision.

"What can I do for you, Suzanna?"

"I just want to get this over with."

"Are you saying you want to terminate the pregnancy?"

"Yes." I had to clear my throat and say it again to make myself heard.

"We're available every day but Thursday and Sunday for first trimester procedures. When do you want to come in?"

"Right now."

She hesitated. I could hear fingers tapping on a keyboard, likely pulling up a schedule. "The soonest we can do is tomorrow at noon."

"High noon," I quipped.

"How will you be getting here?"

"By bus, I guess."

"Okay. We're on Chestnut Hill." She gave me some directions, then asked, "Do you have any questions?"

"Are they going to put me out for this?"

"You have a choice of anesthetics, but we prefer to put you out. It's easier for most women, but the choice is yours."

"Okay. Thanks. See you tomorrow."

"See you tomorrow, Suzanna."

I tapped my foot furiously against the leg support of the chair I was sitting on. Tomorrow it would all be just a bad memory.

I tried calling Chris twice, but he must've been screening his calls because he wouldn't pick up. I didn't blame him.

When Doris came home, she brought some Chinese take-out. As she began eating, I don't know why, but I told her I had made an appointment at the clinic.

"Do you want me to go with you?" she asked.

I was amazed that she would take any interest. I mean, how many years had she spent making sure I knew I wasn't wanted or loved? And now, here she was chumming up to me.

"No. I'm a big girl. I don't need anyone to hold my hand."

"It's just kind of a big thing. I don't want you to be alone."

"I've been alone for the last twenty-two years, and I'm doing just fine."

She grimaced but didn't respond. I heard Dad's keys in the front door and widened my eyes. "Are you going to tell him?" I asked.

"Do you want him to know?"

He came in, knocking his briefcase into the umbrella stand and dropping it to the floor with a loud thud.

"I don't know what I want," I said quietly. Part of me did want him to know—the part that wanted him to hold me and tell me everything was going to be okay wanted desperately to tell him, but with Doris there, I knew he wouldn't give into any emotional displays.

"Whoa!" Dad exclaimed upon entering the room. "What's the occasion?"

"No occasion, just felt like take-out tonight," Doris said.

"I don't mean the food. I meant . . . I just don't remember the last time Suzie ate dinner with us. She's not usually here."

"Yeah, well, I have to stay in tonight since I totaled my car last night."

"You did! Are you okay?" The look of concern on his face was genuine, and it made me feel good. Though he was not overly affectionate, I knew he cared.

"I'm fine, a little sore and bruised, but okay. Thanks for asking." I glanced at Doris to see if she had any remorse for not asking that question at all. She didn't appear to even consider it.

His hand went out for my forehead where the stitches were. "Your forehead . . ."

I dodged his hand. "It's just a scratch, no big deal."

"I'm glad you're okay," he said, then walked to the sink and washed his hands. As he came back to the table, he said, "You know Cue, you ought to give Sam a call next week when they get back from the honeymoon and tell him you're sorry."

"Sorry for what?"

"You know you were being horrible. What would it hurt to apologize? Leaving his wedding for no reason at all, without so much as a good-bye to him, really hurt his feelings."

My throat tightened. I hadn't left for no reason at all. I had been all but kicked out. Didn't he realize what had happened? Didn't he see that I had only tried to help Sam? I reached out for the wine bottle Doris had uncorked and placed on the table, but when my hand touched the chilled glass, I reconsidered and drew my hand back.

"Something wrong?" Doris asked.

"Just . . . probably shouldn't be drinking right now."

"It isn't going to matter," she said pointedly.

"I know. I just feel a little sick. I'm tired. I'm going to bed now."

"Are you sure that she didn't get hurt in that wreck?" I heard my father ask as I made my way down the stairs.

Sleep came heavily upon me, and I didn't wake up until ten o'clock the next morning.

chapter
9

I CALLED IN SICK TO WORK, THEN SHOWERED carefully, scrubbing until my skin was red and hurried through the rest of getting ready. There was no use in bothering with getting anything to eat since the lady on the phone had told me to come fasting. The bus ride seemed to take forever, and my heart felt like I was running the whole way instead of sitting perfectly still on the seat. My knuckles were white from gripping the bar of the seat in front of me. When I came to the stop where I was to get off, the driver shook his head at me as I exited, making me wonder if he knew what I was about to do.

Inside the office, it looked . . . well . . . unexpectedly pleasant. Green plants and serene paintings were everywhere. The receptionist smiled sympathetically at me as I took the paperwork I was to fill out. The form called for my complete medical history and seemed to take forever to complete.

Then I waited. Other women, some teenagers, young enough to still be called little girls, waited with me. Some had mothers, some had a male companion, whether spouse, boyfriend, or simply a guy getting off the hook was hard to discern. Some looked relaxed, as though this were a stroll in the park and that was when it occurred to me that this was a medical facility. Not everyone was here for the same reason I was.

55

But some were. Some looked scared. One in particular sat with her mother, her eyes wide and darting back and forth. She looked like she was fifteen—sixteen tops, her dark hair falling over half of her pale face. She looked as though she was on the verge of bursting into tears.

Did I look like that? I certainly felt like it. Her mother was well-kempt, sitting with back erect and intently reading a woman's magazine. Her face was stony and resolute. And though in any other setting that face would mean nothing, in this setting that face was owned by a woman whose daughter had disgraced her. A woman who was going to take control before it was too late. It was the face of my own mother.

A nurse finally called my name. They took some more blood work and asked for a urine sample for another pregnancy test. Guess they didn't want to start the "procedure," as everyone called it, for a false alarm. Then I was ushered into a room where a woman behind a plain desk introduced herself as Amy. There was no last name given, it was simply Amy.

"Do you prefer to be called Suzie?" she asked.

"Actually, most people call me Cue."

"That's a fun nickname."

"Not too bad, I guess." I focused on keeping my breathing even.

"Why do you want to have an abortion?"

"Why? I can give you a million reasons."

"Okay, I've got time." She leaned back and waited. I couldn't think of one.

"I don't have a husband," I said finally.

"A lot of people don't have husbands and sometimes when they do, those husbands leave anyway. What else?"

"I don't want a baby," I said.

"Have you considered adoption?"

Suddenly, I felt impatient. "Look, Amy, I appreciate your role of devil's advocate, but I made my choice, Okay? Let's just keep going, okay?"

"Okay," she said, sounding not annoyed at all.

She flipped through some charts, explaining the entire procedure. I took deep breaths to keep from throwing up. Amy pulled out some more forms and slid them across the desk to me.

"These are the consent forms. They're to make sure we have your permission to continue from this point."

I nodded dumbly at her instruction.

"And," she continued, "they are to ensure that you are proceeding according to your choice. We need to make sure you are here because this is what you want to do and not because of pressure being put on you by a boyfriend or a parent or anyone else. This is all about you, Cue. It's all about doing the right thing for you."

"The right thing," I echoed. "How do you know what the right thing is?"

She leaned forward. "It's different for everybody."

"But what if it isn't?" I asked. "What if it's the same for everybody and we just consider ourselves the exceptions?"

"Do you want to talk about it? Or maybe go home and rethink this?"

"I . . . no. No. I just want to get it over with."

She didn't move; her unblinking eyes seared through me. *What choice did I have?* I thought. *I could never be a good mom. I wasn't grown up myself, as my mother so often reminded me.* I nodded my head. "I want to continue," I said.

Amy sighed. The flash of concern in her was gone as quickly as it came. She pushed the papers closer. I gulped and started signing.

After the counseling, I was told to undress and put on a hospital gown. Then I was left alone in an examination room. The paper on the table crinkled underneath me every time I moved. When a tall man with wizened eyes entered the room and introduced himself as Dr. Mortimer, I felt my blood pressure go up just a little.

He laid me flat on the table and began gently probing my belly. "Do you have any idea how long ago your last menstrual period was?"

I shook my head.

"I'll have to do an ultrasound to see how far along you are. Do you understand?" I nodded and kept myself from swearing at the guy when he placed the cold paddle on my lower abdomen. The computer screen near my table seemed like a radar detector with little blips and bubbles in it. Red and blue lines moved through a couple of darker circles that pulsed rhythmically.

"What's that?" I asked.

"The fetus's heart. The red and blue are indicative of blood pumping in and out."

"Can you hear it beat?" I asked with wonder. The darker circles pulsed, making the red and blue lines move like a traffic graph.

He paused, casting a glance at a nurse who had joined us. "Do you want to hear it?" he asked.

I hesitated. *Did I want to hear?* "No, no. Let's just get this over with."

He nodded. "From the sonogram it looks like you are about thirteen weeks into this."

Thirteen weeks. That didn't sound so bad until I started adding. Three months. I was already through three months.

"The procedure's a little different for early second trimester, but we can still do this."

I bobbed my head to show I was paying attention. Three months and the heart was already beating wildly.

"Shouldn't I be fatter?" I asked.

"Not necessarily. Everyone's body reacts differently to pregnancy. Especially if you've been sick, it wouldn't be uncommon for you to actually lose weight during this time."

Another man entered the room, pushing a table on wheels filled with instruments. "Your anesthesiologist," the doctor said. "Don't worry; it'll all be over when you wake up."

The anesthetist wiped an alcohol pad over my arm. It was cold like my body. *What was I doing? Was I insane? Was I really capable of killing that heartbeat, stopping it and pretending blood never flowed through it?* I could hear Doris saying I didn't have to ruin my life, and I heard my own voice asking her, *"Did Sam ruin your life?"* Maybe in her mind he had ruined her life, but Sam was my link to reality; he was the only one in the world who came close to understanding me. If she hadn't had Sam . . . where would I be? Sam was a good person; she would have killed him if the option had been given to her. She would have killed me, too. A life. This baby was like Sam . . . like me. It was a life.

"Wait!" I shrilled to them.

The nurse, doctor, and anesthetist recoiled. I sat up on the table. "I can't! I can't do this!"

"No one is forcing you," the doctor reassured me.

I had begun to cry. "I'm sorry. I thought I could. I mean, what difference would it make? But out of all the stupid things I've done in my life, I can't do this, too!"

The doctor signaled the nurse and she left, returning a moment later with Amy, the counselor. Everyone else cleared the room, leaving Amy and me alone.

Amy was prepared. She had pamphlets on my new dietary needs, on the growth of the baby, and what to expect during the balance of my pregnancy. There was a pamphlet on the delivery, and she gave me information on both raising a child as a single parent and adoption options.

We discussed my drinking habits, and she cautioned me about fetal alcohol syndrome and the effects of smoking on a fetus. I made a personal vow to avoid drinking to prevent my kid from turning out like the pictures of sickly infants Amy showed me. Not like it mattered, no matter how bad I wanted to, it seemed I couldn't take a drink without throwing up anyway. Much like I had been forced into getting clean from drugs in that rehab center my parents had sent me to, this baby was forcing me into getting sober. Amy spent a long time talking to me.

As I was leaving the clinic, the girl I'd noticed earlier with her mother in the waiting room was leaving, too. Her face was blank, and she refrained from focusing on anything as the nurse wheeled her out to the car in a wheelchair. Her mother looked exactly as before. I shuddered. I could have been that girl, and instead of leaving armed with bags of information and a second heart beating inside me, I could have been leaving with nothing but that haunted look.

chapter
10

W HAT ARE YOU SAYING, SUZANNA!?" Doris's face reflected a volcanic rage that rivaled any I'd seen in her before.

"I couldn't go through with it," I said. "I don't get why that's so hard to understand."

My father sat on the couch, holding an iced double-bourbon against his forehead. "Doris, please, let's stay calm."

"Oh, shut up! I do not need your criticism tonight. A little support would actually be welcome right now, Franklin."

He flinched. He hated being called Franklin. His friends and associates all called him by his middle name, Tanner, and his response was uncharacteristically strong. "I'm not gonna shut up, Doris. Suzie has a right to make this kind of decision on her own."

"Why? So she can end up like me? Forced to get married and raise kids she wasn't planning on? Forced to cut short her youth because of a moment of stupidity?"

He stood up, glaring at her. "Was I such a horrible choice? Haven't I given you everything you've asked for? You wanted to go to college; I sent you. You wanted a nanny and a career; they were yours. Sorry to hear you feel so put upon!" He slammed his glass onto the coffee table.

It was odd to hear him stand up to her like that. Satisfying, but odd. I knew it wouldn't last. He'd soon back down and tell her he was sorry.

"I'm going to bed," I said, anxious to get out of there before the real fighting started. I was tired of hearing Doris's old complaint that Sam and I were both mistakes that had stolen her life from her.

"It isn't your room anymore, Suzanna," Doris said, barring my path.

"What?" My father and I both said at the same time.

"If you don't want to live by my rules, then you don't get to live in my house," she said.

"You're kicking me out?" The question seemed too absurd to even have to ask. She couldn't be serious, not at a time like this. It was one thing to kick me out for sassing her or taking drugs, but she couldn't really kick me out when I was pregnant. Could she? Even my dad seemed stunned to silence.

"Call it what you will. If you're so eager to go to the school of hard knocks, you might as well get started now."

"But, Doris . . ." Dad's eyes were pleading. She would never get that satisfaction from me.

"Fine. I'm more than happy to leave," I said. "I was through with you people anyway. I'll be downstairs packing; stay out of my way!"

"Don't you take anything that belongs to me!" she shouted as I'd reached the bottom of the stairs.

"Everything you own is tainted!" I yelled back. "No one would want it!"

I threw my clothes into some boxes left over from when Sam moved out. And when I'd run out of those, I dumped two of her Christmas decoration boxes onto the floor and emptied the bathroom drawers into them.

They were yelling upstairs, but that was nothing new. They were always yelling. They had moved to the bedroom to fight by the time I had started hefting boxes outside. It was pathetic how little I owned, but at the same time I was grateful. It was easier to pack.

There was no need to say good-bye or say I was leaving, though I ached to see my father. I borrowed my dad's car to drive myself to Gina's, figuring I could leave a message for him to come and get it. I knew he would do it without resenting me for not asking first.

The apartment was dark, but I used the key she had given me to let myself in. I was exhausted, physically, mentally, and emotionally, and my stomach had a knot in it. It was as though the baby had encased itself in armor to protect it from all the feelings and emotions swirling through my bloodstream.

I patted the knot. "Don't sweat it, kid. I'll take care of you." I didn't bother to wake Gina, who was already asleep, but instead slipped into the guest room and collapsed on the bed.

* * * *

"You and your mom get into a fight again?" Gina asked the next morning. She was pulling her hair back into a ponytail.

"She kicked me out," I said.

"For real this time? Why?"

"Well, 'cause I'm pregnant."

"Shut up!" She whirled to stare at me.

"Serious." I shrugged.

"That bites! How?"

"Don't tell me you really need an explanation," I said.

"Funny, Cue. Why don't you go get rid of it?"

"It isn't a cold. It's a kid."

She stared at me in disbelief. "You're keeping it?"

"Why not? It's mine isn't it?" I was sitting on the closed lid of the toilet watching her get ready.

"How are you going to afford that?" She went back to the mirror.

"I have a job." I said. "I have insurance. I can get by."

"Where you gonna live?"

I sucked in a deep breath. "I was hoping I could live here and split the rent with you."

She had her mouth stretched wide open while she was applying her mascara, yet it actually appeared to fall open wider. She turned to me, her reluctance clearly evident.

"What? And get stuck baby sitting? And getting woke up when your kid cries in the middle of the night?"

"It'd only be for a little while."

She closed her eyes and took a deep breath. Then she pointed her mascara brush at me and said, "You can stay, but don't you dare cramp my style. I'm not looking to be part of some cozy family unit. Got it?"

I shrugged. "No problem. I'm here all the time as it is. Nothing'll change, you'll see."

"Whatever. Another thing, I don't want my stuff messed around, so keep your stuff out of my stuff's way."

"Duh! Like I have much to get in your way anyway." I checked my watch. "I better get ready, too. I have to be to work soon." I stood up.

"So you're really keeping it then?"

"I can't kill a baby. I may be a lot of things, but I'm not some heartless baby murderer."

She sniffed. "I wouldn't keep it."

"That would be your choice to make. This is my choice."

She wrinkled her nose at me in disapproval. "Do what you want."

"That's what it's all about," I said.

11

T HE FIRST MONTH OF LIVING WITH GINA wasn't so bad. Party night was now twice a week since we were both around to take care of the details, and Gina was looking to become the social queen. Her idea of splitting rent was that I pay the vast majority of it, while she took care of the remaining scraps. I was able to swing a deal for $1,500 on another car. With this one there was no starter problem, but it probably had plenty of other problems there, waiting to leave me stranded at some inconvenient point.

During the second month of my stay with Gina, the baby hit a growth spurt. As I watched in dismay, my belly bulged from a flat smooth surface to a small rounded mound. My belly ring now dangled from the edge of the new outtie I had. It no longer looked cool, and I finally removed the star-shaped black stone.

Chris spent a lot of time at Gina's after I moved in, almost like an honorary roommate. Gina, who had always admired Chris's body, didn't mind that he hung around. At least, she didn't mind until it became very obvious that he didn't notice her at all. I wavered between being annoyed to being grateful for Chris's presence. He was a great friend, but sometimes he seemed to be pushing for more, and that bugged me.

Although there was a lot of partying, I stayed away from the alcohol. Sometimes I would pull out a cigarette just to hold it. Having it in my hands seemed to take some of the edge off of my need for one. I didn't ever take a drag on it, knowing full well I would be throwing up within moments afterward. I was still so sick I couldn't even light it without feeling queasy. In all the books I had read the nausea was called morning sickness, and according to the experts it was usually gone by the end of the first trimester. No one bothered to mention that it could be called *all day for forty weeks sickness!* Chris kept telling me that if I would focus on not being sick it would go away. And Gina insisted I was just a hypochondriac trying to get attention. Like they knew anything about it.

One night, about two months into my new arrangements, Chris came over after work and stayed to play a game of Foosball with Gina. As they played, I watched her slither around him like a snake coiling around a rodent and shook my head.

The couch was lumpy, and I was shifting my position, trying to get comfortable, when I felt a thump against my belly. "Oh, cool . . . wicked!" I yelled. Chris pole-vaulted the couch to my side.

"What? What happened?" He scanned my face, looking for signs of damage.

"It moved!" I said in wonder. "The baby moved. I mean, I've felt flutters before, but this . . . this was different."

Chris grinned. "Cool," he said.

"Wanna feel?" I asked, taking his hand before he answered. I held it against my belly and waited. "Did you feel that?"

He strained as though listening really hard. "I didn't . . . oh wait, I felt that! Hey, Gina, come feel this!" he called over.

"Yuck! No! That is so sick. It's like 'Aliens' or something," she said.

She flipped her red hair back impatiently. "C'mon Chris, we're in the middle of a game."

"It can wait," he said, placing both hands on my belly and feeling for the baby to move again. "Okay, Little Angel, move again for me," he cooed to my stomach. He'd started calling the kid Angel as soon as he found out I was pregnant and always referred to it as a *her*. "She's gonna be as feisty as her mother."

"Oh, please," Gina said. "Let's hope she's smarter than her mother."

"Hey, Gina, lay off." Chris said.

She snorted. "If you hadn't been all stupid at your brother's wedding and got in that car wreck, you wouldn't be in this situation."

I laughed out loud. "I hope you don't think babies come from car wrecks."

"No, I don't," she said. "They come from dumb little girls who don't use protection and then don't know how to take a morning-after pill just in case."

"I'm not dumb."

"If you say so." She flipped the foosball bar on her palm and slammed the ball into the net.

"What is your problem?" Chris asked, removing his hands and standing up.

"Nothing," Gina insisted, not looking at either of us. "You two want to cozy up and play Brady Bunch, great. What do I care? I'm going to the Hideaway." She stopped at the door. "Want to come, Chris?"

"No. I'm going to stay with Cue."

"Whatever." She slammed the door.

T HINGS WERE FINE FOR THE NEXT WEEK. Fine, meaning Gina and I didn't see each other much, and when we did, we avoided talking.

"You guys can't give each other the silent treatment forever," Chris said, pulling a bottle out of the fridge and twisting the lid off.

"Well, it's certainly been much nicer since we stopped talking to each other."

"But, Cue, she's your best friend."

"Some friend. She thinks I'm an idiot for not killing my own kid."

"Who cares? I mean, okay, it's a little weird to think of you as a pro-lifer . . ." He smiled. "But I like you this way, and I'm gonna love Little Angel." He patted my stomach.

"Stop it," I frowned.

"What?"

"Touching me. Everyone keeps touching me and patting my belly like I'm some sort of wish troll or something. It's irritating."

"I didn't know it bugged you." He scooted away from me a few inches. I was flipping through the channels on the satellite that came with the apartment.

"Four hundred and eighty channels and *nothing* is on," I muttered.

"It doesn't bother me, normally. I'm just . . . I don't want to be touched right now."

"Fine. Not a problem. I won't touch you then." He scooted a little farther away for emphasis. He took a swig from his bottle then set it in his lap, cradling the long neck with his hand, tapping his fingers against it nervously.

"What's wrong?" I asked.

"Nothing." His chin jutted out defiantly, the hairs from his goatee seeming to bristle.

"Nothing?" At least he had stopped tapping the bottle.

"It's just . . ."

"Just what?"

"Why are you always pushing me away like that? I don't have germs or a contagious disease or anything."

"I'm not," I shrugged.

He took another drink and then stood abruptly. I was secretly glad he had because the smell of the beer made me feel sick. I hadn't had a drink in a long time, and I didn't have the guts to tell him the beer made me queasy. It was like telling someone they had bad breath or something. Of course, bad breath also churned my gut and sent me running for a toilet, so I had learned to look away when talking to people.

He threw back his head, drained the bottle, and then muttered something about needing to go. It was a relief when the door clicked shut behind him. He was gone; Gina was gone; and there was no one left but me and the little alien bulge at my middle.

And yet he left me uncomfortable. I felt vulnerable in a way I hadn't for the last two months. I went to the fridge three times to get a Corona and three times came back to the couch and television empty-handed. Though the smell made me sick, and to actually take a drink made me want to throw up for a week, I really *wanted* a drink and a long drag on a cigarette.

On the fourth trip to the fridge, my fingers on their own accord reached out to snatch up the Corona bottle, hugging the long neck with tenacity. Trembling with the need for it, I twisted the top off, put the bottle to my lips, and poured it down my throat.

I threw up after, and as I held my head in my hands, staring down into the toilet bowl, I wondered if it was worth it. It wasn't, I determined, but the longing for the numbness that came with it buzzed about my head, and I didn't have a flyswatter.

Getting to work late the next day, the back of my throat ached with a desire to be good and drunk. I had been through rehab and knew the steps to getting clean. "Falling" the night previous was starting back at day one. I hated being at day one again and punched in at the clock with a force that could have broken it. Carrie's eyes were wide as she watched me clock in.

"What?" I asked, stuffing my keys into my pocket.

"Mr. Ferguson's looking for you," she whispered.

I cursed. "I'm so not in the mood for that man. What's he want now?"

"I . . . I—"

"Suzie!" his too-high-to-be-male voice barked like a poodle trying to sound like a Doberman.

"Yes, Mr. Ferguson?"

"Meet me in my office." He turned and waddled in that direction, his white tube socks glowing below his too-short dark trousers.

"What's up?" I asked Carrie. She ducked her head, refusing to look at me.

"I don't know," she said.

She *did* know. The lie was written across her face.

I ground my teeth. The need to be truly drunk was increasing and eating away at me like termites at a rotted tree trunk.

"There are some things missing," he said as soon as I was seated.

I shrugged. "Like what?"

"Expensive articles of clothing and large amounts of money from the till have turned up missing over the last two weeks . . ."

"So this has what to do with me?" The knot that was my baby was like a little hard ball again, protecting itself from the panic I felt.

"We've recently run a check into your background, something we should have done when we hired you. It seems you've got a bit of a record."

"That was a long time ago," I said woodenly.

He shook his head. "You should have divulged this information from the beginning."

"I didn't do it!" I blurted. "I haven't taken one stupid thing! You hired that new girl just two weeks ago. Wouldn't it make more sense to look at her? I've been here over a year with no problems!"

"That new girl," he said, his face turning red, "is my niece, and is in *NO WAY* responsible for the theft!"

"But . . . but I didn't," I sputtered. "I didn't . . ."

"I think you're lying."

My emotion switched from panic to fury. I hadn't done anything wrong. I had been clean. Now I was being blamed for someone else's misdeeds.

"Lying? I don't need to lie to a balding middle-aged moron who can't get a real job and has to spend his pathetic life working in a clothing store sorting little girl's dresses! If you don't believe me, then there's no reason for me to stay. I quit!"

He glared at me, then said, "Fine. Get out."

And that was that. Carrie refused to say good-bye to me or say anything at all as she pretended to be involved in paperwork. At the door I turned and shouted, "I am innocent!" The yell rippled through the entire store as I turned again and left.

It took me all day to get back to the apartment. I drove everywhere, trying to figure out what to do. With the job went the insurance. How was I supposed to pay for the kid? With the job went the rent money. How was I supposed to pay Gina? I popped in a CD and cried. It was already dark when I got back.

When I walked in, the party was going strong. "Cue, woman!" a skinny blonde called out with a slur. I tried to smile and say hi, but the smell of party night immediately made me sick. Cigarette smoke, the sweet fermented smell of alcohol, and the tang of weed were heavy in the air. The scene was loud and disorganized, with people writhing wildly to the music and grinning stupidly. It was a far cry from the calm and peace I yearned for at the moment. For the first time party night looked to me like a raging pack of animals feasting on each other's hopes.

"No. I gotta go." I pushed my way through the crowd of people getting high and drunk to my room.

"Get out!" a guy shouted from my bed at the same time an empty can hit the door as I was closing it. A female giggle followed.

"Gina!" I shouted. I scanned the sardined bodies for her, finally glimpsing a bob of red curls from the kitchen.

"Gina!"

"What?"

"Get those guys out of my room."

"You get 'em out."

"Gina, please. I just can't deal with it right now." The smell and the music and the noise were making me dizzy, and tears sprang from my eyes. "I just can't. I'm so sick. I need to sleep. Please, Gina."

"I'm so tired of hearing how sick you are!"

"Please, Gina, don't start. I've had such a bad day. I lost my job and my insurance. I really need some rest. Please." I was begging. Something I'd never done and couldn't even muster the shame to care.

"You lost your job?" Her face flamed to the same shade as her hair. "How do you expect to pay rent, which incidentally is due tomorrow?"

"I'll get another job."

"How? You've got a criminal record. Who's gonna hire you?"

I gaped at her. "How dare you throw that at me? It was your stupid idea!"

"Yeah, well, no one knows that except you, and I don't care what you know anymore."

"Gina, I—"

"Get out!" she shouted. "I don't want a roommate, and I don't need a freeloader. I want you out, tonight!"

"Where will I go?" I whispered desperately, angry with myself for not seeing it coming. She'd hinted at it a dozen times over the few weeks. Now I had handed her an excuse to get rid of me.

"Why would I care? Anywhere I don't have to listen to you whining and crying to Chris about your stupid kid."

That was more than I could take. I drew back my open hand and smacked Gina across the face.

She cursed and slapped me back. I was about to take another swing at her when someone grabbed my arm from behind and dragged me away.

"Yeah! Get that piece of trash out of here!" Gina shouted, holding her cheek.

I wasn't set up right onto my feet until we were outside breathing clean air again. I spun to see who had hold of me. "Chris!" There was no reason for surprise. Who else would it be?

"Let's go to my place, Cue," he suggested softly. I was too tired and battered from the day's happenings to argue. I got in my car and followed him to Cambridge.

"You can sleep in my bed." He led me to his room.

"I can't, you know I—"

"I'll sleep on the couch," he interrupted over my protest.

"Thank you." I slid into the covers without getting undressed, grateful for the soft pillow beneath my head. "Thank you."

I don't know how long he stood there watching me, but I was truly glad to slip into unconsciousness.

13

So I HAVE NOTHING LEFT—no job, no place to live, no insurance, no money, and I swear, Chris, if ever I were going to do a jackknife off a bridge, now would be that time."

He made me toast and poured me a glass of milk for breakfast and then listened patiently for me to unfold all of yesterday to him.

"You could move in with me."

"Oh, yeah, and then what?"

"I dunno. We get married, raise the angel, live happily ever after?"

"Chris, be serious."

"I am serious."

"You're my friend. The only friend I have, but I don't want a relationship. I'm not looking for a husband or for a dad. I just want to make it through tomorrow."

He nodded, seeming to know that would be my response. "How about moving back in with your parents?"

"I can't. Doris would never take me back, and I don't want to go back. Sam always used to say that she . . ."

"That she what?" Chris prompted.

"Sam."

"Yeah, I got that part . . . Sam said . . . Sam said what?"

"Sam . . . Oh, nothing. It's stupid. I just need someone who would understand."

Chris's eyes flashed hurt and indignation. "I understand."

"I'm not saying you don't. I'm only needing some options here!" Exasperation made me snap at him.

"I'm giving you an option," he insisted.

"It's not one I can take! What, Chris? What do you want? You want me to stay here and lie to you and tell you I have all the same feelings you do? Because I can't do that! You'll be able to say a lot of bad things about me, but you'll at least know I never lied to you."

He hung his head in his hands, tugging at his long hair. Then he looked at me glumly and shook his head. "You must think I'm pathetic, following you around, always thinking maybe—"

"I don't think you're pathetic. You can't help what you feel, but I can't help what I don't, anyway . . . look . . . I gotta go now. Thanks for letting me crash here."

"Where are you going to go?"

"I'll work something out."

Once I was in my car and driving, the stupidity of that statement taunted me. *I'll work something out?* What was I thinking? How was I supposed to work anything out? I could go back . . . no. There was no going back. I drove all day until my eyes kept closing with the need to sleep. I parked on the side of the road by a cemetery, locked myself into the car, put the seat back, and slept.

Only when I woke up in the early morning, did my situation seem truly ridiculous. I would have laughed if it had been anyone else, laughed at how stupid it all was, but it was me, and somehow it just wasn't funny.

I was five months pregnant, not really fitting into my own clothes.

I was now homeless, penniless, or near enough no one would argue the topic, and I had just turned away my last friend. *This is crazy,* I thought, getting out of the car to stretch, and wandering the cemetery, looking at gravestones in the growing light. "Mr. Archibald," I said to the tombstone. "Hmmm. Died when you were forty-one. That's what I call a midlife crisis. Mind if I move in with you? Not enough room? Fine, I'll bet Mr. Adamson, three graves down will have me." I laughed at myself, laughed straight to the sky, and then sat down on Tony Archibald's grave to weep. Dead. Now that sounded like a stellar idea.

After using Mr. Archibald's tombstone as a place to have a good cry, I thought about Sam for a long time, remembering all the times we planned our escape from Doris. All the times we talked about taking care of each other forever and ever.

I stood abruptly, went to my car, and started driving, only stopping to get a ninety-nine cent value meal salad at Wendy's. I would have to eat, but eat carefully. Once the money was gone, it would be entirely gone. After a trip to the bank to empty my account of the hundred and fifty dollars it contained, I waited long enough outside Gina's place that I was certain she'd be gone to work and hurried through the apartment to gather all that was mine. Since my possessions were minimal, it didn't take too long.

She had a few nice throw pillows and a lap blanket that went over the couch. I snagged them on the way out, remembering that it had been a little cold sleeping in my car the night before. I figured the little redheaded monster owed it to me. Before locking up, I thought of the food, paid for with my money, left in the fridge and cupboards and went back for it. I took some utensils to eat with and a refill mug filled with water, and as a last minute thought grabbed the small jar filled with change from the windowsill. My money had been tied up the last month paying her bills. I figured she owed me more than the little bit I took from her.

Then I started driving west, stopping once to eat and to refuel the car in the late afternoon and to take a short nap. I got tired easily, and driving long distances sucked the energy out of me. But I was on the road again in less than an hour.

The air conditioner went out just after entering Pennsylvania, and I had to drive with the windows down, enduring the heat and humidity that blew in off the freeway. I ate a cracker to stave off the nausea.

I drove until midnight, then pulled off at a rest stop near Erie, Pennsylvania. After locking the doors and pulling the lap blanket around me, I slept fitfully, anxiously waiting for dawn. All the urban legends of murders at rest stops made every rustle of the trees or dog bark seem like immanent doom. I closed my eyes and begged for sleep.

I finally fell soundly asleep, until just before dawn when the wind blew hard, buffeting my little car, rocking it as though someone were pushing against it. My eyes flew open, and I frantically searched all the windows, certain the ugly face of a toothless, deranged madman would appear in one of them.

After raising the seat back into the upright position, I sat for a time in the growing light, then stared at my reflection in the rearview mirror. Was this rock bottom? Was this how homeless people started out? My face looked sallow in the frame of lifeless black hair hanging around it. My brown eyes looked dead. How had I ended up here?

A shadow passed by the passenger side window and a loud scratch slid along the top of the car. My heart pounding, I looked to see the cause of the noise. I closed my eyes in relief. A tree branch. It was nothing more than a tree branch swaying in the wind. Taking a slow breath to steady my heartbeat, I looked at my watch. It was 5:30 A.M. At least

I'd had a few hours of sleep. Putting the car in drive and continuing would be better than staying and jumping at shadows.

The sun rose sometime after entering Ohio. I turned off the heater and unrolled my window a little to let in the morning air.

Things felt better after the sun had come up, like everything was going okay. Sure things were a little bad, but I hadn't turned to alcohol, at least not yet, and that was good. I patted my belly gently. The baby keeping me sick had been like a forced AA and now that I was really sober, I was glad for the clarity of mind that came with it. The sun burned with the promise of good things as I sang along to the music from the CD player. Lake Erie stretched out from the coast line at the parts where it was visible from the Interstate. I pulled over and studied an atlas of the U.S. to see if there were a road that followed the coast-line so the view could be enjoyed for as long as possible. Finding a route that would do that, I veered off onto Highway 6. At a place where the road bridged over the water, I pulled over at a rest stop and used the rest room to wash up before eating a quick lunch from the remnants of food plundered from Gina's house. The food settled my stomach, and I felt better for a time.

It was only a few short hours after that that the day went from promising to sour. The car started to slow down in Oregon, Ohio, and as I searched the dashboard instruments for some indication of why it would slow down even though my foot was still held firmly to the accel-erator, a cloud of smoke appeared in the rearview mirror.

"No!" I shouted, scanning the dash more fervently, and there it was: the temperature gauge read way past the "it's too hot, turn off the car" mark. The engine sputtered and died as I pulled onto the off-ramp. Luckily, the off-ramp sloped downward, and I was able to coast into a service station on the corner. Blue smoke billowed around the car, making it nearly invisible to anyone outside the vehicle. I cursed and bailed before the thing exploded.

"What can I do for you?" the plain-faced, narrow-shaped woman behind the counter asked.

"My car broke down."

"Oh, honey, I'm so sorry." She didn't look directly at me, but I knew she had taken notice of my black hair with the blue braid and the star-shaped stud in my nose. "Can we call someone for you? Maybe a tow truck?"

After a long debate over what needed to be done, she called her brother to use a chain to pull me to a repair shop.

I sat on an orange, vinyl-covered chair that wobbled precariously if I put too much weight on the left side and waited. After a while, Creighton, the repair shop owner, came in from the garage.

"Engine head is cracked," he said. "Cylinder seized."

"Cracked? Seized?" Though I knew nothing about cars, those words sounded very bad.

"Yep." He ran his hand under his nose and sniffed. "You ran it without coolant."

I grimaced at him. "What does that mean?"

"Means you need a new engine head."

"How much would that cost?"

He whipped out a calculator and his blackened, oily fingers punched the buttons deftly. "One thousand, one hundred and eighty-seven dollars."

"Twelve hundred dollars? Please say you're joking!"

"Nope and that's actually a good deal I'm giving you. I have to order it in and it usually takes a day or two to get parts like that."

That did it. I burst into sobs. It was over. There was nothing left in the entire world for me. I had the eighty-seven dollars and forty-two cents left in my pocket and a few odds and ends that wouldn't raise five bucks at a flea market.

"Do you know anyone that could wire you money?" Creighton asked, looking uncomfortable.

"No," I blubbered. I had considered for a fleeting moment calling my dad and begging for help. But this was his fault, too. If he had ever stood up for us or tried to really protect Sam and me in some way, I wouldn't be on a highway with a busted-down car. Thinking about it made me furious.

"Don't you have any family?" Creighton probed.

"I don't have anyone." The admission felt as bleak as it sounded. I really *didn't* have anyone. If I called my dad and asked for money, Doris would find out. She'd find out and make him miserable for it.

"I'll be back in a minute," Creighton said. He went back into the garage area.

I sat there hopelessly. Things would have been better if I were dead. I numbly wondered about the pills that could be combined to take me to death painlessly. If only I had died in the car wreck. Things would have been better then. It seemed ironic that only a short while ago I was glad to be sober when all I wanted now was to be drunk.

"Hey," Creighton's voice called out. I looked up but couldn't respond to him. "You say you want to get to Utah?"

"Yeah, Utah," I whispered.

"I can make you a deal," Creighton said. He waited for me to respond but continued when I didn't. "I'll give you two hundred and fifty dollars for your car as it is."

"And how will that help me? That isn't enough for a plane ticket." I knew I should have shown some gratitude. The car was garbage when I bought it. But his offer couldn't help me.

"No, but it'll be enough for a bus ticket and leave you a little for food."

"I can't take the bus across country!" I insisted.

"Suit yourself, but it's something to think about." He wandered off, leaving me alone on the orange plastic chair.

I thought about it. Once in Utah, I would be able to find a job, one that offered insurance. Sam would be able to help me. He was a supervisor over some computer corporation. The car was no good to me like it was. But the bus? People like me didn't take the bus!

What did people like me do? And what was so different between riding a bus to get around New England and riding one to get around the country?

I found Creighton lying on a dolly under a car with just his feet sticking out. "Okay, it's a deal," I agreed.

"Good." He slid out and pulled money out of his till. We squabbled over the CD player that I had foolishly spent too much money on. Finally, I ended up with a used Walkman tape player with a small collection of tapes, an old foot locker to put my things in for the bus ride, and a ride to the Greyhound station in Toledo in trade for my CD player.

Creighton dropped me off at the bus station, where I found I had a two-hour wait for a bus to arrive.

THE ONLY VACANT SEAT WAS RIGHT BEHIND the bus driver. I had wanted to avoid sitting there, but it was that or wedge in amongst the unwashed masses on the back seat. It was a double seat, and at least there was no one sitting next to me. I went through the limited selection of tapes Creighton had given me and popped one into the tape player. Simon and Garfunkel. It wasn't something any normal person would listen to, but I put it on anyway and waited for the bus to lurch forward.

America flew past. Ohio was green but not like New England. It was lighter in color and spread farther out. There were great expanses of fields where there were few or no trees. It wasn't like I'd never traveled before; I had just never left the East Coast before. We went for little trips with my mom's friends every year to Martha's Vineyard and to Marble Head to stay in the cottage my mom bought one year in one of her "keeping up with the Joneses" frenzies.

I had also gone to Manhattan with my friends at least twice a year, where the dance clubs were loud and the parties plentiful. But my previous travels hadn't prepared me for what I was experiencing now. The farther west the bus took me, the more innocent and "amber waves of grain" our country looked. I softened toward my music selection as the bus lumbered onward. The song, "Homeward Bound," seemed to fit me. Massachusetts had never really felt like home, and I began to think that in Utah there might be a chance to find that version of home I had always longed for.

More of America flew past. I pulled out my pamphlets and read about pregnancy and nutrition. Even though I knew it would make me sick, I was craving a cigarette. I *needed one,* even just to hold it for a little while. But in my hurry to get out of town and in my newfound poverty, there had been no chance to get one.

At the next rest stop, I bought a prepackaged turkey sandwich out of the vending machine and a small container of applesauce. With that purchase went the last of my money. It would have to do, but when I'd finished eating it, it seemed to only add to the hunger. But the thirteen cents left in my pocket wasn't enough to buy an ice cube. Four states to go, and I would be in Utah. Less than two thousand miles and there would hopefully be a meal and a bed with clean sheets and warm blankets. Hopefully. But there was also a chance that Sam might shut the door in my face.

The rocking of the bus and the droning of the tires finally lulled me into sleep.

I startled awake. It was later evening, maybe seven or eight. I stretched and looked out to the setting sun to try to determine the time. "Well, good morning," a deep male voice said. "I was beginning to think you were never gonna wake up."

I had managed the entire trip so far without having to sit next to someone, and I stared in disbelief at this football jock in a polo pullover.

"Could you sit somewhere else?" I mumbled irritably.

He blinked, looked behind him, and then grinned mischievously. "Nope, sorry. You're stuck with me. The bus is full."

I whirled to stare behind me. It really was full. I felt sick and suddenly extremely claustrophobic. "Great," I hissed between my teeth.

"My name is Rion Evans."

"Good for you."

"And your name is . . ."

"Don't bug me."

"Nice name. Your parents must have a good sense of humor. When most parents say 'Don't bug me,' to their kids, they're sending them away; when yours say it, they're calling you to dinner."

I turned to glare at him through slitted eyes. "Do you think you're funny?"

He cleared his throat. "Apparently you don't."

"Brilliant. Bravo. Now, seriously, don't bug me."

"You got it."

I sat up straight. "Unless . . . you don't happen to have a cigarette I could bum off you, do you?"

It was his turn to give me a slitted-eye look. "I don't smoke," he declared.

"That figures." I slouched back in to my seat as near the window as I could get.

"You shouldn't be smoking in your condition anyway," he said.

I sat up again. "What do you mean in my 'condition'?"

"Aren't you pregnant?"

"Why would you ask that?" It seemed logical he would ask. My stomach certainly looked abnormally large compared to the rest of me. I knew I was being horrible to him and that it was wrong to be so snotty to a total stranger. But he had such a look of . . . completeness. I felt like a pair of mismatched socks next to him. Not that he had done or said anything thus far that seemed snobby, but he *looked* snobby.

"The pamphlet at your feet. *Parenting, from Conception to Birth.*

Either you're pregnant, or you stole that from a bus traveling doctor. It seemed more likely you were pregnant. Am I wrong?" He was tactful in not mentioning my rounded midsection.

"Mind your own business, Rodney!" I snapped, annoyed that he was tactful, and annoyed really that he was there at all.

"My name's not—"

"As if I care!"

He sighed and thankfully went quiet.

I fumed as I picked up my pamphlets and stuffed them in my bag. I snapped the headphones over my ears.

The tape player clicked but wouldn't turn on. Frowning, I tapped it with my hand and tried pushing play again. Nothing. Where were Simon and Garfunkel when you really needed them?

"The batteries are probably dead," Polo said.

"Ya think!"

The corner of his mouth twitched up. He thought this was funny! "Looks like you're stuck talking to me."

"Not necessarily, Roger. I prefer silence. It's restful."

"You don't strike me as the type that enjoys silence."

"Look, you don't have a clue about me." I turned away. He stared past me at the window, remaining quiet for a blessed moment; it wasn't much longer than that.

"Did you know tumbleweeds migrated to North America?"

I grunted in disbelief. "What did you do? Memorize a Trivial Pursuit game to try to make yourself interesting?"

He stiffened. "You could probably be a nice person if you didn't hide behind such a bad attitude."

"Listen up, Ron, you have no idea what I've been through."

"You're right. I don't. Look, how about we start over? My name is Rion, like the constellation Orion, but without the O."

I burst out laughing. "That's the dumbest thing I've ever heard."

"It's not dumb," he defended. "My dad teaches astrophysics in college and my mom designs lenses for telescopes. My sister's name is Cassiopeia. We just call her Cassie, and I have—"

"How sweet," I said dryly. "Is your dog named Pluto? And wait! You've got an older brother named Big Dipper, of course I guess they could have saved that one for you."

"So what's your name? Insufficient Self-Image to Be Polite?"

I grimaced, realizing that I had crossed the line and uncertain where this hostility toward him had come from. I was just trying to defend myself, but it came off as ruder than I had intended. "Look here, O-Rion, I have had the worst four months of my life, and it has all culminated in this one truly wicked awful day. And my self-image is just fine, thanks. My name is Suzanna; my friends call me Cue. So there, we're now clear on what to call each other, should we be inspired to do so."

"So where you headed, Suzanna?"

"Utah."

"Really? Me, too."

"Oh, goody, and I was so afraid you'd be getting off at the next stop."

He smiled, the corners of his hazel eyes crinkling in a way I tried not to notice. "What's in Utah?"

"My brother."

"I'm headed there too, going to school, and getting a job."

"Oh, and let me guess . . . you're a Mormon."

"I am actually."

"Typical," I muttered.

"What's typical?"

"You don't smoke; you're wearing a preppy little Ralph Lauren shirt, headed to Utah with your Disneyland haircut. All you're missing is the sign that says, 'I'm a Mormon, want to go to church with me?'"

"Is that a bad thing in your opinion?"

"I have no opinion. My brother's a Mormon, too."

"Oh, and let me guess . . . you're not."

"You got it."

"Typical," he smirked.

I couldn't help but smile at that. It was the first genuine smile I had offered Rion. "And why is that typical?"

"Black leather jacket with silver studs, nose pierce, black hair, tattoo on your ankle, prissy little eastern accent complete with cynicism and sarcasm. With all that black you look like you're doing an audition for an Anne Rice movie."

I laughed at him. It was refreshing to find someone who could step up to the plate and banter with me. "Hmm, sounds like me."

"So why'd you get the nose pierce?"

"I was drunk."

He laughed. "There's a good reason."

"Is this a confessional?" I couldn't help but smile at him. His open, honest face almost made me want to talk to him. What I had taken for snobbishness a few moments before was apparently nothing more than self-confidence.

"Have you ever been drunk, O-Rion?"

"A few times, when I was young and dumb. Then I realized I was an idiot and went and told my dad and we took care of it."

I snorted at him. "Took care of it? How do you take care of that? Take the bottle out and shoot it?"

"I repented and didn't do it any more."

"Corny."

"Is it?"

"Oh, yeah."

"Everyone's entitled to their opinion."

I had no response to that and stared out the window, hoping he was done with chit-chat for a while.

He wasn't. "So what are you going to do in Utah?"

"Work, live, breathe."

"I'm going to school."

"You already said that, and getting a job, too."

"I didn't think you were listening."

"You make it very hard to ignore you, and believe me, it's not like I wasn't trying."

"Sarcasm again? I thought we were past that." He had an edge to his voice that sounded not exactly offended but unwilling to take banter to rudeness.

I let out a deep breath. "I'm sorry. I have no reason to be such a jerk to you. I don't have a good excuse, really. It isn't your fault. My life just bites, that's all."

"Does it?"

"Like a rabid dog."

"I'm sorry," Rion said, his hazel eyes softening in sympathy. "Anything I can do to help?"

I laughed. "You're kidding. We're on a bus; it isn't like I can send you out on errands for life improvement."

"Maybe not. But I can listen if you want to talk."

"I'll let you know if I need to." The baby kicked me hard. I grimaced, shifted, and mumbled, "I need a little rest."

"You okay?"

"Fine. Stellar. Just need some rest." I did my best to roll to my side and face the window. I must have fallen asleep, and by the way my muscles ached from the position I was in, I must have slept a long time.

chapter
15

"MORNING, AGAIN." O-RION CHIRPED. "You sleep a lot, you know that?"

I winced while stretching. "And you don't sleep at all."

"I got a little bit of a nap in."

I rolled my eyes. "Neat-o . . . where are we?"

"Nebraska, somewhere."

"Where did you get on? Where are you from?"

"Davenport, Iowa. How about you?"

"Massachusetts, Northboro."

"Nice."

"So are you a corn farmer?"

He laughed. "No. I am a programmer or at least I will be if I ever graduate."

"Ah, I see; a computer nerd."

"What do you do?"

"I gratefully have no skills. No one expects anything from people who can't do anything."

"You must have something you can do. Hobbies, things you like, something."

I considered that. "I love to read. I love the ocean. I like swimming

90

and boating. But those aren't exactly skills are they? So I'm hoping my brother will help me get a job."

"What does he do?"

"He's a director over some computerized task force management corporation or something."

"Ah. Think he could get me a job, too?"

"It's more likely he'd want to give you a job over me."

"But you're his sister."

"I am the graffiti that mars the beauty of our family tree." I almost added the words: *at least that is what Doris said,* but stopped myself. No one could understand Doris, and I wasn't in the mood to try to explain her.

He laughed outright. "You're not all that bad."

"You don't know me very well."

"Can I ask a personal question?"

"Is there any way to stop you?"

"What about the dad?" He pointed to my stomach.

"There is no dad," I grunted.

"Uh, that's physically impossible." He said it warmly, with the touch of concern that made it seem like he cared instead of just being nosy, and for a moment a wall crumbled, and I ended up telling him everything about how I found myself on my way to Utah, from the moment I found out I was pregnant after the car wreck to the moment he found me sleeping. I waited, expecting judgment from him that I was expecting a baby from an unknown father after living what he would consider a life of debauchery and sin. I was surprised to find instead understanding and sympathy.

"So aren't you going to preach me a sermon?" I asked.

"A sermon? Guess I could. What kind of sermon do you want?"

"I just figured a little Mormon boy would have something to say about the trail of evil that follows me."

"I do have something to say: No man treads so far into darkness that he cannot return to the light."

I blinked at him, confused by that statement. After thinking about it for a few minutes I asked, "But could he stand being in the light after so much time in the dark?"

He smiled. "Suzanna . . . I think you'd be able to handle it."

His steady gaze made me look away. "So did you go on a mission?" I asked, changing the subject.

"You know about missions?"

"My brother went."

"I went to France."

"I know some French, but you'd blush if I repeated it to you." I said.

"Then you better not repeat it," he said.

"I dunno, might be kind of fun to make you blush."

"So your brother was a missionary?"

"Yep. Sam does everything he's supposed to so that one day his God will call him home," I said, overdramatically.

"Where'd he serve?"

"How would I know? Nigeria, Cuba, Czechoslovakia . . . I have no idea."

"You know each one of those places you named is in a different part of the world?"

"So?"

"You really don't know?"

Shrugging, I finally said, "Japan."

He whistled softly, "Wow, tough language."

"Oh, believe me, my brother's halo is so shiny, mountains move aside simply because he says 'please.' A little language would never get in his way."

"He sounds like a great guy." Rion pulled a pack of crackers out of his bag and started eating them. The twinge in my stomach that was hunger became an ache. The baby rolled like an ocean wave along with the grumblings from my stomach. I looked away.

"He's all right. He was a little more normal before he got baptized, but he seems happy. I'm glad he's happy."

The bus rolled into a city—Grand Island, Nebraska. The driver announced the amenities available at the station, and as I got out to stretch, the smells from the snack bar sang to me. I ignored the taunting scents and headed to the rest room. I washed my face, brushed my teeth, and raked a comb through my hair.

I needed a drink and a sandwich and some chips, and a steak, and some pizza and . . . twelve hundred miles to a meal. I could make it. It was less than twenty-four hours away. I wondered what skipping meals would do to the baby.

I went for a walk far away enough from the station that the smell of the snack bar could no longer plague my nostrils. There was a mostly eaten ham sandwich lying in the gutter. If my stomach were rumbling any louder, I might have considered eating it. The walk back to the station seemed like forever. I got on the bus well before the final call and stared miserably out the window.

"Didn't you get anything to eat?" Rion asked, settling in next to me. He stretched out his long legs after pulling off his Doc Martin dress shoes. His toes wiggled with freedom under khaki socks.

"I'm not hungry," I said, the lie snarling from within my gut.

"Really? It's been a whole day and you haven't even snacked on anything," he persisted.

"I'm fine!"

"If you say so." He shrugged.

The driver was standing outside my window shaking his head at some guy who was pointing at a woman with three small children. He finally agreed to whatever they were arguing about and climbed aboard. I waited. He didn't pull out. Instead the small family climbed on. Where were they going to sit? I wondered. The bus was entirely full with not one seat left over. The woman sat on the top stair by the doors and cradled the smallest child in her lap. The other two squeezed in beside her on the floor. The driver muttered to himself and closed the doors, sending the bus lurching forward.

After a few minutes, Rion tilted his head to the small girl clutching a tattered old Tigger stuffed animal. She had shifted and squirmed a lot on the floor trying to get comfortable. "Hey, there," he said. "Want to sit with us?"

My mouth dropped in disbelief. There was hardly three inches between us, and he wanted to squeeze a kid into that spot?

She smiled and nodded. The mother gave a tired but grateful nod of approval. The girl climbed over and sat mostly on Rion's lap, but partially on mine, too. I shifted to keep her off my belly.

"What's your name?" Rion asked our newest companion.

She ducked her straggly blond head without an answer.

From nowhere Rion produced a Tootsie Roll. "Will you trade me your name for this?" he asked, waving it in front of her.

It took every ounce of energy for me to not snatch it from his fingers, unwrap it, and pop it into my own mouth.

"Joyce," the small voice said finally, twisting a light blond strand of hair into a dirty fist. The other hand shot out and took the Tootsie Roll. She chewed with her mouth open, smacking her lips, and sending a wave of nausea over me. I turned to the window, ignoring the grumble from my stomach.

"Joyce is a nice name," Rion said. "My name is Rion."

Her body bounced slightly with the movement of a nod.

"Where are you going, Joyce?"

"To see my gran-ma. She lives in Col-rado."

"That sounds like fun. You gonna meet your dad there?"

I rolled my eyes at the most insensitive thing I'd ever heard asked. "I don't got a dad," the tiny voice responded.

Rion hesitated at her response for a moment before finally saying, "Well, you have a father, everyone has a father."

I elbowed him to shut up. The world didn't work that way. Some people didn't have two parents, and it was naïve to think they all did. He ignored my elbow.

"You have a Heavenly Father. Did you know that, Joyce?"

I snorted. It was the dumbest thing I had ever heard.

"Who's that?" the tiny voice asked.

"Heavenly Father is God, and he loves all of us."

"All of us?"

"Yep, and he knows us all very well."

"Does he know me?"

"Yes, he does."

"Does he love me?"

"He loves you very much, Joyce."

"Oh, please, Rion—" I turned to reprimand him for filling her with fairy tales, but when I caught his eye, I couldn't say anything. His square jaw was set, resolute and challenging, daring me to refute him.

Fine, I thought. *Let him live in his fantasy.* I glanced to Joyce. Let her live there, too. After all, if it helped her to get through another day, what would that hurt?

And I had to admit, sometimes the absence of a parent is better than having one. If only I'd had a make-believe Heavenly Mother.

Maybe growing up wouldn't have been so bad. As it was, I had Doris and the passive figure called my dad. It was the same thing as not having any parents at all . . . maybe worse. Joyce might be luckier than I had been.

Rion gave the child another Tootsie Roll. She yawned while chewing and nestled further into Rion's lap, leaning her head against his arm. He started singing very softly. I had to strain to hear him. "I am a child of God . . ." his voice lilted. I knew the song. Sam used to sing it, especially after his mission. It was a comforting lullaby sort of song. It was one I had enjoyed hearing Sam sing. I even knew the words.

When Rion was done, Joyce lifted her head and slid a grimy hand around his neck. He didn't flinch away as I likely would have. "Sing me more," she said. He looked around to make certain he wasn't disturbing anyone and started again. I hummed softly along with him, to which he glanced up in surprise. He kept on singing, smiling at me as he did so. He sang all verses, both in English and French many times over before she finally started to breathe deeply and fell asleep in his arms.

"You have a nice voice," I said. "For a guy."

"Thanks. You have a nice voice, too. Only problem with her going to sleep is my arm did too." He tried to adjust her enough to let the blood flow back to his arm.

Joyce woke up and asked if she could give her sister and brother a candy. I watched in envy as three more appeared in Rion's hand and were doled out to Joyce and the others. And then a fourth appeared.

"Want one?" He held it out to me.

For a moment, pride nearly made me say no, but "yes" came out instead. I took it with gratitude, greedily ripping the paper and popping it into my mouth.

In Denver when Joyce and her family got off, Rion did, too. I went for another walk, and when I got back to the bus, Rion was waiting.

"You still haven't eaten," he accused.

"What's it to you?"

"You're pregnant. You should be taking better care of yourself."

"Who died and made you the surgeon general?"

Rather than answer, he shoved a brown sack at me.

"What's this?"

He didn't answer, just flipped open a black leather Bible of sorts and ignored me.

I peeked into the bag—a sandwich from the vending machine, a fruit cup, a can of orange juice, and an apple. My hands shook with excitement. I took two big gulps of air and dropped the bag on his open book.

"I can't take this," I said.

"This isn't open for argument," he said, dropping the bag back into my lap.

"I'm not some charity case," I insisted. "I'm not like that little girl and her family."

He got nose to nose with me. "Look, Suzanna, you will either eat that without help, or I will personally stuff every bite down your prissy, prideful, eastern throat."

"Fine!" I hissed, holding the bag a few seconds longer before opening it and then trying to eat slowly. But each bite made me that much hungrier for the next.

The apple was saved for last. I ate it to the core and around every seed. It was like pouring energy into me. When the meal was finally vanished to my stomach, I stared out the window, uncomfortable in trying to find the courage to say thank you. Gratitude was a new emotion to me. There had never been much reason for it in my life. If anything good happened to me, it was because I made it happen. "Thank you."

The whisper was hoarse and inaudible. I cleared my throat and tried again to make myself heard. "Thank you. I really appreciate it."

He waved it away as nothing. "So tell me more about what your brother does."

"I really don't know. He just works helping companies be more efficient. He travels around a lot from what I've heard."

"I wonder if he needs an IT guy." Rion then droned on about computers and designing Web sites and ram and bytes for another hundred miles. I didn't try to pretend to care, but it didn't stop him.

"So what are your plans?" he asked.

"Haven't we been through this?"

"I mean with the baby."

"I don't know. Maybe Sam will keep it. He's married, has a steady life."

"Could you really give up your own child?"

"Why not? I almost killed it." I said it to shock him, which it did, but he quickly recovered.

"But you already told me you couldn't go through with that. Who's to say you could go through with giving it away?"

"Maybe I won't. I don't know what I'm going to do."

"Could you raise it alone?"

"I don't know. Any other nosy questions, or are you done?"

"I'm just intrigued. I've never been in a situation like yours."

"Being that you're a guy, O-Rion, you aren't likely to ever be in my situation."

He grinned. "I know that; I'm just curious what I'd do."

"Be grateful it isn't a decision you'll ever have to make." I rubbed my temples. "I need a beer," I muttered.

He arched a brow at me.

"Be quiet, O-Constellation. I'm not going to *have* a beer, but there isn't any crime in me *wanting* one."

He shook his head at that.

"You need to lighten up, O-Rion."

"I'm already lit-up, Suzanna."

We stared each other down before I finally broke away to hide my smile. He was as stubborn as I was. That was a likeable trait in him. Trying to avoid his eyes, I found the window to be the only direction to look. We were in Utah now. Red rock and sage lined the landscape; every now and again a lone Joshua tree appeared and vanished in the roadside blur of movement.

It seemed barren earth covered the land. I felt a sense of panic. In Massachusetts, you never saw dirt. It was all grown over by shrubbery and trees. Massachusetts encouraged lush growth; it seemed Utah killed growth, stamped it out by the harshness of the environment. It looked to me like the only things that survived in this desert had thorns. Would I survive or would I get stamped out? Were my thorns sharpened to the needle precision it would take to fight whatever this place had in store? I shuddered. There was no way to know.

In Provo, the trip finally came to the end. I felt grungy—tired and stiff—desperately wanting a bath, a bed, and more food. My backside was numb from sitting so long. "Well, O-Constellation, guess this is it."

"Good luck to you, Suzanna." He stuck his hand out. I arched a brow and gave him mine. "Maybe we'll meet up again someday."

"You must be a glutton for punishment," I said.

He smiled, the crinkles in the corners of his eyes deepening with amusement. "Nah. I really enjoyed sitting by you."

"Sure you did." I stumbled back from him, trying not to notice those crinkles and the warmth that came from his expression. "Bye, O-Rion."

"Bye, Suzanna."

I turned and hurried away to the phone booths lined against the wall, fumbling in my pocket to find the folded up paper with Sam's address. I scanned it quickly and my heart skidded to a stop. No phone number. It was now impossible to call Sam for a ride. I didn't even have enough money to call information for his number, since the plan had been to call him collect. I had no money for cab fare and it wasn't like I could just . . .

"Rion!" I shouted as loud as lungs allowed to get his attention. He didn't turn. I abandoned my trunk and ran after him. "Rion!" He turned a corner and disappeared. My legs pounded harder to catch him as I turned the corner and screamed out one last, "Rion!" and then halted, wishing I could call the yell back into my throat.

He had been joined by a very pretty brunette. She fixed his collar and rumpled his hair, and he turned then to see me. There was nowhere to hide. I was standing out in the open. Rion said something to the girl and jogged over to me. "What's wrong?"

"Nothing, just, I was wondering, hoping actually, that you had access to a car and . . ."

"Sure. I'd be glad to give you a ride. Just give me a second." He went back to the girl, and they put their heads together to deliberate.

He came back and glanced around. "So, where's your stuff?"

I led him back to the phones where I'd left the trunk. He waved me aside when I tried to lift it and carried it to the car.

"Suzanna, this is Cassie."

"Oh! Your sister." I felt a little dumb for automatically assuming they were boyfriend–girlfriend, and seeing them together, the family resemblance was obvious. Both had the same dark hair, his was just shorter, and when they smiled, the crinkles at the corners of their eyes were similar. Both of them had hazel eyes with gold flecked through the swirls of brown and green.

I gave the address to Cassie and then sat back and listened to Rion and his sister banter good-naturedly during the ride to Alpine where my brother had built a new home. There was no need for me to talk, and I had other things to think about. I needed a speech that would convince Sam to take me in.

After driving around a little, we found the address, and Rion helped me to the door, and though I waited for him to leave, he seemed determined to stay with me until someone answered.

"Look, Rion, I really am grateful for the lift, and I swear I'll give your name to my brother for job consideration, but I need to do this alone."

"You're asking me to leave?"

"No . . . more like begging."

"Doesn't your brother know you're coming?"

"It's kind of a surprise."

"Well, Suzanna, if he isn't happy with the surprise, let me know. You've got my number. I'll find someone who needs a roommate, okay?"

"Don't worry, O-Rion, Sam always does the right thing. And, Rion, sincerely, you've been a lifesaver to me."

He grinned and jogged back to the car. I paced the porch as they drove off, then sat on my trunk for a while. What was I going to say? Sam was likely still bothered by what took place at his wedding, though it hadn't entirely been my fault. I stood up to pace some more, and somewhere among all the pacing my finger hit the doorbell button.

It shouldn't have been so unexpected, but it was. When the door opened, April was standing there. She had a phone in her hand that slipped when she saw me, and she had to fumble to catch it. "I'll call you back," she whispered hoarsely into it, her eyes wide and her mouth hanging open in shock.

"Hey, Ape," I greeted, "I thought I'd come for a visit." I hurried past her knowing she was too surprised to stop me, and I didn't want to give her the chance to shut me out.

She followed me in and when she finally found her voice, sputtered, "What are you doing here?"

"I came to visit," I repeated.

She peeked out the window to the trunk out on the porch. "For how long?" I figured she said it more to herself than to me and didn't bother to respond.

"Nice place, Ape." I whistled, walking further into the entry hall. It actually looked a lot like her mom's place in Northboro to me. A large oak staircase going up, a big kitchen off to the side, and down three steps was a huge family room with all the togs of adult entertainment: DVD player, big screen projection TV, and shelves filled with books and DVDs. Apparently, Sam was doing okay for himself. I was going to like it here.

After simply staring at me, April started muttering like she was counting or something. "Unbelievable!" She belted finally.

"What's unbelievable, Ape?"

"You show up unannounced looking for a place to stay and still haven't even apologized." She folded her arms across her chest and waited.

"Well?" she prompted.

"Well, what?"

"Hello?"

"Hi?"

"Unbelievable," she repeated and walked into the kitchen, leaving me alone in the entryway. I contemplated going out and getting the trunk, but feared she might lock me out, so I followed her.

"Apologize for what?" I asked, opening the fridge.

"Are you kidding me?" She closed the fridge. I barely got my hand out in time before it smacked shut. "You ruined my wedding! You didn't show up for pictures, you ruined your gown that cost me a fortune, and then *left* without saying one word to Sam. He felt terrible. I don't think I've seen him that hurt in the entire time I've known him!"

I cringed. April seemed genuinely mad. I tried a joke to ease the tension.

"Since you didn't like the alterations, aren't you glad I didn't show up for pictures?"

She threw her arms up in the air. "Unbelievable!"

I decided it might be best to just ignore her and opened the fridge again. I got out a jug of orange juice and a bowl of strawberries before she could smack it shut on me.

"Just what do you think you're doing?"

"I'm hungry, April. It was a long trip. Do you mind? Man, you are so wicked-tense, lighten-up." I almost cursed her when I turned to face a huge portrait of Jesus looking off over a city. It hung in the open hallway, clearly visible from almost anywhere on the first floor. I frowned at it and turned away. April was on the phone again.

"Sam Quincy, please . . ."

I tried to smile at her, anything to ease the air of contention in the room, but she didn't seem to notice. I bit into a strawberry. She pulled the bowl away in exasperation. "Those are for dessert, Suzie." She said my name like it were something dreaded. I nibbled at the rest of the berry in my hand while scowling at her.

"Sam? You need to come home . . . your sister's here." Apparently that was all that needed saying because she hung up without a good-bye.

"What, no kisses into the phone and sickening innuendos? I thought you guys were newlyweds. Don't tell me the honeymoon's over?" She ignored my attempt at humor.

"How did you get here? You know, your mom's been worried," she said.

I perked up. "Doris called?"

"Well, no. It was actually your dad."

"Figures." I dropped the strawberry leaf into the sink. "Doris wouldn't worry if a terrorist had a gun to my head." It was disheartening to think it was true. Doris really didn't care, and April didn't seem to feel much differently. She was too surprised by my arrival to pretend to be pleasant about it. I felt bad. It was my own fault April felt hostile toward me. And knowing she felt that way made me react the only way I knew how. I was hostile, too.

"I'm sure she worries—" April tried to say.

"Oh, yeah, she's the angel of mothers. Just perfect. Last I heard they were planning on naming her 'Mother of the Year.' Seriously, April, what would you know about it?" I was mad. "Don't try and give me a pep talk about how much she cares when you have no idea what she's really like."

She tucked a blonde strand of hair behind her ear, not letting go of the phone. She held it between us as though it were a weapon to ward me off.

"What happened to you anyway?" I asked. I knew it was wrong to be curt with her, but it was more than I could stand to see her jump to Doris's defense.

"What do you mean?"

"You used to be cool, now you're . . ." I tsked. "Well, just look at you!"

"Sometimes people grow up," she narrowed her eyes at me, "and sometimes people don't."

I hated having April criticize me. It was like having Doris scrutinizing me. My stomach tightened; the baby moved and kicked in protest. I bit my lip to keep from doubling over. We stood there, staring without blinking at each other until Sam came in.

"Suzie!" he boomed, sounding just like Dad. I turned my glare to him, ready for the reprimand and whatever else he had for me. But I wasn't ready for his eyes soft and moist from fresh tears. He threw his arms around me.

"We were so worried," he said, his voice cracking. April's face mirrored my own surprise. "When Dad called and said no one knew where you were, I thought the worst." He pulled away from me to inspect me. "Are you okay? How did you get here?"

I stared at him, shock giving way to exhaustion and hunger. He was still Sam, still the brother that would hug me and help me. I started to cry. "I'm okay." I blubbered. "I took the bus because my car broke down and I didn't have any money! And I haven't eaten. Doris kicked me out. Can you believe she kicked me out? I just couldn't do it, Sam, and she kicked me out for being a nicer person than she ever was. Why does she hate me? Why, Sam?" I was sobbing now. Even April, in the wake of tears and emotions flooding over me, seemed to soften. I couldn't stop crying. It was like a dam bursting free. I was finally with the only person who could understand.

Sam hugged me and smoothed my hair. "She doesn't hate you," he said. "She just doesn't feel good enough about herself to treat others right. She treats everybody like that."

"I'm sorry. I shouldn't have come here," I sniffed, "but I didn't have anywhere else to go."

"I'm glad you came," Sam said. "You're welcome to stay as long as you need to, isn't she, honey?" Sam turned to April. Her face was full of turmoil. Then she was composed as if a decision had been made.

"You can stay as long as you need to," she echoed Sam's words. "Are you hungry?" her voice had softened.

I nodded numbly and wiped my eyes on my sleeves.

"Dinner will be ready in less than an hour. Sam, Suzie has a trunk on the porch. Why don't you go get it for her and put it in the guest room."

Sam went to do as told. April glanced at my belly, a tired and sad look crossing over her face, and turned to the stove. I remained standing there, shifting uncomfortably from foot to foot, until Sam pulled on my arm to show me to the room. It was spotless; a white lace coverlet over the bed and white lace and navy blue throw pillows adorning the head of it, a white dresser and nightstand, yet another portrait of Jesus, and a framed, hand-sewn, blue and white sign that said "Families are Forever." It was very homey in a trite sort of way.

"Suzie," Sam started after placing the trunk at the foot of the bed.

"Yeah?"

"I'm glad you came, I really am."

"Thanks, Sam. I appreciate you taking me in. I really didn't have anywhere else to go." I hesitated "Would it be okay if I take a shower? I haven't washed up in almost a week."

"Oh. Sure. The bathroom is right next to your room. Towels are in the closet by the sink."

"Thanks." I kept waiting for the lecture. Sam and April knew the whole story; they had to. There was no way my dad wouldn't tell every scrap of information he had. They had to know I was going to have a baby. Even if they didn't know, there was no hiding the bulge in my midsection. But the lecture never came.

I decided to take a bath. It felt like heaven. Warmth enveloped me with only my ever-growing belly peeking out over the bubbles. The baby was moving. It seemed it was always moving when I wasn't, making it difficult to sleep. As heavenly as the bath was, I hurried so I wouldn't keep April and Sam waiting.

chapter

17

W E WERE SEATED AT THE TABLE, and I was reaching for a roll when Sam cleared his throat, "We need to say prayer first, Suzie."

"Prayer?"

"You know. Thank God for the food." Sam bowed his head.

"Why? Did he come down and help make it?" I couldn't stop myself from saying it even though everything in me knew I shouldn't.

April's bent head popped up, and I could've sworn I heard her say "unbelievable" again.

"Suzie . . ."

"No, Sam. I apologize, go ahead and pray or say grace or have Hanukah or whatever you do. I'm sorry. I didn't mean to be disrespectful."

Silence ticked by. Sam finally bowed his head again. "Our Father in Heaven . . ."

Were they going to pray at every meal? Sam thanked God I was there and that I was safe. He asked God to protect my baby and to help me through whatever I would face in the future. I rolled my eyes and tapped my foot. Absurd. That's what it was. Did he really believe some all-powerful being was personally going to insure a healthy child and prosperity for me? Absurd. But at the same time it was *nice*. It was nice that someone cared enough to ask for good things to happen to me.

"So, do you have any idea what doctor you'll see?" April asked.

"Doctor?"

"For the baby," she said.

"Oh. Not really. I—uh . . . don't have insurance. I need to get a job with benefits."

"You know, Suzie, insurance might not cover a preexisting condition. Have you considered that?" Sam poured vinegar and oil over the whole bowl of lettuce.

"I haven't really thought about it. But I was wondering . . ." I cleared my throat. "Do you think you can help me get a job?"

Sam pursed his lips and steepled his fingers against them. "What can you do?"

"I can tie a cherry stem into a knot with my tongue." I grinned at his smirk. "What do you mean what can I do? Who do you think handles all of Dad's billing and stuff? I know my way around the Internet. I can type fifty-six words per minute—no mistakes. I understand most dumb little office programs because Dad insists on buying every new thing that comes out, and if I write a letter to you to collect money, I can almost guarantee you'll send it. I can do anything I need to. Put me anywhere, and I'll get the job done."

"I'll see what I can do. It won't be easy though, considering you have a record."

"I was a minor. My record is clean unless someone is digging for information, and it isn't like I'm applying for the FBI or anything. C'mon Sam-Halo, cut me some slack."

"I'll see what I can do," he repeated. "They might have something opening up where you don't need a college degree. I'll check it out first thing tomorrow."

They talked about Sam's day, about April's calling in Young Womens, whatever that was, her job at some mortgage institution, and about the next day's responsibilities. While I was not excluded, I felt that I didn't belong, like a *Sesame Street* lesson on things that matched. *One of these things is not like the others.* April had changed, and as I watched her, I had to concede . . . she had grown up. Did that mean I hadn't? *One of these things just isn't the same.* Did I belong anywhere?

I slept in late. When I awoke, Sam and April were both already gone. A note left on the counter gave phone numbers if I needed anyone and a half-hearted suggestion to make myself comfortable. I fixed myself pancakes and ate them with a bowl of fruit as I flipped through stations on their satellite. I watched TV, napped, ate lunch, and watched more TV. It was like going to heaven. Even the baby seemed to approve as it tumbled and rolled. I poked at it with a grin.

I may have been a disappointment to my family, my friends, and all who knew me, but I was doing something right. I had made a life and let it keep living. Whatever else I had done, I could at least feel good about that.

When April came home, I heard the word "unbelievable" a few times from the kitchen. "Suzie!" She stomped down the three stairs to the family room.

I didn't respond—just looked up and waited for her to say whatever was boiling in her.

"The kitchen is a disaster," she finally spit out.

"I was going to clean it," I shrugged.

She heaved a deep sigh and stomped back up the three stairs. The water in the sink was running, dishes bumped and scraped against each other loud enough to stifle April's murmurs. I really had planned on doing the dishes and cleaning everything up. I hadn't realized she would come home so early. It wasn't even four o'clock yet. After she threw her little tantrum, storming around the kitchen, I decided it might not be a good idea to try to go in there to help.

The rest of the week stayed consistent with my first night; dinner conversations that floated around me distantly, days of fallowed bliss, followed by not-so-silent tantrums from April. I tried to clean up once, but put something in the wrong place in the dishwasher and melted a plastic bowl on the heating element. The smell had sent me into sickness that rendered me useless for the rest of the evening and left me sitting on the couch to moan. I had gotten up and was on my way to my room when I overheard April fuming as Sam cleaned out the charred plastic.

"Get her a job, please, Sam," she begged.

"Doing what, April?"

"Anything, I don't care, sorting mail, making copies, or sending faxes. I just can't handle my job all day and coming home to a disaster every night!"

It irked me that she thought I was only capable of making copies and sending faxes. It irked me that she talked about me at all.

"I'm waiting to see how some things pan out. We hired a new guy last week, and he might need a secretary; we just need to see if he works out."

"I'm serious, Sam. I know she's your sister; I know she needs help, but she doesn't do anything all day. Pregnancy is not a license to be lazy."

"Why don't you try being her friend?"

I heard April slam a cupboard closed and smack a cup onto the counter.

"What?" he asked.

"I seem to remember a time when you told me your sister was nobody's friend."

"That was before . . ." he started.

I went to my room and put the headphones to my tape player on, turning the volume as high as it would go. So he told her I was nobody's friend, huh? What did he know? I was a good friend. When we were teenagers, I had taken April in when she didn't have anybody. Granted, I fired her when she decided she was too good to party with me, but that was a long time ago. I had changed. Hadn't I? I fell asleep with Simon and Garfunkel blaring in my ears.

The phone rang. I had no idea how long it had been ringing, but it didn't show any signs of stopping. "I'm coming!" I growled, rolling over and out of bed. I picked up the cordless and wandered to the kitchen.

"What?" My head ached. I subconsciously opened the fridge to find a Corona, frowned at the milk and jug of juice, and slammed it shut again.

"Morning, Suzie, sleep well?"

"Do you need something, Halo?"

"Yes, an employee. Get down here for an interview and some tests."

"You are so lame, Sam-Halo. How do you expect me to get there, ride my broom?"

"Does it work?"

"Funny. Ha-ha."

"I'm actually sending someone to pick you up."

"Why can't you pick me up?"

"I have meetings."

I smiled. "Well, aren't you the hotshot?"

"Yes, I am. Lighten. If they hire you, you'll get benefits for the baby immediately. I checked into it."

My mood brightened. "Thanks, Sam, I appreciate it." I really did too. I had been worried about insurance. I had put off seeing a doctor entirely out of necessity. I just assumed that as long as I could feel the baby moving, everything was fine. I knew the assumption was wrong to make, but without money, there wasn't much choice. There was always that nagging fear in the back of my head that the alcohol and smoking I did before I knew I was pregnant might have stunted the baby's growth somehow, making me uncertain if I really wanted to find out something was wrong. Especially if it was because of something stupid I did.

"He'll be there any time, so be ready, okay?"

"Sure thing, with bells on."

"Suzie?"

"Halo?"

"No bells, okay?"

I laughed at him and hung up. He must have been afraid of me making a bad impression. I cleaned up, put on some makeup, and pulled my hair back, tucking the dyed blue strand into the black strands so it wasn't so visible. As I was buttoning my blouse, the doorbell rang.

I OPENED THE DOOR WITH A SMILE that dropped when I saw Rion standing there.

"What are you doing here?"

"Hey, Suzanna."

"Hey, yourself. Seriously, what are you doing here?"

"Sam sent me to pick you up."

"You're the new guy?"

He straightened his broad shoulders. I looked away, determined not to be distracted by his shoulders. "Is that not okay?" he asked.

"What? That my own flesh and blood hired a stranger before hiring me? Oh, no problem, why wouldn't it be okay?"

"Suzanna?"

"What?" I snapped.

"You should probably wear a dress."

"I don't have a dress. And the only skirt I own is short enough it would set off pacemakers if I wore it in public in Utah. Besides, I'm fat now and can't fit into it anymore. The pants are gonna have to work."

"Sam's wife probably has something . . ." he slipped past me into the house.

"Hey! You can't just come in here!"

He ignored me, tromping up the stairs to the master bedroom.

"You know, I could have you arrested for breaking and entering."

He flung open the closet doors and started sifting through hangers, pulling out a black dress with a red floral pattern. "Don't be silly; I didn't break anything, and entering isn't a crime. Here, put this on."

Without knowing why, I took the dress, muttered my way to the bathroom, and did exactly what I was told. I loosened the ties at the waist to make room for the baby. The sandals I was already wearing didn't look too bad with it.

When I exited the bathroom, Rion grinned. "Wow!"

"Don't wow. My brother would kill you if he knew you just stole one of April's dresses."

"He told me to."

"He told you to?"

"Yeah, he said if you weren't in a dress, that I should make you put one on even if I had to hog tie you to do it."

"I can't believe this! You're all tight with my brother, and I haven't even told him about you yet."

"Yeah. I figured with everything you had going on you might forget, so I got proactive. I called on my own the day after we got to Provo. They were in the midst of an IT crisis and I helped fix it while being interviewed. It's what you call being in the right place at the right time, and they hired me."

"Yippee," I said. "I'd do a back flip, but I'm pregnant."

The ride over to Sam's office was quiet, which was odd since the constellation boy had been anything but quiet up to now. We walked in together. He had to swipe a badge over a security plate to get the door to unlock and let us in. He put an arm through mine and slowed my pace to whisper in my ear. "I think you should lose the nose piece, Suzanna.

This is a pretty conservative company." He nodded toward the ladies' room, and nudged me that direction.

Again, without any reason why, I obeyed. Without the studded star, I felt naked. It was as though my identity had been stripped from me. After breathing deeply to keep from crying, there was nothing left to do but go out and get through the moment.

Rion was waiting. "Do you know what you're being interviewed for?"

I shook my head.

"You're being interviewed for the job of monitoring a new program we are implementing in several of our subsidiary companies. You would be orchestrating breaks, days off, and holidays for about two thousand people. Think you can handle that?"

I snapped my gum in his face. "I can do anything, O-Rion."

"Good. Convince them of that, and lose the gum!" He nudged me toward another door. Stepping forward, I felt like the person in a game show choosing a door. Behind the door was either a perfect prize or a pie in the face. I opened the door. A woman shook my hand and immediately pulled me to a table of paperwork.

It took nearly two hours for me to complete the paperwork and finish the tests. The woman, whose name was Sandee, went through all my test results, sifting and sorting and making me start to fidget with nervousness. There were other applicants I had passed while going from test to test. They all looked professional. There was no way I was getting this job.

"So, Suzanna," Sandee was eyeing my application, "What makes you think you would be an asset to our company?"

"Well, I'm a hard worker . . ." I began reciting other typical things you say at an interview but realized Sandee wasn't having any of it. She wasn't impressed. With all the other professionals in power suits applying, who could blame her? I needed the job enough that courage took the place of my regular apathy.

"Sandee, let me explain to you why you should hire me. You know my brother, Sam, who has an unarguably exceptional work ethic; I try hard to follow that example. But more than that, this company needs me much more than I'll ever need it. I'm innovative, a self-starter, proactive, and I thrive in the dynamics of an environment that's always changing. I'm not afraid to speak up, and you can count on me to fix what needs fixing and take accountability for everything I do. In short, Sandee, I'm exactly what you are looking for. Am I right?"

She smiled and after the clock ticked off five seconds said, "You're hired."

"Just like that?" I blinked.

"Just like that. You see, Suzanna, we're in a bit of a crunch right now and need bodies to fill spaces. I've been interviewing all day, and you are the only person to stop and take charge of the interview. It's a quality we need, someone who will take charge. So you're hired. Can you start Monday?"

And that was that. I could scarcely believe it. In my entire life, it was one of the few breaks I had ever gotten. Sandee showed me to Sam's office where I had to wait to get a ride home.

Sam's large, black leather chair swiveled and reclined. It was impossible not to want to try it out and see what it could do. I made myself so dizzy, I had to twist the other way to keep from throwing up.

"Having fun?" a deep, pleasant male voice asked.

Cursing and slamming my feet to the ground for brakes, I stood up. "Rion! You scared me!"

"Sorry . . . so, you got the job."

"No kidding."

"I was wondering if you wanted to celebrate and go to dinner with me tomorrow night."

"What? Like a date?"

"Not a date . . . more as friends." He cocked his head and grinned. "So?"

"Are you kidding me? Aren't you Mormon?"

"Yeah, I am . . . but—"

"I thought there was some rule against Mormons hanging out with pregnant girls. You might turn into a pillar of salt or grow horns or something."

"Would you rather not?"

I hesitated. "It isn't that, I mean, yeah . . . I'd be happy to."

"Happy to what?" Sam asked absently, whisking in past Rion to the desk where he dropped his leather satchel on the shiny mahogany surface.

"I have a date," I announced.

"Sure, Suzie. You haven't been here long enough to get a date." Sam didn't even look at me as he flipped through messages.

"I'm going out with Rion, Halo."

Sam's hands froze in mid flip of messages and his head lifted slowly to notice Rion standing there next to me. Confusion creased his forehead. "Rion, could you excuse us for a minute?"

For the first time, Rion was heeled, looking nervously from me to the brother who looked very much like the father.

"Sure, Sam . . . sure." He stepped backward, almost tripping, and left, closing the door behind him.

Sam waited until he could see out the glass partition that Rion was ten steps from the room before folding his arms across his chest and sitting on the corner of his desk. "I don't think I like the idea of you going out with Rion."

I folded my arms across my chest in imitation of him. "Why? Afraid he'll knock me up?"

"C'mon, Suz! Be serious a minute will you?"

"I am serious. I would've thought you'd approve of this guy," I snapped back.

"It isn't the guy I have problems with. It's just that . . ."

I ground my teeth down hard. "Oh, I get it. It's me that's the problem. You're afraid I'll taint the boy. You are such a jerk, Sam! It isn't like I plan on dragging him to a tattoo parlor and a mosh pit. Give me some credit!"

"Does he know you're pregnant?"

"Duh! Look at me! It's a little obvious!"

"I just don't think it's a good idea." He scowled.

"Like I care what you think. You didn't even congratulate me for getting the job. Anyway, he didn't really call it a date. He said he wanted to go as just friends."

Sam smiled weakly. "I'm not trying to be mean, Suzie, but you're in a delicate situation in your life right now. All I want is to see you making good choices." He scrubbed a hand over his head. "Look, as much as I'd love to, I can't sit here bantering with you. I'm meeting with the district manager in five minutes. Congratulations on getting the job. I really am proud of you for that." He patted my shoulder, pulled out a file from his desk, and hurried off.

"Nice pep talk," I muttered. Since Sam was going to a meeting, there was no reason to hang out in his office. I went to find Rion. When I caught up with him, it seemed Sam had beaten me to it. I ducked behind a rubber tree plant and listened.

"I appreciate your concern, Sam." Rion looked flushed. "Really. But I do like Suzanna. It isn't charity or a missionary effort. She's funny and pretty and stubborn. I'm not asking her to marry me; I just want to get to know her."

"And that's great to be her friend; she needs friends. I'm only concerned about her having too much on her plate right now. She's in a vulnerable situation and I just don't want—"

"To see her get hurt?" Rion finished for him.

"Yeah. Exactly."

"Well, it's like I said; I just want to be her friend. No strings."

"Just be careful. Besides it isn't a good idea to date people from work."

"Sure thing, captain." Rion looked past Sam and noticed me. "Hey, Suzanna," he said.

It was Sam's turn to look flushed. "Hey, Suz, see you later." He ducked his head and hurried off.

"So, did he change your mind?" I asked.

"No. You ready to go?" he allowed a beaten smile.

"Go where?"

"I told Sam I'd drive you home since he's going to be at least another hour and I'm off already."

"Great. Let's get out of here, then." I cast a long look back at where Sam had disappeared down the hallway. It bothered me he was being bossy about my life and butting in like that, but at the same time, it was nice. He had always looked out for me.

chapter

19

S O IS HE ALWAYS LIKE THAT?" Rion asked once in the car.

"Who?"

"Your brother."

"Yep. He's always looked out for me."

We rode in silence for a minute. "So Sandee was real impressed with you. What did you do to make her hire you?"

"Lied."

"Lied?"

"Lying is a very useful job skill."

"I somehow doubt that," he laughed. "So what was the big lie?"

"I told her I was a goddess."

Rion chuckled at that. "That isn't too big a stretch. You're the only person I've ever done a duet with on a bus of "I Am a Child of God." That's goddess status in my book."

"Now *you're* lying," I grinned.

"I never lie. Anyway, I'm glad you got the job. You'll like working there. It's a good environment."

"High praise from the man who's been there less than a week."

He ducked his head sheepishly. "Good point. So, tell me something about yourself."

"Like what?"

"Anything. What do you want out of life? Where do you want to go? How do you feel about the stars? Anything."

"What do I want out of life . . . no one has ever asked me that before. I don't think I've ever thought about it. I guess I want what everyone wants. I want to grow up and just live. I want to—" The words *love* and *be loved* stuck in my throat. It sounded ridiculous, but sitting there in his car, it was true. I changed the subject. "Let's see, and how do I feel about the stars? I think they're great considering they're nothing more than the result of the nuclear fusion of hydrogen and helium millions of light-years away."

His jaw fell. "Say that again."

"What, you figured that since I was all tattooed and everything that I had to be an airhead, too?"

"I never figured you for an airhead. Most people just don't know little tidbits like that."

"Did you know it?"

Rion smirked. "My parents named me after a constellation, remember? It isn't like I have a choice in knowing things like that."

"I learned it from *Discovery* magazine. My dad subscribes to things he never reads. I skim through them every once in a while before Doris throws them away."

"Now you really are at goddess status in my book. What else do you know?"

"I know we're home already."

He pulled into Sam's driveway. "Then I'll be asking later. I'll be by tomorrow at five. Okay?"

"Sounds like a plan."

Though Sam was not too thrilled about me going out with Rion, April was actually excited. She did a complete one-eighty with me.

Maybe she was just relieved I had a job and would be out of her hair. Either way, she fussed over going to get me some maternity clothes that she insisted on paying for. I stayed with clearance stuff, feeling uncomfortable with her spending any money on me. "So do you think he's cute?" she asked after handing the clerk her debit card.

"He . . ." I was going to lie and say he was just okay, but it seemed unkind. "He's nice to look at. But I'm not interested in him as anything like you're thinking. A guy like him is too *not* like me. Oil and water."

"Still . . ." she mused with a half smile.

"Still, nothing. He's too Mormon for someone like me."

Her smile broadened. "You know, Suzie . . . I used to say that about your brother."

"Well, you were right. Sam's too Mormon for anyone. I still wonder why you decided to hook up with him."

"Sam is the very best. The kind of guy who makes you want to be better, just by being around him. I tried not to like him, tried desperately not to love him, but sometimes things don't work out like you think they will."

"Tell me about it! You got baptized for him?"

She smiled, her eyes seeming to focus on something far away. "Actually, I got baptized for someone else. But I converted for the right reasons. I did that for me. Sam was a bonus."

When we got home, I promised to pay April back with my first paycheck. She waved me away and told me not to worry about it. She seemed pleased to have done me the favor.

It felt good to be wearing something that fit me without cutting into my middle. It was nice to know I looked normal by Utah standards, so that when Rion came to pick me up at five, I was assured I wouldn't embarrass him.

We went to an Italian restaurant. The tablecloth was made of paper, and there was a can full of crayons in the center of the table. I took a blue crayon and traced my hand on the paper, then took the red crayon and gave me painted fingernails. With a twist of a grin, Rion did his hand right next to mine so they were touching. "Look, we're holding hands." He pointed to the paper.

"Are you flirting with me, O-Rion?"

He shrugged. "I just want us to be friends."

"Why?"

"You make me laugh. And I don't really know anyone else here in Utah, aside from my sister. Anyway, you said you'd tell me more about you tonight."

I shifted in my seat. "Well, I've been thinking about that, and I don't think I should."

"Why not?"

"I don't throw eggs at people."

"Excuse me?"

"It's an analogy I heard in a high-school class once, it just means . . . We all carry around baskets of eggs, and these eggs are precious, they represent information about us, our concerns, our needs, our lives, our downfalls, everything. As we meet people and become more comfortable with them, we toss some of our eggs to these people and they, in turn, place those eggs in their baskets. But, there are times, when out of desperation, or immaturity, or whatever, we throw too many eggs at once, and the recipient can't catch them all, and a few get broken, and we then find out that this other person knows too much about us, or at least more than they wanted to know, and that then destroys the ability to truly be friends."

Rion leaned back in his chair and stared at me. "You sure aren't like other girls," he said.

"Is that good or bad?"

"I don't know yet. Jury's still out."

"Am I on trial?"

"Not like that." He tapped his straw and knife on the table like drumsticks. "I will make you this promise; I'll always catch any eggs you care to toss my way."

My eyes shifted to the slate floor tiles. That had not been the response I expected. The truth was, I was pretty certain I had already thrown too many eggs at Rion, and I was pretty certain he *had* caught them all. He was like no one I'd ever met, a fact that made me uncomfortable.

"So do you have any siblings other than your sister, Cassie?" I asked, changing the subject.

"I have a little brother on a mission in Texas and a younger sister living with an aunt in California, trying to be an actress."

"Are they named after the stars too?"

"Andromeda, we call her Anne, and Ammon, he's just Ammon."

"I've never heard of Ammon."

"He isn't a constellation. He's actually named after a hero in the Book of Mormon."

"Doesn't he feel left out?"

"I don't think so. He's pretty proud of his name."

"I hate my name." I declared.

"Why? What's wrong with it?"

"It sounds ridiculous . . . Suzanna. Do you know how many people sing, 'Oh, Suzanna, don't you cry for me' to me? I cannot tell you how annoying that is. Then there's the nickname *Suzie*. Makes me sound like an eight-year-old girl with blonde ringlets and a sucker in my mouth."

"Is that why people call you Cue?"

"Yeah. It's a good nickname. Short, undemanding, yet still cool."

He tilted his head to view my stomach. "Pretty soon someone will be calling you mom."

"Does that bother you?"

"Why would it?"

"Since you're sitting here with me, maybe people think we're married and that this kid is yours."

"Naw, that doesn't bother me."

"What if they thought we weren't married and that it was yours? Would that bother you?"

"I don't care what people think. People have opinions about everything, but until they've walked in my shoes, their opinions of me are just opinions."

I liked that he said that, and I liked the way the crinkles formed in the corners of his eyes when he smiled. I liked that he agreed to go up the canyon to look at stars with me, and I liked knowing there would be no expectations when we got there. I had never been with any guy that didn't have expectations of something physical. I liked that he didn't pat or touch my belly the way everyone else did, and I liked that he laughed at my jokes. I also liked that he listened when I told him all I knew about black holes and other things I'd learned from *Discovery* magazine. I liked it when he pointed out Orion, "The Hunter," to me in the stars.

"So do you feel cool being such a big part of the sky?" I asked.

"Not really. It was there before I was here."

"Well, I think it's cool."

He smiled. "Now that's a surprise. I recall you telling me how lame it was."

I felt my face flush and was glad it was dark so he couldn't see. "People can change."

His head tilted, washing his face in the sliver of moonlight that shone down. "So they say."

He dropped me off at a quarter of three in the morning with a "thanks" and "see you at work Monday." No kiss and no attempt at one. It seemed he was true to his word that he only wanted to be my friend. It was a new concept: a male friend that wanted nothing but friendship. I smiled all the way up the porch and into the house, entering quietly, knowing they'd be sleeping. But Sam was at the island in the kitchen. He was playing Solitaire, slapping cards on the counter harder than necessary. The assumption he was angry came easily. I braced myself.

"Have you been up all night?" I asked.

He jumped from being startled and whirled with fury to me. "Where have you been? I told you to be home early!"

I glanced at the clock and shrugged. "Three o'clock is early, Halo."

"That isn't what I meant! I've been up all night worrying about you!"

"Worrying about me, or him?"

"You, you egg-head! I don't know him very well. He could've been an ax-murderer for all we know!"

"C'mon, Halo, he's a nice guy."

"Nice guys don't stay out all night with girls!"

"You're going to wake up April if you keep yelling like that," I said.

"Too late. I'm awake." April's voice came from the stairway.

"Sorry, honey," Sam said.

"It isn't your fault," she consoled him while glaring at me. It appeared her excitement over my "date" had waned with the passing night.

I rolled my eyes at the pair of them. They were angry, but it was out of concern. It was kind of cute to see them worry like that. But I was tired and really needed to go to sleep. "I'm going to bed," I announced. Both of them gaped at me as I walked away from them to my room. I wasn't there long, however. At 7:00 A.M., Sam was there calling for me to get up.

chapter

20

Go AWAY, SAM! I'M SLEEPING." I swatted at him and rolled away.

He pulled the pillow from under my head.

"Hey!" I growled. "I'm using that!"

"Not anymore you aren't. I told you as long as you live under my roof, you'll have to live by my rules. Last night was totally unacceptable, and now I—"

"Don't, Sam," I interrupted, anxiety over what he might say next overwhelming me. "Don't tell me I have to leave." I could feel the tears building and had lost the pride to care if they fell. "If you kick me out, there's nowhere left, and I can't go back to Doris and Dad. Please don't tell me to go, because once I left . . . I—"

"What are you talking about?" It was Sam's turn to interrupt. "I'm not kicking anyone out. I'm just saying I was up all night and don't get to have decent sleep until after church. Neither do you."

I stamped out the panic that had welled up into my throat. "Church?"

The argument was long and nasty. Church—and they meant it. Since I already had April's dress, they'd decided I could use a little religion. April's look of stubborn insistence, mingled with Sam's "as long as you're under my roof," assured them victory. I would be going to church. The very thought was abhorrent to me. I'd never been to church in my life.

"I'm not gonna be a Mormon," I declared to no one in particular as we got into the car.

Church? Were they crazy? They must be, I decided as soon as we'd entered the building and filed into a room with long pews lined down the length of it. A large picture of Jesus took up the wall behind the pulpit, and three men in suits sat on the dais, to the right of the pulpit. A woman sat on the other side, holding a man's hand while whispering to a teenage girl. Organ music was playing. Sam nudged me into a pew, pulling me to sit on the padded bench. I scowled but sat. The baby pitched and rolled, making me uncomfortable in the sitting position. I grimaced. Sam poked me and whispered to quit being so cranky.

"You have no idea what I'm going through," I hissed back.

One of the men seated on the stand stood at the pulpit and began making announcements.

I tried to stretch out to get the baby's feet or hands or whatever it was that was in my rib cage out. Tired hit hard. I was exhausted to my toenails and leaned on Sam as a pillow while the meeting droned on. Sam nudged me to stay awake, but when I shoved back, he finally left me alone until the meeting had adjourned.

"Can we go home now?"

"Not yet," April said, almost laughing at how annoyed I seemed. So she thought this was funny, huh?

"You know it's not good for the baby to get no sleep," I pointed out.

"You should've considered that when you stayed out so late last night," she countered.

"You're not my parents, you know."

"Thank heavens!" she muttered. We went to Sunday School, where we read from the Old Testament and everyone discussed what the things they read meant. After that April stopped me. "You have a choice here. You can come with me to my Young Women's class or go to Relief Society."

Not wanting to be left alone, I said, "I'll go with you," and followed her down a hall to a large room.

A girl no older than fifteen stood up. "I'd like to welcome you all out to Young Womens today . . . it looks like we have a visitor," she said. "April, could you introduce your friend?"

April stood up and pulled me to my feet. "This is my sister-in-law, Suzie Quincy. She'll be staying with us for a while." She emphasized the words "in-law" as if to make it clear there was no blood relation involved.

Everyone looked at me, smiling nervously, only just then aware of my rounded midsection. "Welcome," the girl said with an encouraging grin.

"Thanks," I grumbled. They sang, said a prayer, read a scripture, and then one of them stood up and asked, "Who will stand for truth and righteousness?"

They all stood and together recited a motto of sorts. I was surprised and impressed. They all rattled off this motto with so much certainty and conviction that I wondered if they had been brainwashed into playing the parts their parents had chosen.

At that moment, a familiar need slammed hard enough to take my breath. The need to hide. I didn't belong here, could never belong here. This was a place where kids could stand up in front of people and act like adults, comfortable in their own skin. I could never be like that. *One of these things is not like the others . . .* the only times in my life where I had been like the others was when I was partying with my friends. But now . . . I didn't fit with them anymore, either . . . *one of these things just isn't the same.*

They dispersed to separate classes. April led me and nine other girls to a different classroom and took her place at the front of the room. "What is a testimony?" she asked. I had only heard the word *testimony* when someone was giving a testimonial for some new gadget on an infomercial, or in a courtroom drama on TV. I'd never heard of a testimony being something spiritual. April was well-prepared and comfortable engaging the class members in a discussion. I was impressed with her, but the whole thing left me uncomfortable and that discomfort made me hostile.

"I'm never doing that again," I declared once we were home. I kicked off my flip flops and dropped heavily into an easy chair, elevating my swollen feet on an ottoman.

"Doing what?" Sam was putting his scriptures onto the bookshelf.

"Spending three hours on hard chairs being bored!" It hadn't all been boring, but I wasn't about to give them an inch.

April rolled her eyes.

"Aw, Suzie, it couldn't have been that bad."

I glared at him. "You can't tell me you really enjoy doing that every week. It was boring enough to drive me to drink."

"I *do* like doing that every week," April said. "If you listen next week, you might get something out of it."

"I already told you, I'm not going next week or ever again." April and Sam sighed and frowned in unison. I sighed, too.

"I'm going to bed," I announced. I got up and waddled to my room, grateful no one protested. April came in some time later and tried to get me up to eat dinner. The only response she got was a wave of my hand and a grunt that would have been "get out and leave me alone," if I could've mustered the strength to utter it.

At three A.M., my eyes opened. The sleep had relaxed me to the point of bliss. My body felt heavy and warm amidst soft rolls of comforters, sheets, and pillows. I rolled over and stretched languidly. Then I got up and went to the kitchen.

There wasn't much to eat in the fridge but some leftover chicken meat. I pulled it out with a large jar of Miracle Whip. Dipping a strip of meat into the jar and gnawing on it, I caught sight of the large portrait of Jesus in the hallway. It was likeable . . . almost. I dipped another couple of pieces and walked over to inspect it more closely. "O Jerusalem," the caption read. He was looking off to the city. Was he sad over what he saw? Maybe. *Maybe he was just thinking of where the skyscrapers would go,* I joked to myself. Somehow, that didn't seem funny. He did look sad, like the city had disappointed him; and that seemed sad to me.

Had that city all turned against him? Even friends and family? April had spoken a lot about Jesus in her lesson on testimonies. She had talked about his betrayal, even after all the mighty miracles he had wrought. She had even cried when she told the class that she knew he had sacrificed his life for her, that he had born the weight of her sins so that she could be forgiven.

Sins and *forgiveness.* It was puzzling. Everyone in this state seemed consumed with those two words. And it seemed like everything to these people was a sin. The oppressive eyes of judgment trailed after me everywhere I turned, and it was maddening. The baby rolled and kicked sharply. Taking that as the cue to go back to bed, I went to my room for more sleep. *Sins* and *forgiveness.* The words tormented me in my dreams, too.

c h a p t e r
21

WORK WAS NOTHING LIKE I'D EXPECTED. My first day was multiple meetings that seemed to seep into each other forming one long meeting. I was handed the URL to the Web site, given a password that I was to change immediately upon entering the site, and set loose to work. During one of the meetings, they pulled what they called a brown bag forum, meaning, somehow, that lunch was involved. The free food was great but left me with the dreaded pregnancy disease called heartburn.

The paperwork at their Human Resources department to get my insurance up and running was a mile high.

Things at home were much more pleasant once I began working. Since I wasn't at home all day messing up April's things, she relaxed around me. On a few occasions, she was actually quite friendly.

Except for a quick smile and a hello in passing during the week, I didn't see anything of O-Rion. But I was kept so busy there wasn't really time to even think about him until the day was over and I was on my way home. It was nice to be busy. It was nice to feel useful. Every day represented new challenges at work that I'd never had before at a job, and I liked puzzling them out. By the end of the week, I had made new friends and was learning to be efficient. It felt good.

There was no Saturday night date, which I figured meant that since

I was home at a decent hour, I wouldn't be forced into church that Sunday . . . I was wrong.

The fight was short and bloody. At least on my side. Sam and April took no prisoners, and before I knew it, I was in a dress, buckled into the backseat of Sam's car, and headed toward the meetinghouse.

I scowled at the bread and water Sam tried not to pass to me. I grabbed a little plastic cup of water on its way by despite him passing it around me.

"At least the Catholics serve wine," I grumbled.

"You shouldn't be taking any at all," Sam whispered. There was no reason for him to be so cranky; it was just a lousy sip of water. They announced a fast and testimony meeting, though there was nothing fast about it. It was an open forum, and people went to the pulpit and cried and blubbered over the craziest things. A couple of children even got up and giggled into the microphone and said they loved their parents. It was all pretty boring until the man who was the organist stood up. He didn't cry, ramble, or giggle, but he made me sit up straighter.

"Brothers and sisters, I'd like to bear my testimony . . ." the man began. "I *know* this church is true . . ."

He was an older man, gray-haired, tall and bony. He spoke softly but with conviction.

" . . . most of you wouldn't know this, but I've made some real mistakes in my life. Before I found the gospel, I was on a path leading to nowhere, and I not only hurt myself but also those who should have been able to trust me."

I wondered what kind of mistakes he was referring to. He was well-dressed and didn't look like some kind of deviant person.

"I don't wish to burden you with a catalog of my sins, but the truth is, I've seen some awful things and done some awful things."

Now, he had my attention.

"When the missionaries found me, I wasn't much of a prospect. In fact, I don't know why they bothered with me. But they did. By then I had pretty much lost everything that I should have valued in life—my wife and family, my business, my self-respect, and any hope."

Even though he was pretty much spilling his guts, there didn't seem to be any shame, or even sorrow. I wondered where he was going with his story.

"When the elders began to teach me about the Atonement, I had no idea what they were talking about. But when it finally sunk in, that no matter what I had done, the Savior was willing to forgive me and that he could heal even someone like me, it was like a light went on. At first, it seemed too good to be true. I had hated myself for so long, that I couldn't imagine anyone could love me."

As I listened to him, it was as though everything around me had disappeared. All I could see was his face and the light shining from it.

He slowly raised a bony index finger and pointed it first to his chest, then across the crowd and directly at me. " . . . I am so grateful to know my Savior sacrificed everything for me . . . and for you."

It was as though he had whispered a secret I had known but forgotten, and I felt a thrill go through me.

"Life is short," he continued. "Make good decisions. Don't make selfish choices because I promise, all sin is selfish, and you'll never be happy like that."

Then he closed and went back to the organ.

Life is short. Make good decisions. Well, I hadn't done so well thus far, but that didn't mean I couldn't fix things to be a little better. *All sin is selfish.* What did that mean? I spent the rest of the meeting wondering about things Mormons called sins. Upon inspection, they *were* selfish things. The thought made me uncomfortable. I had never thought of myself as selfish before and was glad to see the meeting end to allow me to get my focus elsewhere.

Sunday School wasn't so bad, and April's lesson to the Young Women was quite enjoyable, though I had no intention of telling her so. One of her girls walked in late. Immediately I knew her. Not personally, but she had that look. It was the look of a girl who was learning to use her body to get what she wants, the look of a girl who was involved in what that man in testimony meeting had called "selfish sin." I knew that look. It had greeted me every morning in the mirror since I was fourteen.

The class seemed to go morbidly quiet upon her entrance. April smiled and welcomed her to class, then went on.

"Does anybody know how big the galaxy is?" April asked. She looked surprised to see me raise my hand.

"It depends on which scientist you're asking, but in general the galaxy is believed to be 100,000 to 120,000 light-years across, give or take a light-year, and 3,000 light-years deep. Kind of long and skinny." I shrugged at the questioning glance she gave me and muttered, "*Discovery* magazine."

"Wow . . ." April exclaimed. "That's right actually."

The new girl frowned. "So?"

April stammered a bit at the girl's belligerence. April appeared to want to please this girl, wanted to somehow impress her, though I wasn't certain why. "Well, the point I'm trying to make is that big questions have big answers, and sometimes the question may seem too big for an answer. But God has provided us with the knowledge and ability to receive an answer, no matter how big the question." April smiled gratefully at me. "As Suzie has shown us, sometimes the answer isn't as difficult as we thought it was."

I GRUMBLED ON THE WAY HOME FROM church out of principle. I felt as though my defenses were crumbling, and it made me uneasy. I was about to go to my room and sulk in private when April touched my shoulder. I turned to face her.

"Yeah, Ape?"

"Would you be willing to help make dinner?"

"You want me to cook?" The idea was more ludicrous than me going to church.

"We'll do it together. It'll be fun."

"Is this some twisted sort of joke? You do realize that by putting me in a kitchen to cook, you risk getting food poisoning, don't you?"

Sam laughed as he walked upstairs. "Don't worry, Suz, we'll bless it first."

I didn't laugh but grudgingly followed April into the kitchen and perched myself on a bar stool at the island and waited. April pulled a few seasonings from the cupboard and some items from the fridge.

"So what're you making?"

"You mean, what are *we* making?"

"Right."

"Navajo tacos."

"Come again?"

"It's a taco on a scone; haven't you ever had one?"

"Can't say that I have." I tried not to swallow in distaste. "Well, what do you want me to do?"

Before I knew it, I was pouring cups of flour into some sort of mixer. "No." April said as she took the measuring cup from my hand. "You need to do it slowly so it mixes evenly; otherwise you'll get flour bubbles in the dough."

I stepped back and threw my hands in the air. "Maybe you should just do it!"

"No. You can do it. If people always do everything for you, you'll never learn to do anything for yourself."

"Maybe I don't want to do anything for myself."

"Well, that would give you an awfully sad future."

"My future couldn't be any worse than my past."

"I know your past wasn't easy."

"You couldn't know. You never had to deal with Doris."

"No, I didn't, but Sam did, and it wasn't easy for him, either. He struggled a lot with his problems from childhood. He still struggles."

Heat boiled up into my face—from anger, embarrassment, and regret. "That's all I've ever heard: Buck up and be more like Sam. Sam has all his stuff together. Sam is perfect. Not like me. I'll never be good enough. . . . I'm sick of it!"

Her hand flew to mine and gripped it tightly. I tried to pull away, but she held on. "Oh, Suzie! No! That isn't what I meant at all!" She sighed and pulled me into a hug. Tears built up behind my eyes, but they didn't fall. That kind of vulnerability wasn't allowed. I stood woodenly in her tight embrace, awkward and wanting to return the affection but not certain that would be acceptable. It was something I didn't . . . couldn't do.

She finally released me. "I'm not saying Sam's perfect." She chuckled. "I'm married to him. Believe me, I know. He's got his faults too. My life wasn't so hot growing up, either, but you deal with it and make whatever changes are necessary to make it better. You've already started making those changes. I'd say your future is looking up already."

She asked me to chop some tomatoes and shred some lettuce. While I did that she was deep-frying the scones.

"Hey, guys, is dinner ready?" Sam came down the stairs and tried to sneak some grated cheese, but April slapped his hand.

"Not yet," she said, turning back to the skillet, "but soon."

"Is that *soon,* as in real people time, or *soon* as in April's time, meaning another two hours?"

She laughed and shook her head. "Oh, is poor little Sammy hungry?" she teased. "It will be ready a lot quicker if you give us a hand. Why don't you set the table?"

"Gee, I dunno. Do you think you can trust me with that?"

"I think so. You are beginning to handles knives without cutting yourself . . . right?"

I liked the comfortable way they bantered back and forth. At home, Doris and Dad never did that. Everything there had to turn into a fight, but April and Sam seemed to enjoy just kidding each other.

She turned from the stove and set a stack of scones on the table. Then she went to the fridge.

"Oh, heck!" It was her version of a swear word.

"What?" Sam asked. I snorted at her inability to articulate anything stronger than, *Oh, heck.*

"We're out of taco sauce."

"Oh." Sam looked disappointed.

"So?" I shrugged. "I'll run to the store."

"Can't. It's Sunday," April said, as though that meant something I should understand.

"Your point being?"

"We don't go to the store on Sunday," Sam explained.

"Why?" I scoffed. "What if you need something?"

"Well, that's why you try to plan ahead. And if you didn't plan well enough, you go without."

"But the stores are going to be open regardless. They're just waiting there to help you."

April shrugged. "Learning to keep the Sabbath day holy was a toughie when I got baptized. My parents went to brunch every Sunday and pitched fits when I told them I couldn't join them anymore. It's just a choice I had to make. If people stopped going to shop in stores, then those people forced to work could go home and enjoy their Sundays too."

"That's the dumbest thing I've ever heard! Those people are working so they can put food on the table and make car payments. They don't care what day they work. They're just glad to have a job. And the rest of us are glad for the convenience."

"It's the 7–11 convenience mentality of this world that is making society irresponsible," Sam declared. I thought he was joking, but he kept a straight face.

I threw my hands in the air in exasperation. "You people are insane!"

With the table set and everything ready, we sat down to eat. After the usual prayer, I piled tons of glop onto the fried scone, minus any taco sauce, and took a tentative bite. The flavor was not as expected. It was much better. It earned April a smile from me. She really was a good cook. There was also some degree of satisfaction in knowing I had helped and that it still tasted good.

"So do you have your OB/GYN appointment set up yet?" she asked.

"Yeah. For Tuesday, during my lunch hour."

"Do you want me to come?"

I hadn't thought about taking anyone with me. It was one of those things that seemed personal, a thing done alone. But the more I considered, the more I liked the idea of not being alone. I had been alone at the women's clinic, and I didn't really want to go through anything like that again.

"Sure, if you want." I tried to keep the nonchalance in my tone, but I really did want her to come and was glad she had offered.

"Okay. I'll pick you up. Where is it?"

I told her and settled into the first family dinner I had in Utah where I was a part of it instead of just watching it. We had some things in common now to talk about. We had work and church, and the conversation included me instead of floating around me.

chapter

23

I HAD BECOME COMPLETELY IN TUNE with this baby. I could almost hear it breathing. I knew when it was sleeping and when it was awake and when it was ticked that I had eaten too much garlic. And though in my heart I knew the baby was fine, I really wanted a doctor to confirm it.

April and I were asked to sit down in the comfortable waiting area. The office had a warm feel to it. Framed prints of women with children done in imitation of the impressionists hung on the walls. An arrangement of silk flowers in a huge vase sat on a round table, which was littered with parenting magazines.

My foot tapped in a steady rhythm that I wasn't even aware of until April put her hand on my leg to make me still.

"What is taking so long?" I demanded.

April smiled and turned a page in the magazine she'd picked up. "You're in a doctor's office, Suzie. You always have to wait."

"But look at that sign over there."

April looked to where I was pointing.

"It says if you are more than ten minutes late you have to reschedule! That's crazy! They aren't going to be ready for you in ten minutes anyway! What difference would it make?"

"Calm down, Suzie."

"I am calm!" The hiss was loud enough even the reception desk people turned to look. Wouldn't it be lovely to strip away the barriers that age puts up and stick your tongue out at the whole world? I harrumphed and slid down into my chair to sulk.

"Suzanna Quincy?" A tall, redheaded woman in a pale pink scrub outfit called my name. I pushed myself out of the chair and followed her.

She showed us into an examination room and gave me a hospital gown to put on. While April studied some medical diagrams on the wall, I changed, then sat on the examination table and waited.

It took another twenty minutes for a doctor to come. He said his name was Doctor Roth, and he was all smiles in glasses too big and too round for his face. "Oh, Suzanna, no, don't you cry for me . . ." he sang as he flipped through the chart. Did he think he was clever?

He had me lie down on the table and pushed on my belly softly and then took out a measuring tape to measure it. "So this is your first doctor's visit since learning you were pregnant?" he asked.

"I had to get insurance," I said.

"Well, let's take a listen to the heartbeat and see how Junior's doing."

I held my breath. A sound I was desperate to hear filled the room. It wasn't the slow *thump-thump, thump-thump* I was expecting to hear, but something much faster and more furious, like the beat of hummingbird wings. Fat tears gathered in my eyes. That heart was still beating. April's eyes were misted over, too.

"Oh, my heck, Suzie, that is so awesome!" she said.

"Wicked," I breathed.

The doctor timed the beats to his watch. I felt a stab of dismay when he pulled the device away, and the room fell into silence again. "Fast heartbeat," he observed.

"Is that bad?"

"No. No. It's fine. Could be a girl with a beat like that."

"You can tell the sex from a heartbeat?" I asked.

The doctor chortled softly. "No, but a girl's heart tends to beat faster. It's a trait they carry into womanhood, and men spend their whole lives trying to catch up." He laughed at his joke and again pushed up his too big, too round glasses. "Are you taking prenatal vitamins?"

"I try to. I bought some over-the-counter kinds at the drugstore. It was hard at first since even the smell of them made me sick."

"Well, I'll prescribe you some, and I have some samples you can take with you. Good nutrition is very important."

He glanced at me. "Have you had a lot of morning sickness, then?"

"I was sick almost every day, until just recently. It seems to have tapered off."

He marked something on my chart. "From the size of your abdomen and from what you said they determined your date at the women's clinic in Boston, you are approximately twenty-six weeks into this deal. The good news is you're over halfway there. The bad news is there are still fourteen weeks left." Dr. Roth asked more questions and when he appeared satisfied he'd pulled anything he could learn from me, he stood.

"At this point, we'll want to get you in for an ultrasound to make certain everything is going okay in there."

"Great, when can we do that?"

"Let me check to see what they've got. We might be able to do it today."

Today. I might catch a glimpse of the person within today. The excitement was almost too much to stand. My heart raced with the same furiousness as the one I'd just heard.

Dr. Roth came back after just a few minutes. "Well, I can't get you in today, but we have an opening at five o'clock next Wednesday. Are you interested?"

"Definitely!"

"As you leave, make sure you set up the appointment with the reception desk; also, we'll need to see you back here in four weeks; you'll want to make that appointment, too. I deliver at the Utah Valley Hospital, so you will, at some point, want to check it out and preregister."

I nodded.

"So do you plan on having an epidural or are you going to try it natural?"

"Natural? Do people still do that? Why would anyone do that? That's insane. No. I'll be getting the drugs, the more the better."

He checked off something in my file. "Even with the drugs, Lamaze classes can be helpful. You're also far enough along that the next time you come in, we'll need to take a test for gestational diabetes. Now will you be breast-feeding or using formula?"

"Excuse me?"

"Will you be br—"

"No!" I shouted to stop him from saying that word again. It made no sense that that word, spoken by a professional, should make me so uncomfortable, especially since I hung out with what Sam called the cesspool crowd, and we said things that were far worse to each other.

"I heard what you said. I think I'll be using a bottle."

He checked off another mark in the file. "Do you have any questions?"

I knew I did but couldn't think of any. I shook my head.

"Okay, great, we'll see you in four weeks. Take your prenatal vitamins and call if you need anything. I'll let you get dressed now, and I'll be back with those samples in a minute." He closed the door behind him.

April inspected the medical diagrams again while I changed. "Oh, my heck," she said.

"What?"

"Look at this." She pointed to a diagram of circles. There were ten circles and each was labeled, from one to ten centimeters. They depicted how dilated a woman had to be to deliver, and there was simply no way! The one that was labeled ten was huge. Not just huge, but astronomically huge. The circle on that graph looked big enough to drive a truck through it.

I gaped at the ten-centimeter circle and then cursed more articulately than April had. "It isn't possible for a body to get that big," I declared. "I don't think I want to do this anymore." I gulped down the panic.

April put her arm through mine. "Well, it's too late for you, but I think I've decided *I'm* never going to."

Dr. Roth came back, handing me a bag of samples for the vitamins and another sack filled with little Enfamil formula packets. As we left the room, I tossed another distressed glance back at the dilation chart and shuddered.

chapter
24

"Hᴇʏ, Sᴜᴢᴀɴɴᴀ." Rɪᴏɴ ᴡᴀs ʟᴇᴀɴɪɴɢ ᴀɢᴀɪɴsᴛ my cubicle wall.

"Hey," I smiled. I hadn't seen him except in passing since we went out. "What's up?"

"I've heard some good reports on your work. I just wanted to congratulate you."

"Thanks, just doing my job."

I waited.

He waited.

Seconds ticked by.

"So . . ." he finally said, "I was wondering . . . do you like the symphony?"

"The symphony?" I asked.

He nodded.

"You mean like flutes and violins?"

He nodded again.

"Sure, they're okay. Why do you ask? You taking a survey?"

He grinned. "I was just wondering if you'd like to go with me tomorrow night."

"What time?"

"About five-thirty. We'd have to drive to Salt Lake."

"Oh, can't. Got plans."

"Oh." He fidgeted. "I was just . . . I . . ." He looked disappointed.

"I have a doctor's appointment at five," I explained.

"Oh, how long will it take?"

"I don't know. It's an ultrasound. I don't know how long they take."
He perked up. "An ultrasound? How cool! Can I come?"

"Oh, please, like you'd want to come."

"Yeah, I'm sorry. That's kind of a personal thing; I shouldn't have
asked. But . . . I could pick you up after."

"Wait a minute. Is this like a date?"

"Not really. Just as friends."

I nodded. "Okay." I told him where the clinic was and grinned long
after he was gone. Even as friends, I liked his attention.

He was so . . . attractive. Not just in looks, even though he was nice
looking, but he was . . . a good person. And *that* was attractive. His
smile was always just under the surface, ready to spring up at any provocation.

April called me at work the next day. She was stuck going to a meeting and couldn't take me to my appointment. "Yikes," I said aloud and
then hurried over to see if I could catch Sam in his office. I did . . . just
barely.

"Knock-knock, Halo."

"Hey, what's up?"

"April can't come to my ultrasound, and I can't drive myself since I
don't have a car yet and—"

"What time?"

"Five, but we need to leave at 4:40. They don't let you in if you're
late."

"I can't take you, but I can meet you there after I'm done with my
meeting."

"So how will I get there?" Frustration welled up in me.

"Is there anyone on your team you can catch a ride with?"

"Maybe . . . I'll think of something, but you'll meet me there? I really don't want to go in alone."

"Yeah, I'll be there with bells."

"Sam?"

"Suz?"

"No bells, okay?"

He laughed. "I'll see you there."

I ran to Rion's office. "Hey, O-Rion, can I ask a big favor?"

We slid into my appointment at exactly 5:09. Twenty seconds later and we would have been rescheduling.

"Are you nervous?" Rion asked as I waited for the radiologist.

"Yes," I answered honestly. It didn't help that I'd had to drink two quarts of water before the appointment and had strict instructions that I couldn't go to the bathroom until it was all over.

"Are you going to find out if it's a boy or a girl?"

"I hope so. They said sometimes they can't tell."

Rion watched me shred my appointment card. "I could tell you a joke while we wait." When I didn't respond he launched into the joke. "What happens if you eat yeast and shoe polish?"

I stared at him. When I realized he refused to tell the punch line until I actually responded I said, "What?"

"You'll be able to rise and shine every morning!"

He laughed. I raised my eyebrows.

"Okay, how about this one? What do you get when you throw Daffy Duck into the ocean?"

"What?"

"Saltwater Daffy!" He laughed again.

I rolled my eyes.

"One more. This is a good one; I guarantee you'll laugh. What does an agnostic, dyslexic, insomniac do at night?"

"Do tell."

"Lie awake in bed and wonder if there really is a dog!"

I couldn't help myself. I had to laugh. He had succeeded in taking my mind off of being nervous *and* proven he was as big an adorable goofball as I thought he was.

"Suzanna Quincy?" A short man with a trim goatee and a white lab coat called my name. I stood, but Rion didn't. "You can come, too," the man said to Rion. I looked around the waiting room, wondering where Sam was.

Rion waited, not looking at me while I decided. "Yeah. You can come," I agreed. What it boiled down to was that I didn't want to be alone.

"Are you sure you want me tagging along?" he whispered as we followed the goatee doc.

"Sure, why not?" I said, not at all sure I wanted him in the room with me. I wondered again where Sam was.

Before I knew it, my belly was exposed to the world, or at least to everyone in the room, which was only Rion, the radiologist with the goatee, and me. It certainly felt like the whole world.

Goatee doc moved the paddle around, causing the fuzzy screen to sort itself into vague images. "Okay, great," the radiologist said, pointing to a tiny pair of dark circles. "There's the heart." They pulsated rhythmically. "Looking healthy," he said.

The doc clicked his mouse and froze the picture on the screen, and then entered in a few points and a line between them. The letters CRL appeared by the line.

"What's that?" Rion asked, awed by everything.

"CRL stands for the crown–rump length. It gives us an accurate estimation of the gestational age."

"That's cool you can do that," Rion said.

I said nothing. I couldn't take my eyes off the screen. It started running again. Every time the screen was still, Rion and the goatee would talk about what was going on. I didn't care what was going on aside from the frustration I felt when the screen froze and I could no longer see the movements I was also feeling.

"What did you say? I propped myself up on my elbows.

"She looks like she's coming along fine," the goatee repeated.

"She?"

"You did want to know, didn't you? I thought you'd marked in your chart that you wanted to. Most couples do."

"It's a girl . . . " I breathed. "She's a girl." My heart pulsed past my ears in a roar that drowned out everything but my own thoughts. *A girl. She's a girl.* It was at that moment a profile of a face and a hand stretching up came onto the screen. He froze the picture and took a snapshot.

At that moment, Sam entered the room. "I made it!" He looked at me with a smile that faded as soon as he saw Rion.

I opened my mouth to explain Rion's presence when the goatee said, "Uh-oh."

Rion's head shot up at the same instant that my heart stopped.

"What?"

"Um . . . oh, it's nothing." He pointed to the screen.

"What is it?" Sam said, stepping over to the table and edging Rion out of the way.

"Nothing to worry about. Trust me."

"Trust you?" I questioned.

The goatee stretched his collar away from his neck. "Really, it isn't anything. I thought I saw something, but I was mistaken. Sorry if I caused you alarm." He looked confused as he glanced from Sam to Rion.

I blinked at him, feeling sick. *What did an "uh-oh" mean? Was there something wrong? Was she having a problem? If she were having a problem, was it my fault? Was she in some way less than perfect because of something stupid I did? And if she were perfect, would I be able to raise her?* The questions churned and tumbled in my mind. I wanted to scream and cry and stamp my feet. *What did an "uh-oh" mean?* Sam put his hand on my shoulder. I felt calmer with that touch.

The doctor wiped the goop off me and pulled my shirt back over the large bulge. I hopped up to run to the bathroom. At the sink, I ran cold water over my face. *A girl.* I was thrilled and horrified. A girl. And what did an "uh-oh" mean? If the "uh-oh" meant nothing, what would *that* mean? What did I have to offer a baby girl? When I came back, Sam and the doc were talking quietly. Rion stood apart from them, looking uncomfortable. "You ready to go home?" Sam asked.

"Actually," Rion cleared his throat and stepped forward, "we were going to the symphony . . . if that's okay."

"Oh . . . sure." His eyes tightened like it might not be okay, but he didn't say it. "How about having her back at a decent hour this time?"

Rion flushed. "I will." Then he nudged me and said with a smile, "Aren't you going to tell him the good news?"

"It's a girl," my voice squeaked. I was bringing a girl into this world, and I was in no position to be any better of a mother than the one that brought me into the world.

Sam smiled wide and hugged me. "Well, congrats, Sis! With a little luck, she'll be . . ." He paused for barely a second, but I jumped in.

"Nicer than me? A better person than me?" I whispered it.

He frowned. "I was going to say as pretty as you." He looked hurt, making me feel bad.

"I'm sorry, Sam. I didn't mean that. I just . . . Thanks for showing up."

Sam darted a quick glance to Rion with a slight scowl. "It's no trouble. *I'm* here to take care of you."

He said it with that no nonsense "dad" tone, obviously trying to let Rion know who was in charge. I almost laughed at him; I *would* have laughed were I not so grateful to have him there. "Don't worry, Halo. I won't let him do anything shifty." I winked. "Let's get going, Rion. See you tonight, Sam." I herded Rion out the door and to his car.

Y OU OKAY?" HE ASKED FOR THE EIGHTH time once we were in the car
and headed toward Salt Lake City.

"Sure. Stellar." I looked out the window.

"You're a bad liar."

"Aren't all liars bad?"

He ignored the bait. "Want to talk about it?" he asked.

"I just feel guilty leaving Sam like that after he came all that way to
be with me."

Rion's face fell. "I could take you home . . . "

"No. It's okay. But we're going to be late."

"Yeah, I know." He glanced at the clock on his dashboard. "We
could just skip the symphony."

"Didn't you already buy the tickets?"

"I got them free from work."

We agreed not to go to the symphony, and Rion parked under the
covered parking at the ZCMI mall.

As we walked through the mall food court and out onto the street,
Rion asked, "Have Sam and April ever taken you to Temple Square?"

"Are you kidding? Sam hasn't taken me to the grocery store."

"Nobody should come to Salt Lake and not see Temple Square." He walked me across the street and onto a walkway leading through some beautiful flower gardens that opened into a plaza that provided a view of a large, ornate building with several spires and a gold statue on top of one of them.

"That's the Salt Lake Temple," Rion explained.

It was like a huge palace and towered above a pond that captured part of its reflection.

The temple was surrounded by a high wall that made it look like a fortress. We entered the grounds through a set of tall, black iron gates.

"What's it for?" I asked, pointing to the temple. "Is it like a cathedral?"

"No. It's a place where we do religious ordinances for ourselves and for the dead."

"For the dead? That sounds a little creepy, O-Rion."

"No, not like that. We take the names of our ancestors who have already passed away and act as proxies for them to get baptized or sealed together as families so they can be together forever."

"Now there's a crazy notion," I said. "Why would anyone want to be sealed forever to their family? I always thought death would be a nice excuse not to have to see them again."

Rion smiled at that. "Do you want to go into the Visitors' Center?"

"Sure. Why not? This is your tour." I followed him down the sidewalk past a building with a domed roof and through some electric doors that opened with a satisfied sigh.

"Let's go upstairs." He took my hand and without giving me a choice dragged me to a ramp that spiraled upward. Walking up it made me dizzy and left me on the verge of throwing up.

The closer to the top we got, the further my jaw dropped. It was like walking into the stars. My heart beat faster at the idea. The walls were painted to depict stars, clouds, planets, and galaxies against a dark backdrop of every shade of blue. In front of this wall was a huge, white marble sculpture of a solitary figure in a flowing robe.

As we continued up the ramp, all I could see was his back, until we rounded the last turn and we came into full view of the statue.

I stopped short as though my feet were cemented and my breath had been knocked from me. It was beautiful.

A larger-than-life statue of Jesus stood before us. But where in April's painting he looked like a noble but tormented man, here, there was no doubt, he was a god. From the angle we stood, it looked as though the planet Earth rested in the crook of his outstretched arm. Soft music played in the background.

"Wow," I whispered.

Rion looked at me expectantly. "Awesome, isn't it?"

I tried to shake off the feeling of what? Reverence? Why should a piece of stone have such power? It was illogical. I refused to be dragged into whatever the Mormons were trying to create in this room.

"Can't you feel the Spirit?" Rion asked.

"What spirit? I don't know what you are talking about with spirit. I was just thinking the architecture and painting is pretty cool. I'll leave the detection of any ghosts to you."

A deep, rumbling voice began to speak. In surprise I looked to the statue to see if it had moved; it hadn't. Yet it felt very much like this god was speaking to me.

"Behold, I am Jesus Christ . . ."

I started.

" . . . learn of me . . . behold the wounds . . . I have suffered these things for all if they would repent . . ." I stared in mixed curiosity and awe at the statue, wondering if it would move, tilt its head to view me better. If it moved, should I be afraid and run and hide, or would it hug me? I didn't know and the not knowing paralyzed me. "Let not your heart be troubled . . . If ye love me . . . keep my commandments."

When he'd finished speaking, and the other people in the room had started to move around, I remembered to breathe. Did he know my heart's troubles? No . . . no, of course not. No one did. No one understood what I'd been through.

"Can we leave now, O-Constellation? I'm sure you feel at home here among the stars, but we can't stay forever looking at stone that doesn't move." *Or would it move if I stayed long enough? No! Ridiculous.*

Rion looked disappointed but followed me out the other side and down a hallway lined with religious paintings and murals.

By now my feet were killing me, and my back was aching from waddling everywhere. "Can we go now?" I asked.

Rion shrugged. "If you want to."

Once we were outside again, Rion glanced at his watch. "It's seven-thirty. Why don't we go get something to eat?"

Just outside the temple grounds, an older woman wearing layers of tattered coats held out her hand. "Can you spare some change?" she said. I pulled a few dollars from my purse and handed them to her. "Bless you!" she called after me.

Rion watched but didn't comment until we were on the other side of the street. "You never cease to surprise me," he said.

"That woman could be me if Sam kicks me out," I responded and entered the door he held open for me to the Joseph Smith Memorial Building.

"Wow," I said again once we were inside. It was like stepping back into a Victorian age. Heavy, green marbled pillars stretched from the elaborate lobby up to the other floors. The center of each floor remained open, creating a vaulted ceiling four floors high where a glittering, crystal chandelier hung. A large, round-topped table in the lobby held a huge vase of gorgeous flowers, and a man wearing a black tuxedo was playing the grand piano in the corner.

Rion smiled. "It is a wow, isn't it?"

"There's food here?" I asked in disbelief.

"Yeah, on the tenth floor. There are actually two restaurants."

I took his arm, stopping him from heading to the elevators. "Rion, I appreciate you trying to be nice and all, but this looks really expensive, and I'm not sure I—"

"Don't worry about it. It looks expensive, but the prices aren't that bad. Trust me, I'm a college student. I don't spend what I don't have."

"But I have a job now; and we're more like friends, so let's just go Dutch, okay?"

"Even just as friends, the guy should pay!"

"Don't be so archaic."

He scowled. "Fine, Dutch it is then."

Our waitress, a bubbly, happy sort of girl who identified herself as Donna, handed us menus and welcomed us to the Garden Restaurant. We were seated by the windows on the west side of the building. I was facing the temple. Though it wasn't exactly dark yet, the lights of the temple had been turned on, bringing back the impression of a palace.

Donna came back. "Are you ready to order?"

Rion waited for me to order: "I'll have the Raspberry Chicken Salad."

He then ordered the Grilled Chicken Medallions.

After Donna left, Rion laughed. "You're such a girl!"

"What?"

"A salad? I thought you were different from the other females."

"I am different, bonehead!" I insisted. "I'm pregnant. Ask me here again after I have this little girl, and I'll be ordering the prime rib and mashed potatoes."

He laughed some more. "It's a date, then."

I scowled, frustration and agitation welling up in me. Frustrated he was talking about us in future tense. Did I want that? He couldn't really want to date in the future, not a pregnant girl, not a girl who was going to have a baby she couldn't take care of.

As we waited for our food, Rion leaned in on his elbows. "Do you want to talk about what's bugging you?"

I unfolded and refolded my napkin. "No," I said without looking at him.

He grinned. "Okay, tell me about your home in Boston."

"I didn't have a home in Boston. It was just a place I lived. There was never any more to it than that." He fell silent, twirling a spoon in his fingers slowly.

"What about you?" I asked.

"Boston wasn't my home either."

I smiled. "Ha. Ha. I meant Iowa. What was your family like?"

"Like everybody's family. I was the second of four kids. Cassie's the oldest, and Ammon and Anne a few years younger. We fought and made up a lot. Mom used to make us hug and say we were sorry. We hated hugging. We lived out of city limits where we could see the stars, and we all spent a lot of sleepless nights when Mom and Dad would get excited over a meteor shower or an eclipse and pull us out of bed to see it." His eyes shone.

It sounded like a dream. I used to have dreams about a family like that, but reality had taken over. Reality had won.

"That's not like everybody's family. We never hugged in my house, and my parents were always gone. If we were sleeping, there would be no way they'd wake us. They were glad to be rid of us for a little while. Doris hated us. When she was around she was always h—" I paused. Telling him she hit us all the time would be throwing too many eggs, even for a guy who said he could catch them all. "Sam and I were the reasons her life is so horrible. She could've been something great if she hadn't had us."

"You don't believe that?"

"Of course I do. Some people should never have children."

"But you can change that. You can be different in the kind of mother you are to your child."

"Oh, yeah, I'm real different. She hasn't even been born yet, and I've already ruined her life." I dropped my head into my hands.

"C'mon, Suzanna, why would you say that?"

"You are so naïve, Rion. I'm having a baby with nothing to show or give her. A little girl is going to be born, and there is nothing but poverty and psychosis ahead of her."

"Where did all this come from?"

"I dunno," I shook my head. "Just seeing her move and hearing she was a girl. I thought it would make me happy to see her, but it only made me realize what a screw-up I am."

"Be serious. The fact that you're so worried about her is enough to prove you're going to do great raising her. You'll be fine."

I wanted to believe him. I really did. I threw my hands up in the air. "You Mormons!"

"What?"

"You're an annoyingly optimistic people."

He leaned back abruptly with a grin. "What gives with that anyway?"

"What?"

"How is it Sam's a Mormon and you aren't?"

"One of his friends gave him a Mormon bible and he read it, liked it, and went down to the water to get dunked."

"Were you ever interested in it?"

"Are you kidding? Fairy tales are for kids, O-Rion. God is as much a fairy tale as Santa Claus and Seven Dwarfs. Sure . . . a nice enough fairy tale, but—"

"But you don't buy into it?" he finished.

"Do you?"

He didn't blink. "I do." His look of resolution and surety melted into the smile, the crinkles appearing in the corners of his eyes. "But I understand where you're coming from. I didn't always believe, either."

"Do you hang out with me so you can preach to me?"

"No." He looked offended.

I pursed my lips, surveying him. "Isn't it a violation to hang with harlots in your church?"

"I don't think you're a harlot."

"Then you don't know me very well."

"I might know you better than you think I do."

I shifted uncomfortably under a gaze that felt very much like he did know me better than I thought. I couldn't respond around the boulder resting in my throat. Looking away, I asked as nonchalantly as my rapidly beating heart would allow, "So you're the kind of guy that believes in fairy tales."

"I am. And you're a girl that believes only in the here and now."

"When you're pregnant with a baby girl and living with your brother, planning for here and now seems like a safer bet."

"Maybe safer . . . maybe not. What are you going to name her?"

"What if I'm not naming her?" I asked carefully.

"What are you going to call her? Hey, Kid? Oh, no, no, no, wait! Lemme guess! You're going to name her 'Don't bug me!'" He guffawed at his own joke.

I smiled, in spite of myself.

We fell silent for a moment. "Actually, I'm thinking about

adoption." I wasn't sure where that came from, since I hadn't been really thinking it. But maybe I had, on a subconscious level. And now I had said it.

His brows knitted together over the bridge of his nose. "Could you really go through with that?"

"Why not? I'm a mess. I'm not married. My life is going nowhere. I have nothing to offer her."

"You're smart, beautiful, and stubborn. You can get married."

"I'm not in the market for the father of my child. I wasn't when I created her, and I'm not now."

"I see. Some women raise kids alone you know." He took a sip of his Sprite.

"She'd do better with a mother *and* a father. Even I know that."

"She'd have a Heavenly Father. We all have that."

"Fairy tales again, O-Rion?"

"Nope, simply reality, Suzanna."

T HE WAITRESS BROUGHT US OUR FOOD. I stared at it, not really seeing it. Rion's optimism had given me something else to think about. Could I raise her on my own? Lots of women did. Then again, maybe I could woo Rion, make him fall in love with me. He'd be a good father. But Rion's friendship was important to me. He seemed genuine about wanting to only be my friend, and that was worth more than I could ever repay.

"Something wrong with your food?" Rion asked.

"It looks fine; I've just got a lot on my mind."

"I'm sorry." He really did look sorry.

"It isn't your fault I've been such a loser all my life." I tried at a chuckle that ended with a scowl.

"Oh, c'mon! You're not a loser. A goon maybe, but not a loser."

"April uses that word all the time. What exactly is a goon?"

"Not sure. I think they were those big guys with long noses and grass skirts on *Popeye*."

"So you think of me as a long-nosed big guy dressed for a hula?"

Rion sputtered at the sip of Sprite he was taking. "No, Suzanna," he said after he had stopped laughing. "I think much more of you than that."

*Did he think much more than that of me? And how much more was
much more?* My heart quickened. I stared out the window to clear my
mind of those thoughts, taking in the lights of the city and the fading
sunset beyond the lake. The spires of the temple continued to glow in
the gathering darkness.

"Hey?" I nudged Rion's hand with my arm. "Is that a real train station?" We were sitting right in line with a street that ran into a large
building with a huge Union Pacific sign on it.

"Not anymore. It's called the Gateway. It's like an outdoor mall. It's
actually pretty cool. If you want, we can go see it after we eat. We should
probably hurry though if we want to have time."

We shoveled our food in quickly and hurried downstairs. As we
walked through the lobby, we passed a huge marble statue of Joseph
Smith. I stopped in front of it to admire the workmanship and read the
caption: "If any of you lack wisdom, let him ask of God . . ." I frowned
at it. "I thought your prophet's name was Joseph Smith."

"What do you mean?" Rion edged closer to see what I was
looking at.

I pointed at the plaque and read aloud, "It says here: James 1:5."

Rion laughed heartily and shook his head as we left the building to
find his car. "What's so funny?" I asked, to which he only laughed
harder in response.

The Gateway Shopping Center covered several blocks and featured
all kinds of stores and restaurants. The sidewalks were made of red sandstone, and there was an artificial waterfall cascading over the sandstone
to a small pool and stream at the bottom. We stood at the top of the
waterfall and looked down onto a large flat surface where jets of water
were spouting up, timed to the classical music that was playing over a
loud-speaking system. Some children were running among the geysers,
laughing and squealing as they would get blasted by the waterspouts.

We wandered along the sidewalks that were crowded with shoppers and loitering teenagers.

"Hey, let's go in here!" Rion pointed to a store window.

I looked at the sign. "Build-a-Bear"?

"Yeah, let's get the baby a present." He dragged me into the store where a young, enthusiastic store clerk named Jeff greeted us.

"Can I help you?" he asked.

"Yes," Rion said. "We need a present." He pointed to my belly with pride. "We just found out today she's having a girl."

Jeff grinned. "Well, congratulations! What do you have in mind to get?"

"We haven't ever done this before. Tell us what's available, and we'll go from there."

"Well, you pick out a bear or any other animal you'd like and we make it right here. We stuff it, give it a heart, stitch it up, and give your bear a bath. Then you take it home."

I looked at the prices on the various animals. The animals themselves seemed reasonably priced, and even the outfits were affordable, but I could see Rion getting carried away and buying all the extras. I felt a little guilty he was spending anything at all.

I tugged lightly at the soft, cotton shirt Rion was wearing. "Rion, no . . . you're in college . . . this is too much."

"Hey, c'mon. You already saved me on having to buy you dinner, so I can at least do this. It'll be fun. What kind of animal do you want?"

There were many to choose from: dogs, rabbits, elephants, lions; but the light brown bear seemed the best choice.

Jeff pulled a light brown bear "skin" from a barrel and went to work blowing it full of stuffing. Then he inserted a red satin heart inside the body and sewed it up.

"What kind of clothes do you want to put on her?" Jeff asked.

"Yeah, what do you want your little lady to wear?" Rion asked, eyeing the rack of clothes.

The way Chris had continually called the baby "little angel" before I left him and Boston behind flared up in my memory. "That one." I picked it off the rack decidedly. It was a white dress with matching bonnet and white lace bottoms.

"Cool." Rion exclaimed. "You could almost use that outfit for the baby's blessing dress."

"Blessing?"

"Yeah, when you give her a name."

"Like a christening?"

He grinned. "Like that—yeah."

After the bear was dressed, Jeff asked me what name I wanted to put on the birth certificate.

"Name?"

"Yeah, for the birth certificate," he explained.

That was more than I could think about, so we skipped naming the bear and just had it put into a little cardboard bear house and left.

On the walk back to the car, I couldn't think of anything to say. Even though the evening had been fun, I felt depressed and sad.

"You okay?" Rion asked.

"Yeah."

"Are you lying?"

I smiled. "Yeah."

"You do know everything's going to be fine, right?"

"I hope it will."

"Good. If you've got hope, you'll be okay."

I shook my head in wonder at how nice he was to me. I'd never met anyone like him before. All the guys I'd ever known all wanted something *from* me. But Rion seemed to want to do things *for* me. In a way,

I didn't know how to handle it. It was good, having a friend, but it was so different from anything I had ever known that sometimes I didn't know how to act.

On the drive home, I kept thinking about my baby. For some reason, I thought about Doris and how she had always pounded into me the fact that I had ruined her life. Would this little girl grow to hate me the way I hated Doris? Would I resent her and hate her like Doris hated me?

I was suddenly scared for my baby. I thought about what the doctor had said during the ultrasound exam. *What did, "uh-oh" mean? Maybe nothing.* But there would be an "uh-oh" when she was born. She was coming into my life, and I was nothing. Doris's words, *You're ruining my life!* echoed again and again in my head. I could picture me being like that. I could picture me being resentful of a life I could have had, but worse I could picture having a child that would say those words to me, bringing my life full circle. My mother had said those words to me my entire childhood; my child would say those words to me my entire adulthood. And it would all be true. If I tried to raise this baby, I would be ruining her life. The thought made me want to crawl into bed and never get out.

As soon as Rion pulled into Sam's driveway, I reached for the door handle to let myself out, but Rion put his hand on my arm. "Hold on. Let me get it."

"I'm not helpless, O-Rion."

"I know. It's just something I want to do."

I stayed where I was, waiting for him to walk around the front of the car and open my door. His little act of kindness left me fumbling and vulnerable in a way I'd never been in my life.

"M' Lady," he smiled as he took my hand to help me out of the car. At the doorstep he released my hand and stuffed his hands into his pockets. He seemed at ease, proving further to me that he saw me only as a friend. The surprise was from within when I realized I saw him as much more. I blinked at him, unable to hide the shock of my own desire to lean in and kiss him.

"I . . . I need to go in now. Thank you, for everything. It was a great night." With that I opened the door and slipped inside the house without saying more. I leaned against the closed door and let out a breath I hadn't realized I'd been holding. He had been wonderful. He was a wonderful guy and I . . . I was nothing.

I pulled myself away from the door.

Following the sound of the TV into the family room, I found April and Sam curled up together, watching a movie. "How was your date?" April asked at the same time Sam paused the DVD.

"It wasn't a date," I said, feeling the dejected hollowness at the words. "He bought her a present." I plopped down on the couch next to them, grateful to rest my feet, and held up the box for them to see. I kicked off my shoes and rubbed my swollen ankles.

"That is so cute!" April cooed after I'd pulled out the bear.

"Rion said we could use the dress as the baby's blessing outfit if I wanted."

April seemed delighted by that. "I think that's a great idea."

My lip trembled. "It would be, if we get that far."

"What's wrong?" Sam asked.

"I don't know . . . something's not right with me." *You're ruining my life!* Doris screamed in my mind. "I don't know if I can do this."

"What?" Sam probed.

"I dunno." *You're ruining my life!* my daughter's voice would yell as she grew up.

"Something's bothering you."

I closed my eyes, fighting back my tears. "What if I end up like

Doris?" I whispered. One fat tear slid down my cheek. I hadn't meant
to say it out loud. I hadn't meant to incriminate myself so wholly, but
there it was with no hope of recalling it.

"Oh, Suzie . . ." April said, sliding out of Sam's grasp to sit next to
me on the couch and hug me. "Don't worry; everything will be fine,
you'll see. You aren't—" she cut off. She was going to say I wasn't like
Doris, but she couldn't lie. We all knew I was more like her than anyone
cared to admit.

Sam joined us on the couch and put his arm around me. "You *are
not* like her. You've made choices that are so opposite of who she is, there
is no chance you'll be the kind of mother she was."

"It doesn't matter. Either way, I'm not raising her."

"What are you talking about?" Sam asked.

"Why don't you two adopt her?" I said in a rush. "You have a nice
home and a stable family and then I'd still get to see her."

Sam and April's faces mirrored each other for shock.

"Suz, you know we can't do that," Sam countered slowly.

"Why not?"

"It wouldn't work," April said. "You'd still feel like her mother; we'd
always be at odds, fighting each other for parental rights. Things like
that never work and never end happily."

"I think you're wrong," I insisted. "I think sometimes those things
work out fine for everybody."

Sam scrubbed a hand over his head. "And maybe you're right, but
April and I just got married, and we're not ready to start a family yet."

I hissed at them, standing as fast as my tired, sore legs would let me.
"Well, that's fine; you're not *ready* to have a family. But I am? Look at
me! I only have three outfits that fit me properly because *you* had to buy
them for me! I have no house, no car, and no money. I don't even have
a cradle to put her in when she gets here. But because *my* belly is

growing, that must mean *I'm* ready! Fine!" I grabbed the box with the bear and stomped to my room, hating all the extra hormones that were making me act like a deranged escapee from a mental hospital. *I'm going to ruin her life just like Doris ruined mine. If her life turns out to be drugs and teen pregnancy, it will be my fault.* As soon as I fell sobbing to the bed, I realized how stupid I was. Sam and April were right, though it ached to admit it. If they were to take the baby, I'd never really let them be in charge of her. A time would come when I'd want her back and would cause them grief to get her back. I waited a while, wondering if Sam would come to smooth things over. When he didn't come, I stepped quietly out of my room to find him and say I was sorry for treating them like that.

They were still in the family room. I sneaked to the corner to peer around and hear what they were saying. Sam was pacing; April remained on the couch where I'd left her. She had been crying too. "Stop pacing! You're making me crazy!" she said to him.

"What if she's right? What if we should be taking the baby in and raising her. I mean—at least then she'd be raised in the gospel. She'd have a chance."

"We've been through this," April said. "We've prayed; we've fasted! We got the same answer. We know that isn't what we're supposed to do."

"So what are we supposed to do?" He fell to his knees beside her. "Tell me, April, what?"

"I don't know."

"She's my sister. I love her, and I want to see her happy. How do I do that? How do I help her?"

"I don't know that, either. Just give her some time. She needs to make her own choices, and I don't know Sam, but I think she'll be okay. She's come so far. She's made so many good decisions."

"Can we have a prayer?" Sam asked.

"I was going to ask you the same thing." April scooted off the couch and knelt next to Sam. They held hands; their heads bowed.

"Our Father in Heaven . . ." Sam's voice cracked with the threat of a sob. "We are so thankful you've brought my sister to us. We are grateful for the choices she's made that have given us the chance to know her and be close to her. Please bless her to continue making good choices. Bless her to know she's thy daughter and that she has a purpose. Bless her to know that we love her . . ."

I stepped back into the hall. They weren't angry with me. *They were praying for me.* As odd as it was, the thought comforted me. I went back to my room and sat on my bed, shuffling my swollen feet. I frowned at them, wondering if I'd ever see my thin ankles again. *They were praying for me.*

And they had already discussed and prayed about the possibility of taking the baby as their own. The fact they they'd already considered it bothered me at the same time it lifted my spirits. It meant they cared, in a world where I thought nobody cared. I waited a while longer.

If I prayed, would someone answer me? Would that stone god amongst the stars at Temple Square tell me what I needed to do? Or maybe it would be the god in April's painting in the hall; maybe someone else. I shook my head. More likely it would be no one at all. *If there is a god, would he have sent me a little girl I can't take care of?* I waited some more. Sam never showed up. I stood and walked to the door twice before deciding it could wait. I'd apologize in the morning.

chapter
27

"SUZIE? SUZIE?" SAM'S VOICE cooed softly.

"Go away, Halo! I'm sleeping!"

"You need to get ready for church."

I tried to swat him away. "I'm not a Mormon; why do I have to pretend that I am every Sunday?"

"Consider it rent." He patted my leg. "Get up."

I got up, grumbling only a little. The memory of them praying for me a few nights previous dampened most of my better arguments.

Sacrament meeting was intolerably long. I amused myself by drawing hearts on a notepad I found in April's Young Women bag. I started writing an R to begin Rion's name when I realized what I was doing and quickly scratched it out.

April's lesson in Young Women was on forgiveness. When the girl who came in late last time entered this week just as late, she sat by me. April again smiled at her with love and encouragement. I wondered why this obviously misfit girl kept showing up in a place where she must have been uncomfortable. I knew I didn't fit in, either, but April and Sam had not given me a choice. She appeared to be there of her own free will.

173

I was grateful when church was finally over. Sam was staying after for something, and April drove us home.

"I'm not going back," I declared upon entering the house.

April groaned, "Not again, Suzie. Why do we have to fight about this every week?"

"Because every week Sam makes me get up and put on this flaming dress and sit for three hours listening to people tell me stuff that doesn't mean anything to me."

"It's important that you're there."

I kicked my shoes off. "Important to who?"

"You know the girl who has come in late the last few weeks?"

"Yeah."

"She hadn't set foot in my class until the week you showed up. She always went to sacrament meeting because her mom made her, but she skipped the rest as soon as her mom wasn't looking."

"What's that got to do with me?"

"One of her friends told me she said you looked like someone she could relate to."

I scowled, annoyed that I had thought the same thing about her when I had first seen her. "So? She hasn't even spoken to me."

"She's been through a lot, things you'd understand, but things that make her scared to talk to people, especially at church. She feels comfortable with you there. I hope you'll keep coming for her sake. She needs to be there."

"Yeah, well, I can't help her. I mean look at me!"

"Maybe you could give her some advice on things to avoid. Help her to see a way out of some of the things she's involved in. Just being there so she doesn't feel alone seems to be helping her."

I softened at that. What if someone had been around to help me?

"What's her name?" I asked.

"Alison."

"I guess I could go a few more times."

April's eyes glistened. "Thank you, Suzie." She grinned, real and genuine, not the tight-lipped, I-have-to-accept-this-girl-in-my-home twist of her mouth she had been giving me. I smiled back. It was a strange feeling to think that for the first time in my life someone might actually need me and that I had the ability to be useful in some way.

In all the years of my life, I had never "helped" in the kitchen before. My idea of cooking had always been spreading peanut butter on bread or pouring milk over a bowl of cereal. Milk was optional in the cereal scenario since Doris always forgot to buy more when the old went sour. But with April's help, I was almost becoming profficient in my new domestic skills.

With dinner over, I was putting in another attempt at doing the dishes, when two women from Relief Society came by to see me. Their names were Jan and Roberta, and they were about forty years old. They introduced themselves as my visiting teachers.

April seated them in the family room and ushered me in to sit with them. April sat, too.

"We've been looking forward to getting to know you better," Jan said.

I nodded dumbly, not sure what to say and wondering why I was pleased to have visitors.

"So, when's the baby due?" Roberta asked.

"In December . . . sometime."

"We just found out it's a girl," April volunteered.

"How wonderful!" and "Oh, perfect!" they said.

After a lesson from Jan on following the teachings of the prophet, out of a thin magazine called the *Ensign*, I asked, "You do know I'm not a Mormon, right?"

"April told us," Jan said, smiling warmly.

"So you don't have to feel obligated to visit or anything, 'cause . . . I mean I'm not on your quota or anything."

Roberta grinned, "You're not a quota, Suzie. We wanted to come meet you."

Jan chuckled. "No one's considered a quota! We owe each other all the support and friendship we can give." She reached out from across the table and touched my hand. "We all need each other."

"I'm not exactly a prime candidate for joining your church," I said, making a last-ditch effort to relieve them of feeling as though they needed to pretend to care about me.

Jan laughed good-naturedly. "Oh, we're not worried about that. We just want to be your friends." She gave my hand a squeeze and released it.

Roberta nodded her agreement. Why they cared was beyond me, but I was moved nevertheless. "Thank you," I whispered.

They stayed only a few minutes longer and left after making me promise I would call if I needed anything. I would have taken it as a vain offer, except that they gave me a slip of paper with both their names and phone numbers on it. I couldn't imagine myself actually calling them, but the offer was like a spoonful of warm soup on a cold day.

The next night after dinner, after April, Sam, and I had settled in to watch a movie together, the phone rang. Sam paused the movie while April answered it. She handed the phone to Sam. "It's for you."

"Hello? . . . Oh, no . . . Sure, I'll be right over. . . . No, don't worry about it. I have oil." He hung up.

"What's the matter?" April asked.

"Mary Stiles is really sick. She needs a blessing."

"A blessing?" I asked, turning to April for a definition since Sam looked like he was in a hurry. The only time I'd heard about blessings were for babies when they got named. I'd met Mary Stiles at church and knew she was an older woman.

"Yeah, why don't you come along, Suzie?"

"What for?"

"So I can spend some time with you," he said, pulling me up and toward the door before I could think of a proper protest. I came up with tons of excuses once we were in the car as to why I couldn't go, but by then it was too late.

It was just a short drive to the Stiles's home. When we arrived, Sam insisted I come in with him.

Mr. Stiles answered Sam's knock immediately. "Thanks for coming, Sam. Mary asked me to call you." His face was lined with worry and fear, but something more . . . hope? He apparently believed Sam could help with his wife in some way.

We entered the living room. Mary was on the couch. I stifled a gasp when I saw her. Her hair was dull and greasy, hanging in her face. Her skin was so pale it was pearlescent with the sheen of sweat glistening in the dim lamplight. Her smile was thin and forced and with it came a wince of pain. Sam was at her side only a step behind Ted. "How you doing, Mary?" he asked.

"It's good of you to come, Sam." Her lip trembled and a tear trailed down her cheek.

"Hey, no tears; we'll get you fixed up in no time."

Sam pulled out a little wooden cylinder attached to his key ring. He detached it from the keys and unscrewed a tiny cap, revealing an even smaller plastic tube inside. Curious, I peeked over Sam's shoulder to see what it was.

"What did her doctor say?" Sam asked.

Ted sighed, the lines deepening in his forehead. "Things are just not going well. The pneumonia has filled both her lungs. She's had a shot of antibiotics and has been on a Z-pac for three days, but nothing's changed. If anything, it's just gotten worse. She can't stand up at all. I've had to carry her to the bathroom. The doctor said if we can't break her fever in another couple of hours, he wants her back in the emergency room."

Sam touched the older woman's forehead with his palm. "Oh, Mary," he murmured, "you are really warm." The words expressed tender concern and did not reflect the alarm in his eyes. "Would you want me to bless or anoint, Ted?"

"Please do the blessing. I don't think I could. I don't trust myself to submit to the Lord's will."

Ted took the plastic tube and dripped a drop of oil onto Mary's head, then placed his hands on her head and said an odd sort of prayer. Maybe it was just my imagination, but in spite of the sickness, I felt a peaceful feeling in the room, and I watched Mary's face go from pain to calm. Then Sam placed his hands on Mary's head and began to pray. His voice was deep and clear, reminding me of the statue at Temple Square and the deep ethereal voice that seemed to whisper to my very soul.

This was a different Sam than I had always known. In his prayer, he promised Mary a quick recovery and strength to bear the pain until recovery came. I peeked open an eye to look around. Tears were rolling down the cheeks of both Mary and her husband, Ted. Through the peace, I could feel the love they had for each other, and it occurred to me that Sam and April shared that same kind of love.

While growing up, I had never experienced anything like what I was seeing. How lucky these people were. Was it their faith that gave them the courage to open themselves to so much love? Or were they too foolish and naïve to know that love causes pain?

Sam bent and hugged Mary gently when he was done praying, and he shook Ted's hand. I wiped my eyes before anyone noticed they were moist and stood to go.

"Want to stop and get a bite to eat?" Sam asked, once in the car.

"What about April?"

"We'll get her something."

"Sure."

We stopped at a Wendy's, went in, got our order, and sat in a booth. The restaurant was empty aside from the teenager behind the counter and another teenager sloshing a mop over the tiled floor.

Sam surveyed me from under the dark eyebrows arched over his chocolate brown eyes. "You still dip your fries in your Frosty?"

I grinned. "You still disgusted by it?"

He shook his head and bit into a beefy burger. I chewed thoughtfully on my chocolate-covered fry and finally blurted, "What are you, Sam?"

"Hmm. Good question . . . an undeniably perfect specimen of the male species."

"You do realize that pregnancy makes women more prone to vomit, don't you?"

"What did you want me to say?"

I frowned into my Frosty. "Do you think that woman will get better?"

"I know she will," he shrugged.

"Why? Because you told her she would?"

"No, because the Spirit told me to tell her she would."

"So, what are you? Some kind of witch doctor or something?"

He chuckled. "No, I'm not a witch doctor. But I hold the priesthood."

"Doris always said you'd joined some crazy cult. After tonight, I almost believe her."

"You never agree with Doris. And you shouldn't in this case, either."

"Don't worry, out of principle, I simply can't agree with her. I swear, I hate that woman."

"Hate? That's a strong word, Suzie."

"Are you going to tell me you love her? Sam, look at us! We raised ourselves! Where was she our whole lives? The only times I recall her *being* around was when she was *smacking* us around and telling us how stupid and worthless we were—how we had ruined her life. So, yeah. I hate her. Don't you?"

Sam looked away. I'd struck a nerve. Sam's halo did have a crack, with Doris's name written all over it.

He suddenly looked up, his eyes shining with tears. "Do you remember the last time she hit me?"

"I've tried to block it all out; so to remember one instance would be difficult."

"I swear, Suz; sometimes I can still feel the burn across my cheek and hear the ringing in my ear from that last time. You don't remember?"

I shuddered, cringing against the images that haunted me when I looked too far into my past. I could see Sam lifting his arm to shelter his face from her bejeweled hand as it swung down again and again over his head. He continued. "It was when I told her I was getting baptized. The best decision of my life, and she gave me the beating of a lifetime for it. And just when she lifted her hand to take another shot at me, you stood in the way and blocked it." His voice cracked slightly. "My little sister to the rescue. You told her you were done with her, told her if she ever raised a hand to us again, you'd call the police and humiliate her in front of all her friends. You told her to let me go so I could have a decent life. And you know what, Suz? She did. She left me alone after that." His jaw worked angrily against the memories.

"I have every reason to hate her, but I don't. I really don't, Suzie."

"How is that possible?"

"Because it didn't hurt her to hate her. It only hurt me. I had to let go." He locked his eyes on mine. "You need to let go, too."

I bit my lip to keep it from trembling. "I can't. Sam, she wanted me to kill my baby! If abortion had been an option when she found out she was pregnant with us, we wouldn't be sitting here right now. And I couldn't do it, Sam. I couldn't. For all the times she said we'd ruined her life, I couldn't see us as anything that bad. When I went to the abortion clinic to get rid of the baby, I looked into the ultrasound they were doing; it was like it was us, and I couldn't kill *us*."

"I'm so sorry you had to go through that, Suzie."

"It isn't your fault."

"Some of it is. I should have been the one to block a blow for you. I should've been there to help you."

I stood up and scooted into the booth seat with him and threw my arms tightly around his neck and hugged him. "You did, Sam. The day I showed up at your door and you hugged me and told me you were worried and that I was welcome to stay because you loved me . . . You blocked one for me that day." We sat in the booth blubbering and hugging each other for what seemed like forever—long enough that I hoped Sam could face his tomorrows without the memory of the burn from Doris's last blow to him. For me, I wasn't sure such a day could ever come.

chapter
28

WE HAD JUST FINISHED OUR WEEKLY staff meeting, and I was on my way back to my desk, when Rion caught up with me.

"Nice job, Suzanna," he said quietly. "You really put that mousy little brown-noser in his place."

"Who? David? He makes me crazy. I don't know why Peter puts up with him."

The meeting had gone long; my swollen feet were killing me; I had a dull ache in my lower back; and I desperately wished someone would fire David. How I hated corporate politics. I knew I had developed a reputation for controversy, and I sometimes worried about being too outspoken. Some in management liked it and would shake their heads and say with fondness, "It's always something with you, Cue." Others, like David, felt threatened by me and would try to quell my ideas before they could get a fair hearing. At least they tried. But I was from Boston, and the thickness of skin that came with my heritage made me hard to quell.

Rion walked with me to my desk. "I loved your comments. It's nice to see David get slammed."

He hesitated for a moment, then asked, "So, would you like to hang out with me and my sister on Friday?"

"I don't know, Rion . . ."

"You don't know what?"

"I don't know how I feel about hanging with people I don't know. Look at me. I look like a cow."

He smirked at me. "You do not look like a cow. You look perfect."

"Perfectly fat," I scoffed.

"Hey, you don't have to come, but I figured you could stand to meet some new friends."

"Why are you so concerned about me having friends?"

"Everyone needs friends. Do you want to, or not?"

"Yeah, I'll go." I relented. It wasn't that I didn't want to, but more that I was afraid of how *much* I wanted to. It was something that had grown gradually, but I was feeling bad that Rion thought of me only as a buddy or a pal. It hurt to admit it, but I felt much more strongly toward him than he did toward me.

That he was only trying to be a friend was reinforced by the fact that he dated other girls. I knew that just that week, he had twice taken another girl from the office out for lunch. There was no reason why he shouldn't see other people, but it hurt to see how hard this girl was working to impress him. An unfamiliar yet all-encompassing wave of jealousy flooded my emotions.

I had never really experienced jealousy before. I had never cared enough about anyone to be jealous. Even Chris, whom I had considered one of my closest and best friends, failed to make me jealous when he brought other women around. At times I was annoyed and provoked to cynicism and hostility, but never jealousy. The idea of this new emotion bothered me almost as much as the emotion itself. I frowned at the feelings, so . . . unlike me.

On Thursday night, Sam and April took me out to dinner and to a movie. When we got home there was a phone message from Mary Stiles, thanking Sam and announcing she was well and that the fever had broken almost as soon as we had left. She had not needed to go to the emergency room after all. Sam didn't seem to think it was a big deal, but I wondered about it. How sick had she really been, and had the blessing Sam given her actually made any difference?

The next day I came home from work and quickly changed clothes. As I waited for Rion, I sat uncomfortably on the couch. My belly was expanding pretty rapidly, and I really did feel like a cow—bloated and huge. Over the last few weeks, I had also begun experiencing a kind of dull ache down low in my abdomen. The pain worried me, especially when I recalled the doctor's "uh-oh" during my ultrasound exam. But since the baby was continuing to do aerobics, I tried to put any concern out of my mind.

Upon entering the little restaurant, it became apparent that we were meeting more than just Rion's sister for dinner. Two other girls and three other guys were already crowded around the table, eating from a bowl of tortilla chips. Rion edged me in next to a guy with a shaggy haircut and then slid in next to me. Sitting across from his sister, Cassie, made me grossly uncomfortable. She was a beauty, perfectly manicured and wearing preppy clothes. It seemed highly unlikely that I could have anything in common with her.

"Hey, Kiddo." Cassie smiled at Rion. Then she turned that smile to me. "Nice to see you again, Suzie. Looks like things worked out okay for you with your brother, huh?"

I shrugged. "Yeah, I guess so. It's been a good move for me."

She made the introductions, and everyone said hi. Then their discussion continued.

"Can you believe that pop quiz he gave us? the shaggy-haired kid exclaimed.

"He only did that because that nerd, Adam, challenged him. You don't tell professors they don't know their own material like that. It just makes the class worse for the rest of us," chimed in a thin, brunette girl.

"The little weasel!" a girl with her hair all tucked under a bandanna, exclaimed. "To tell the professor that there is no mathematical language in nature is suicide! Anyway, he totally disregarded the concept of the Fibonacci Sequence, which proves Doctor Mann's point. I can't believe he would pick a fight with the guy who determines his grade."

"Mann did have an interesting point, though," the guy with the shaggy hair reflected.

Rion leaned over and whispered in my ear. "Sorry," he said, "sounds like we got in on study group, huh?"

"No problem. It's actually pretty interesting," I whispered back.

He raised a brow at that, but it really was interesting to listen to the group bantering about their opinions of how mathematics was the language of nature. The longer they talked, the more heated their opinions became. Cassie called out the shaggy guy, who was now talking very loudly, "If you don't think nature is mathematical, then why is it that random mathematical exercises seem to predict nature so perfectly?"

"I don't think math is the language of nature," I cut Shaggy off before he could respond to Cassie. Everyone turned to stare at me. Since they were silent, I continued: "We need to remember that mankind created math. Nature has provided us with the boundaries and limits that we hold to as the hard and fast rules of mathematics, and we took things from there. Mathematicians identified the Fibonacci Sequence and the concept of phi, and it does help explain why the universe is so much more organized than anyone would imagine at first glance. But that doesn't necessarily mean math is the language of nature. It just means it provided us the framework for math and left us to our own conclusions. So looking at it that way, math is just a representation of nature, like someone taking a picture. The picture isn't actually the subject being photographed, but is simply a representation of that subject." The more I explained, the warmer my face got. Everyone remained quiet, and Cassie was gaping at me.

"Wow, Rion! This is the first time you've ever brought someone around who can think. What's up with that?"

Rion made a helpless gesture with his hands but said nothing, looking at me in a new way. He was smiling, but it was a puzzled smile, as if he were measuring me.

"You sure impressed Cassie," he remarked as he pulled into my driveway at the end of the evening. "How did you know all that—about the difference between pi and phi?

"I don't know that much about it, really."

"You could have fooled me."

I rolled my eyes. The truth was I only knew the basics. I had been sick one day when I was in the fifth grade and stayed home from school. It was a day when Doris had something to do, and she made my dad call in sick so he could watch me.

Dad was fun to be home with all alone like that. He sat next to me on my bed and taught me number games to keep me busy. Then he told me about the Fibonacci Sequence. The concept seemed uncomplicated to me, and the way Dad explained it made it easy to grasp. I understood it immediately, but then it got more complex. Dad spent forever going over equations that looked like the scrawlings of a foreign language. I think he was a little disappointed that I didn't get the finer details. His love of numbers was what led him to being an accountant. He knew that I was naturally good with numbers and seemed to take it personally that I didn't make the effort to pursue that talent.

"I can only tell you the basics. All the technical stuff you'll have to learn on your own. The sequence is actually pretty simple. It's the basic rule that if you want to get the next sum in the sequence, you just add up the two numbers just before it. The first number is zero. Next comes one; now you have two numbers, so you add them together and get one again. Then you add the two ones and get two. Then you add the two to the one right before it and get three. Add the two and the three you get five."

Rion grinned. "Then you add the three and five and get eight!"

"Right! See, it isn't so amazing after all."

"It's amazing enough. Where did you learn all that? I was blown away."

"I read a lot." I shrugged, not wanting to share the pains that the memory of my father stirred. My heart sank a little. I had wanted to impress Rion, not surprise him. "Anyway, why so surprised? Just because I'm pregnant and have a tattoo doesn't mean I'm stupid."

"I didn't mean it like that."

"Well, it sounded like it," I broke in crossly. I expelled a deep breath. "Look, I'm sorry. There was no reason to snap at you. I must be tired."

"I really didn't mean anything by it. I think it's really cool you know things like that. Have you ever thought about going to college?"

"Oh, right. My grades in high school were barely good enough for me to graduate. There's no way I could get into college."

"You could go to a community college."

College. Me? It seemed crazy to even consider it. I wasn't the type. But a part of me had to admit, I had enjoyed being with Cassie and her college buddies. It was fun to be a part of their discussions and to have them pay attention to my ideas. Who knew *Discovery* magazine and a few sick days with dear ol' dad would turn out to be social tools?

"Thanks for inviting me out. It really was nice to be around some new people." He had helped me out of the car, and we were standing at the front door.

"I had fun. And it was neat to find out about this other part of you and the stuff you know," he said.

"Neat?" I repeated. "Neat to be surprised that I'm not so dumb after all?" I had tried to say it like a joke, but it came out as bitterly as the thought made me feel.

"Hey! I never said that!" Rion complained. He appeared baffled by my short temper. I was, too. Completely baffled. I tried smiling, but it came off more like a grimace. I mumbled an apology, repeating that I must be tired and hurried to get in the house before he could say anything further.

After turning out the lights and getting into bed, I wondered why I allowed myself to get angry like that. But deep down, I think I knew the anger had to do with Rion. Every time I was with him I realized even more that I cared more for him than he did for me. And it bothered me also that he seemed so surprised whenever I proved I was smart. In spite of what he or anyone else thought of me, I wouldn't act dumb just to meet their expectations. *College.* The more I considered it, the more I liked the idea.

chapter
29

SUNDAY, I DIDN'T GRUMBLE AT HAVING to go to church, at least not where anyone could hear me. When Alison came in late to Young Women and took a seat next to me, I made a point of smiling at her. She gave me a little smile and sniffled in a few places during the lesson. I was intrigued that she would feel anything to drive her to tears during the lessons. I mean, sure, April did a good job and was entertaining and everything, but what was there that would make Alison *feel* like that?

I tried to talk to her after class, but she was reluctant to stay and hurried away as fast as her legs would carry her. The other girls were beginning to grow on me. They were lively and fun and filled with an enthusiasm that seemed to have passed me by. I didn't ever remember having that kind of spark to me when I was a teenager. I could see why April enjoyed teaching her class.

At work on Monday, Rion found me and apologized for being insensitive. I told him I was sorry for being cranky. He then asked me if I wanted to hang out on Friday. He always referred to time spent with me as "hanging out" but never as a date. It was frustrating to me that I noticed little nuances like that. How was it I had come to care? That question occupied my mind for the rest of the week until Rion came to get me on Friday.

"So, what are we doing?" I asked as he pulled his car into a spot in the Orem High School parking lot.

"Going to a play," he responded. "Don't touch your door." The command was strong enough to hold me in my seat until he came around to let me out.

A teenager with a drama letterman's jacket hung over her shoulders handed us a playbill announcing the play *My Fair Lady.* Soon the lights were dimmed, and the spotlight shone on a young girl with a very convincing Cockney accent.

The scenery, music, and dance numbers were all impressive, and even though I was uncomfortable sitting, I found myself enjoying the performance. I had never attended the plays in high school. High school for me was a fuzzy haze of pot, alcohol, and ecstasy. I experienced a pang of regret. All the years I wasted being wasted, times I could not recall, let alone go back to and fix in any way.

Rion laughed at a line in the play. I wondered, if he knew my past in long and sordid detail, would he run away? Or worse, would he look on me with pity or disgust? He knew a lot about me. My ever-growing belly made evident a good deal of who I was and where I'd come from without me ever having to say a word, and he hadn't run away yet. I had come so far, it seemed my old life was a million years ago. I hadn't had a hit or a drink in so many months, it may as well have been years. I was far enough away from it now to realize I had been a fool.

When Eliza and Professor Higgins were finally reconciled, the final bows had been taken, and the enthusiastic cheers and applause had been silenced by the dropping of a heavy curtain, Rion turned in his seat and gazed at me.

"Stop looking at me." I scowled.

"Why?"

"Because I told you to."

"Sorry, all directions must be in writing and left in the suggestion box."

"Well, you're making me nervous."

He grinned at that, the crinkles around his eyes deepening. His perfect teeth were framed by his perfect mouth. I wondered if he was going to kiss me. I wondered why the idea of such a kiss made me all fluttery. I had been kissed by lots of guys, but never had I felt such intensity of emotion as I did with him, and he hadn't even come close to kissing me. With everyone else it had been so mechanical . . . something to do to idle away time. I knew with him, were he to kiss me, it would be entirely different.

The people around us were getting up and leaving. "Tell me something about you. Something I don't already know," he said.

"I've served time in jail," I said without thinking. I had always loved shocking people, and it just came out. Immediately, I regretted it. He laughed out loud. "You did not!"

"I did." I shrugged.

"For what?"

"Murder."

"Oh, really? Where'd you hide the body?"

"Uruguay."

"Oh, that makes sense. I heard that Uruguay is a good place to hide a body," he joked. "Seriously . . . what for?"

"Embezzlement."

He grinned. "Nope, sorry . . . try again."

I didn't know why I felt compelled to go on. "Really. It was embezzlement. Corporate theft."

"What did you do?" His incredulity made me laugh.

"When new shipments of DVDs came in, I didn't inventory them. Instead, I loaded up my friend's jeep, and we sold them on eBay and some to pawn shops. I also found ways to get money from holiday pay. The company I worked for was terrible at keeping track of our hours. I added a few to every pay period. Throw in a bereavement day or a holiday or vacation leave every once in a while, and it never occurred to them to check to see if I had really accumulated that time. Well . . . it never occurred to them until I got caught."

It made no sense. Here I was, telling him the worst things about myself.

"You're serious?" If his eyes were open any wider, they'd have bugged out of his head.

"Serious as a heart attack, O-Rion."

"So what was jail like?"

"The first few days, before my parents posted bail, I was in a real cell. There was nothing but a bed with a cot that was less than two inches thick and a metal toilet that was so cold, I was afraid to sit on it. I was afraid my hind end would freeze to it."

"Did you have a cellmate?"

"Nope, just me, a cot, and a can. They wouldn't even give me a magazine to read. I've never been so bored in all my life. I counted bricks for entertainment."

"Bricks?"

"The bricks that made up the outer wall. It was the worst three days of my life."

"Oh, come on. Boredom can't be the worst thing in the world. It could've been worse."

I bit my lip. "There were other things besides boredom that made it really bad. Things you could never understand."

My heart was racing, trying to decide if I should tell him everything or leave well enough alone. The quickened pulse pumped blood furiously through my already throbbing head. I put my palms against my temples to try to ease the headache that was building. Rion's earnest expression—open and wondering—waiting for me to tell all, encouraged me to continue. For reasons I didn't really understand, I wanted him to know how horrible I had been. Maybe I was testing him—trying to see if he would run away. I was tossing all my eggs to him, wondering if he would catch them.

"For those three days, I was drug-free. It was the first time in almost two years that I'd gone longer than twenty-four hours without being high or drunk or both. I had been forced into detox, and it hurt, and it was scary."

"Explain it to me. What does that feel like?"

"When you go so long doing drugs and getting tweaked all the time, it dulls your senses. It's like being numb and frozen and then thawing out too fast. All of a sudden, the numbness began to wear off, and I could feel the pain. Sort of like when your feet have gone to sleep and begin to wake up and tingle—only a thousand times worse. I couldn't stand up. I couldn't do anything but cry. Well, cry . . . and scream at the guards."

"It sounds awful," he said softly.

"So do you hate me now?" I looked away from him. The auditorium was nearly empty, aside from stage crew readying the stage for the next night's performance. I tried to focus on them, not wanting to hear Rion's reaction to my drug addiction.

"Why would I hate you?"

"For being such a bad person."

He put his hand on my chin and turned my face toward his. I could see by the look in his hazel eyes that he wasn't going to condemn me. "Look, Suzanna, the events in people's lives are just patches; every event is a different color or texture that gets sewn into a big elaborate quilt. I think it would be sad and very boring if all of us had perfect, uniform quilts. The color and variety is what makes us interesting people. That one patch in your past isn't who you are. It's just a part of the quilt. The whole quilt is who you are."

"Do you really believe that?"

"I do. My dad wrote me that in a letter after I'd had a few failings in my mission. I was feeling pretty bad about them and was completely down on myself. What he said made sense, and I knew he was right. Those few bad days didn't define the kind of missionary I was; they were just patches. And tomorrow there will be a different patch. The goal is to someday edge the entire quilt with the gold thread of understanding and growth and hand it to God and say, 'This is what I got out of life . . . thanks.'"

I thought about that a moment—thought about handing my finished quilt over to that being with the resonating voice at Temple Square. Would He want it? Would I dare hand it over? "That doesn't answer my question. Do you hate me now?"

He chuckled softly. "No, I don't hate you. You'll have to try harder than that."

He had caught the eggs—once again. My head was still aching, and my hands were still trembling, but I felt safe with him.

I took a deep breath. "So tell me something about you."

"I'm not that interesting. I haven't really done much in my life."

"There has to be something," I said.

"Hmmm . . . well, I jumped out of an airplane once."

"Why would you do that?"

The lines around his eyes deepened as he laughed. "For the thrill. It was so cool."

"You know, people break legs and other important body parts doing stuff like that."

"Yeah, well . . ." He stopped, frowned, and looked at my hands. "Why are you shaking? Are you cold?"

"No. I just feel . . . nervous. It sounds crazy, but I feel almost like you feel when you have to do an oral report for school. That sick dread sorta feeling."

"Is this about work?" He looked really concerned.

I shrugged. "No. I don't know, maybe . . ."

"Well . . . maybe you're hungry. Let's go get something to eat." He stood, pulling me up with him. The ache in my abdomen that had been intermittently causing me discomfort, suddenly slammed through me.

"Ow!" I cried, doubling over. I would have cussed if I could have found the breath to utter it.

Rion held me up. "What happened? What's wrong?"

The pain subsided after a moment, and I stood upright. "Nothing, just a little pain. It's gone now." I shook my head to clear the black flecks and pinprick bursts of light that had spotted my vision. My head was aching, like I had a hangover, only worse.

"You sure you're okay?"

"Yeah, I'm fine . . . really."

He acted as though he didn't believe me as he gingerly led me to the car and eased me into the front seat. "I'm fine," I repeated, more to myself than to him. The baby was still moving, so I was sure I really was fine . . . almost. I gauged everything by her. It worried me when she didn't move for longer than an hour. But since she was moving now, I had to be fine.

We stopped to get a burger and some fries. There were tacky orange and black decorations pinned up to celebrate the up-coming Halloween season. The colors were sickening if colors could be such. I was feeling more jittery by the moment. My hands were now trembling so violently I clamped them together in my lap to keep Rion from noticing.

"Would you ever marry a girl with a kid?" I asked.

He leaned back, apparently stunned.

"That wasn't a proposal or anything, O-Rion."

His laugh was higher than usual. "Oh, I know that."

"So would you?"

"I dunno. My hope has always been that when I get married, the girl I pick will have waited for me to start a family. But I s'pose I might, if I really loved her, and if I knew it was the right decision in the Lord's eyes."

"How would you know if it were the right decision?"

"I'd pray and then I'd know."

I didn't bother to tell him that sounded perfectly absurd, and I didn't bother to ask him if he would ever consider putting in such a prayer about me. It seemed insane to think he would. My heart sank. I was in love with a guy who couldn't love me back. Now I knew how Chris had felt.

I could no longer shake my head to clear the spots dancing through my vision because it ached too much. Instead I blinked rapidly and trained myself not to focus too long on anything. The twinges in my abdomen were constant now, and I had gone from feeling dull anxiety to near outright panic.

"I need to go home," I said, quickly standing and setting off another shower of sparks inside my head. My peripheral vision seemed to be caving in on itself, and I experienced a sudden dizziness and a wave of nausea. Leaving Rion to dump our trash, I beat him to the car, where I leaned my forehead on the cold metal. The night air was cool, and I breathed in the frigid air, scented by the smell of burning wood.

Rion was right behind me. He quickly unlocked my door and helped me into the car. He drove fast. *Was he worried?* I was worried. I thought I heard him say I should get home and get to bed. *Was he mad at me?* The ring on my hand had been bugging me earlier and now seemed to be pressing into my skin like a clamp. My finger hurt. Were my hands swelling? It figured that they would. My feet and ankles had been swollen for almost a month. Why not everything else? The way I was going, I'd look like the girl who turned into a swollen blueberry in *Charlie and the Chocolate Factory,* the one the Oompa Loompas rolled away.

When we pulled up to Sam's house, Rion got out quickly. He didn't tell me to not open my own door. I opened it and climbed out of the car, not certain why the jittery, something-was-wrong feeling had taken over so completely. The flecks turned into holes again across my vision. My body was shaking and I was falling, and I caught Rion's arm and fumbled at his jacket to hold on. *Why was I shaking? Why was I falling?* My peripheral vision caved in entirely this time, and the world suddenly faded to black.

chapter
30

S<small>UZIE!</small>" I<small>T WAS</small> S<small>AM'S VOICE, BUT IT</small> was muffled and seemed to be coming from a long way off. My heart was racing, pumping the blood too fast through my brain to be of any use. The pain in my stomach was worse, and I could feel it tighten around the baby. Something was dreadfully wrong.

"Sam?" My voice sounded horribly high-pitched to me.

"It's okay. Let's get you in the car." Sam was carrying me. He slid me into his backseat where Rion was waiting. My head sank gratefully to Rion's lap, and his hand smoothed over my hair. Sam and April were in the front, and we were driving. *Where are we going?*

I must have voiced the question because Rion cooed soothingly, "To the hospital."

"Something's wrong," I said. "Something's wrong with her." I was wailing. Panic flooded through me and carried all reasonable thought away with it. "Don't let her die," I pleaded.

"Sshhh. Don't even talk like that. Everything's okay," Rion soothed.

April twisted in her seat to reach behind her and take my hand. "Oh . . . she's shaking!" she said. *Was I shaking?* Yes, I was.

At the hospital, Sam and Rion gingerly lifted me out of the car and carried me through the doors that opened with an electronic swoosh. I was crying, the pain in my stomach getting worse. I totally panicked. I felt like a claustrophobe locked in a coffin.

"She's dying, Sam," I sobbed as attendants took me from Sam and Rion and eased me onto a gurney.

There were people around me now. I could see them around the spots hazing my vision. "She's dying." My words were lost to the crowd.

An emergency doctor looked at me. My body was trembling as though I were freezing. "Let's get her up to the women's center," he ordered. As they wheeled me away, my head hurt so badly I wanted someone to cut it off to stop the pain.

Someone was taking my blood pressure. She patted my hand as the wrapping around my arm squeezed tighter, making my head hurt even more. "We need a urine sample," she said. "Can you do that?"

I nodded and was helped to a rest room where I lost all decorum, not caring that my hands had become too twitchy to pull my own pants off. The woman who'd taken my blood pressure helped me through the moment, asking me questions in a soothing calm tone. "Your blood pressure is high," she observed, causing my anxiety to double. "Tell me what else is happening?"

"I can't see," I blurted. "And my heart is racing so fast I feel like I'm running. I can see it pounding through my shirt. And my head," I groaned. "My head hurts so bad; and my belly keeps hurting here." I pointed to the middle. "But then sometimes it hurts really bad here." I pointed toward the bottom of my belly. "Help her," I pleaded to the nurse.

The nurse patted my arm again. "How far along are you?"

"Thirty weeks."

I was left alone in a bed for a moment, wondering why Sam, April, and Rion had left me. More nurses came in to stall my wonderings and strapped belt-like things around my midsection. The sound of the baby's heartbeat echoed into the room from a speaker in a monitor by my bed. I cried when I heard it. She was still okay. But I could feel . . . tell that she was fighting. Something was wrong. I was losing her.

"She's contracting," one nurse said to another nurse. "Get the on-call doctor in here."

"I'm contracting?" I wailed.

"Sshhh. It's okay. We need you to try to calm down. We have to get an IV in you so we can give you medication that will stop the contractions. The best thing you can do right now is be calm."

I tried what she suggested, but I could feel the baby slipping away. My head pounded like horses hooves on a racetrack. How could I stop her from fading? How could I fix this?

"It's unusual," one of the nurses said. "Pre-eclampsia is much more common in young girls."

"How high was her protein count?" another nurse asked.

"Two."

The doctor came in then. He grabbed a chart. "One-seventy over one-ten. What did the protein come out at?"

"Protein is at a two. She's complaining of a headache and vision distortion. Her feet and hands are swollen, and she's experiencing some hypertension. She's also fairly spastic."

I listened to the nurse's assessment with horror. I had no idea what she was even saying, but it sounded terrible.

The doctor looked at the baby's charts that were scrolling out from the monitor. He frowned. "She needs nifedipine. It should bring her blood pressure down." In a lower tone, he added, "Do magnesium sulfate, too . . . just in case."

Just in case what? I wanted to shout, but the idea of shouting made me stifle a sob for the pain that would bring to my head. He did a very invasive check on me and then pulled off the rubber glove, pitching it to a hazardous waste trash can. "You're dilated to a three and twenty percent effaced."

"What does that mean?" I managed to squeak out.

"You're in labor with toxemia. It's serious. We need to get your blood pressure under control." He left. Nurses injected things into my IV bag, frowning when they read my charts over again. Panic was all-consuming. She was fading; couldn't they see? Didn't they know? *She was dying!*

April entered the room just as I let out a wail of despair. Her eyes went wild with fear as she rushed to my side and clasped my hand. "What's wrong? What's happening?"

"Where have you been?" I demanded.

"They wouldn't let us in until just now. We had to fill out the paperwork and insurance forms."

I clenched her hand tighter as another contraction came, and I pulled her close enough our noses nearly touched. "She's dying, April! My baby's dying. I can feel her slipping away, and I can't hold onto her. Get Sam. He needs to help me. Please, get Sam!"

She gave a short nod of understanding and hurried from the room. It seemed I had barely taken two breaths before all three of them were standing next to my bed.

Sam put his hand on my forehead and with his other hand took hold of mine. "What do you need? What can I do?" he whispered.

"Fix me like you did Mary Stiles. The baby's dying! You have to save her. I swear, if she dies, I will too. Please fix this!"

Sam rolled his eyes in frustration and desperation. "I can't," he said.

My anger was overwhelming. "What do you mean you can't? I know you can . . . I saw you!"

He ran a hand through his dark hair, and his dark brown eyes locked with mine. "That wasn't me, Suz. That was God. It was His power." He leaned closer to me, whispering. "I didn't do it; God did." I was sobbing now. "Please help me. Don't let her die. Ask your god to fix this."

April sniffed. Tears slid down Sam's perfect nose and dropped onto my hand. Was he crying because the moment was hopeless? I looked over at Rion. He was crying, too. Did they all know something I didn't? Was I so far past repair that they were already mourning?

"*You* have to believe He can. It isn't enough for me to believe. You have to. Do you, Suzie? Do you believe that in Christ's name, God can heal you?"

Time froze.

The baby's heartbeat thundered in my ears along with the pounding of my own, and all other sound was drowned by it. *Did I believe?* Sam believed; April believed, too. I looked at Rion. His face was a mask of terror and hope. He hoped. What was it he hoped for? He believed; *did I believe?*

What did I believe? I believed I was losing the baby. I believed Sam could bring her back. I believed he could fix it, but I also believed him when he said he couldn't. Did I believe that God could? My life spiraled in my mind—images I had drowned out by alcohol, guys I'd spent the night with, lies I'd told, the bars slamming shut on my cell door, rehab in all its white sterility; the moment in the women's center in Boston when I realized I couldn't kill this baby. Could my baby die anyway, after all of that? I saw Doris's angry face when I told her I couldn't do it.

Doris . . . the idea of being such a selfish mother made my teeth clench and my muscles tighten. If I kept this baby, being the person I was, would I be like Doris? I knew the answer was yes. But the thought of her dying wasn't acceptable, not even to escape a future with me, a future like mine.

What did I believe? The statue at Temple Square with the god holding the world in the crook of his arm. *Did I believe in him?*

"Behold . . . I am Jesus Christ . . . learn of me . . . let not your heart be troubled . . ." It was like I was there again, in that starry room, standing before the white statue of Jesus. The memory stood out so much in my mind; it was almost as if I could reach out and touch the pierced stone feet.

"Do you believe in me?" The voice asked in my mind. I was delirious. I had to have been.

"Who are you?" my mind demanded.

"You know who I am . . . but do you believe?"

"I don't know . . . Wait! Don't leave! Yes, I do believe . . . " I thought; *"I believe and I'm so sorry . . . so sorry. Please save the baby. Don't let her die."*

"Save her for what?" the voice wanted to know.

"I'll do anything . . . everything to make her life good. Just don't let her die."

"She isn't yours to keep; do you understand? Her future lies with others. Can you sacrifice that?"

I could feel my body convulsing, her heartbeat mingling with mine in a crescendo of ache. Could I sacrifice that? I could; I had to. And somehow it seemed I had been expecting that answer. "I can. I will . . . I do believe."

I must have uttered the last out loud. The frozen moment ended. Sam was now pulling out his keys—the vial of oil. Rion stepped forward and their hands were on my head. I don't remember the words, but the feeling was so intense that had I been standing, I would have collapsed to my knees. *"Don't worry,"* the statue said. *"She'll be fine."*

Then He smiled at me. It had to be delirium. Statues don't talk; they don't smile.

My heart was still pounding in my rib cage, but as Sam ended his prayer it was as though it stopped altogether, suspended in the space of two regular heartbeats. And then it thumped in my chest. The beat was now regular. It left me exhausted, as if I'd been running and now could finally rest.

Rion kissed my forehead, not seeming to notice the sheen of sweat there. Sam hugged April. They were both crying. As Rion edged away, I caught his shirt. "She's okay now," I offered weakly. He smiled, his beautiful hazel eyes framed by those sweet crinkles.

"I know," he whispered, his square jaw set in confidence of this truth.

chapter

31

I MUST HAVE FALLEN ASLEEP, OVERTAKEN by exhaustion. I didn't remember dreaming. But when I awoke, I was in a different room, in a regular bed instead of the one in the labor and delivery room. My throat was dry, my tongue swollen. There was a sensation of pain where they had taped the IV to my arm. All of the other pain was gone, or at least dulled to where I could barely feel it.

April was asleep in an easy chair next to my bed, a white hospital blanket tucked under her chin. There were still the Velcro belts holding the paddle that monitored contractions and the baby's heartbeat. All seemed quiet and peaceful.

The anxiety I'd felt before was completely gone and my body lay still, not trembling at all. How long had I been there? I must have been really tired if I couldn't remember changing rooms. Where were Sam and Rion?

"April?" My voice was a squeak, strained by exhaustion and thick with sleep. I tried again. "April!"

She mumbled something and turned in her chair a little more toward the windows. I picked up a Styrofoam cup filled with half-melted ice chips and flung a few at her.

She sat straight up. "Sam!" she yelled, looking around. I snickered that she thought Sam was the one torturing her in her sleep.

"Sam's not here."

"Oh . . . You're awake. How do you feel?"

"Actually, kinda numb. I don't feel anything."

"Good." She stretched deeply and yawned, which made me yawn.

"What happened? How did I get in here?" I asked.

"You went to sleep right after they gave you the blessing. The doctor said your heart rate had calmed down and that your blood pressure was stabilizing. He was planning on delivering the baby, but your condition changed so dramatically, he couldn't justify it. After the contractions stopped, they decided to move you in here."

"So everything's okay?" I knew it was but had to ask to be sure. I wanted confirmation.

"Everything's okay. But you're going to be on bedrest for the rest of the pregnancy."

"Bedrest?"

"Yep. You're allowed to get up to go to the bathroom only. You won't have to here." Her eyes flickered to the lower part of my bed. "Here you're on a catheter. You might end up having to spend the rest of the pregnancy in the hospital anyway."

"I can't be on bedrest. What'll I do about work?"

"Sam said he'd see what he could find out. Don't worry about it. Everything will be fine. The doctor said you weren't allowed to be under stress of any kind."

Some people from the office pitched in and sent flowers. Rion sent flowers, balloons, and sneaked me in a Frosty with fries. He stayed a long time and seemed to be beaming at me for reasons I didn't understand. I felt a little relieved when he left, mingled with a strange emptiness that only his presence was able to fill.

The doctor from the previous night came in and congratulated me on a narrow escape. He told me they had almost decided to take the baby early, but upon reentering my room had found the baby and me both to be infinitely better and in no immediate danger. He had taken a chance and let the pregnancy continue. He reaffirmed I would be on bedrest and gave me a list of things I needed to do to keep my blood pressure down. Nurses filtered in and out, checking my temperature, changing IV bags and catheter bags, and checking my feet and legs for heaven only knew what. By that night, I had decided it had been the most bizarre day of my life.

32

Getting any sleep in the hospital is impossible. Though they called this new phase "bedrest," there was nothing restful about it. Every two to three hours, some new shift nurse would come in to take my blood pressure and check my feet and legs. When I grumpily asked one of the nurses what she thought she was doing, she muttered something about blood clots and hurried away. The only good thing about my present status was the direct and constant link to the baby. They still kept her monitored by the paddle that echoed her heartbeat to my ears. She was okay now, and I had to decide what to do about that.

It was a little after twelve-thirty in the afternoon that Jan from the Relief Society came to visit me. She brought me flowers in a vibrant and cheery splay and a small package wrapped in shiny paper with a real daisy and a red rose nestled in the ribbons.

"How are you doing?" she asked, settling into the easy chair near my bed.

"I'm good. Tired, but good." I bit my lower lip, surprised that she had come but very pleased that she had.

"Heard it was quite a miracle the way you pulled out of it."

"It was," I agreed.

We sat in the silent space of seventeen heartbeats. It seemed

I measured every moment by heartbeats. I could count them as the monitor on the baby dutifully kept track. "Well aren't you going to open your present?" she asked. "It's from Roberta and me."

"Oh . . . yes." I tore the wrapping, indiscriminately ripping it to uselessness but careful to take out the flowers and set them aside. Jan stood up and busied herself with putting them in a foam cup with water while I turned the dark blue, hardbound book over in my hands. The Book of Mormon.

I hesitated, wondering what to say to such an odd gift. Opening it just to be polite, I found a hand-written letter tucked between the pages, and I glanced at the opening lines in the first chapter: "I, Nephi, having been born of goodly parents . . ." I snorted at that. "Well, it's nice to know someone in this world was," I quipped, closing the book again.

"Try to be more positive, Suzie. You'll soon have a child that will be able to say just that."

I turned away as much as the tubes and wires attached to me would allow. "I'm not keeping her," I finally said out loud. I didn't turn back to face her, not wanting to know how she would react to such a statement, but it felt good to say it to someone.

"You're not?"

"I sort of promised I wouldn't." There was really no more to it than that. Though the thoughts from the other night had likely been the result of feverish delirium, there was no denying the peace that came when I promised that I would make her life as good as possible. And there was no denying the force of the voice telling me she wasn't mine to keep. I *wanted* to deny it . . . it was insanity after all, but I *couldn't* deny it.

If I kept her, I would love her, but she would have a mother like mine. I had changes to make in my life and the realization that I had to *be* somebody *before* I raised somebody slammed home hard. That, along with the words from the voice in my head before the blessing, had convinced me: *"She isn't yours to keep; do you understand? Her future lies with others. Can you sacrifice that?"*

"Who'd you promise that to?" Jan got up and sat on my bed where I would have to look at her.

"Your God."

Her face froze, suspended in surprise, and then crumpled as she held back tears. Then she smiled and said, "And I thought I was just crazy . . . " She reached for her bag and pulled out a file filled with papers and pamphlets.

"I woke up this morning fully intending to visit you," she started, "and on my way to the hospital I had this incredible impression that I should stop and get you this information." Tears had welled up in her eyes as she handed the file to me. "By the time I'd gotten back in my car to come here I decided I had just imagined it all and had made up my mind to not give these to you . . . but now . . ." She wiped a tear away. "If you truly believe in this promise you've made, then this is the very best choice you have."

I looked at the file with wonder. LDS Adoption Services. My eyes burned as I shut them defiantly. No! There would be no tears today. Not about this. It had been all I'd thought about for a day and a half, and I knew it was the right choice. Maybe it wouldn't have been for another girl in my situation, but for me . . . it simply was the right thing to do. And Jan showing up with this information was the confirmation I needed.

"Thank you." The whisper was hoarse. "I wasn't sure how to get started, and . . . I've been afraid to tell Sam and April."

"I'm sure they'll understand. They're some of the best people I know."

I laughed, holding back the partial bitterness I felt. "Yeah, me too. I used to tease Sam about the mountains moving out of his way just because he said please. I wish I could do that . . ."

Jan patted my hand. "You're doing that right now. Beginning the day you decided to stand up for yourself and for this little baby." She wiped her eyes. "Well, I'd better go." She stood up.

"Thanks for all of this." I moved the folder. "And for the book. I'm not much of a reader, but . . ."

She laughed. "With two and a half months to stare at the ceiling, you'll probably find time to do some reading." She hesitated for a moment, then added: "I love the Book of Mormon. I hope you will too."

With that, she was gone.

After she'd gone and I'd sifted through the paperwork from LDS Adoption Services, I opened the book she gave me and pulled out the pretty paper folded up inside.

She'd written in a purple ink to match the petals pressed into the paper. It was by far the prettiest letter I'd ever received.

Dear Suzanna,

I heard a speaker at a fireside once say that women are either roses or daisies. Each is beautiful and perfect in its own way, but they are very different from each other. The rose is formal, graceful, and elegant; the daisy casual, cheerful, and perky.

Sometimes daisies have a hard time fitting in when they get planted in a rose garden. And roses would seem to be out of place in a garden of daisies. I hope this book will help you discover who you are. Whoever it is, know this, either one is a grand thing to be, and one shouldn't try to pass for the other. Be happy and know you are loved by Heavenly Father.

Love,

Jan

I read the letter through once more before looking at the rose and daisy Jan had placed in a cup together. They did make an odd pairing, yet together like that they seemed to complement one another. "I'm no rose," I said bitterly. I pulled the daisy out and inspected it for lack of anything better to do. It *was* cheerful, too cheerful, too sunny. I wasn't a daisy, either. "I'm a weed," I snorted. "Nothing but a weed."

April and Sam came that night and went through a succession of reactions to my decision to place my baby for adoption: surprise, concern, hesitation, and finally—support. The last was what I needed from them.

Rion and Cassie dropped in as they were leaving. Rion shook Sam's hand and hugged April as though they were long-lost friends. He had brought more flowers and a kid's meal-sized Frosty but no fries. "I didn't want to upset your blood pressure," he explained, handing me the miniature shake. His hazel eyes shone, and his smile seemed genuine. Cassie was her normal gorgeous self and seemed to be fascinated by all the bells and whistles I was hooked to. We made small talk about school and work until Rion suddenly checked his watch. "Oops. Can I borrow your phone, Cassie?"

"We're in a hospital, dummy. You can't turn on a cell phone. There's a phone right here. Or use the phone in the waiting room if you need privacy."

He hesitated for a moment then said, "Maybe I'll use the phone outside."

As he left the room, Cassie gazed after him then turned back to me with a fond shake of her head. "He's such a nut."

"But a likeable one."

"Do you like him?" She asked it directly, from the point of view of a big sister looking out for her brother.

I frowned. How do you tell a guy's sister that he is the only male in the world capable of making your heart race? "Who wouldn't like him?" I hedged.

"Well, if it makes you feel better, he likes you, too." I had to grin. It was all so juvenile—like having someone in grade school confide that a certain boy liked you. But, still, hearing it made my heart leap.

While I savored the news, Cassie added, "But he does have concerns."

"Concerns?"

She hesitated for a moment then went on, "I don't know exactly what he plans to do, but there's this whole church thing to consider. From the time he was a little boy, he was always taught that the only way to get married is in the temple. It means everything to him. So it's a big deal to him that you aren't a member."

"I suppose it doesn't help that I'm going to have a baby, either."

She laughed. "Yeah, there's that, too."

She sighed. "Suzie, I swear I'm not telling you all of this to dissuade you from liking him and I'm not saying anything to him to dissuade him from liking you. I'm only saying don't be surprised that he's being careful and don't be surprised if he decides to do something different from what seems expected."

"I don't have any expectations," I lied. I almost told her I had decided to give the baby up for adoption, in hopes that it would increase my favor with her brother, but realized it probably wouldn't make a difference. I still wasn't a Mormon. I glanced at the book Jan had given me and wondered what Mormons got from that book that made them so different from everyone else.

Rion came back into my room and the two of them stayed another hour. It was fun to listen as he and Cassie talked about growing up together, even though it made me jealous to think about all the love they had experienced in their family. Cassie also asked me about Boston and my schooling and seemed genuinely surprised that I hadn't had any formal education beyond high school. She was even more surprised that I had barely managed to graduate. When they left, the empty space, that only Rion seemed to be able to fill, returned.

It was hours into the next day before I realized it would be hours longer before I received any visitors. Everyone was at work. Boredom finally lured me to open the Book of Mormon Jan had given me. "I, Nephi, having been born of goodly parents . . ." I wondered if Nephi had any idea how lucky and how unlike the majority of the world he was.

By the time Sam and April showed up, I was most of the way through first Nephi. They either didn't notice the book, or they chose not to mention it. I chose not to mention it, either, not needing the over-exuberant enthusiasm that I had witnessed whenever Mormons got the idea someone was even remotely interested in their religion.

The next morning, a nurse came in to check up on me. "Glad to see you're doing so much better!" she beamed. "It was quite the miraculous recovery, I hear. Going into preeclamptic labor is a scary thing."

"Does it happen a lot?" I asked.

"Often enough. Though it's mostly common among girls who smoke or drink or do drugs . . . you know the type." She waved a hand absently, entirely unaware that the type of person she was describing was lying in the bed in front of her. I tried to comment, to agree in some way that would not incriminate me, but when I opened my mouth no sound came out. *So it* was *my fault.* The baby I had been so valiant to save at the abortion clinic was almost killed by my stupid choices. It was all my fault.

"Oh, and youth. You're young. That's probably why it happened to you," the nurse continued, still unaware that I was the drugged-out teen she was describing. "Pregnancies in younger girls and older women are statistically more likely to end up in preeclampsia. Of course, it isn't so much that the girls are doing drugs or whatever they do, but more that they just don't take proper care of their bodies and so when they get pregnant their bodies can't handle the extra load. There's also a genetic factor . . ."

She barely paused for a breath as she prattled on. "If your mother had eclampsia, you'd be more likely to have it. Older women get it, too. But no need to worry about any of the whys. You pulled out like a plane from a nosedive. You're doing just fine now and should stay that way if you're careful from here on out. Just make good choices."

Make good choices. It was something the man at the organ had said at testimony meeting. *It was my fault!* My choices had been anything but good. There were gaping holes in my memory, caused by the times when I was drunk or high. How many guys had I lured into the bedroom thinking I was the exception?—that diseases and pregnancy happened to other girls? My baby had almost died! *And it was all my fault.* Guilt was a new emotion for me. Until now, there had never been anything in my life important enough to feel guilty about.

Thinking about these things made me despondent and sullen. It was to escape those feelings and pass the time that I found myself reading the Book of Mormon.

I looked forward to the evenings when Sam, April, and Rion would come to visit. I tried to act chipper and to hide my guilt and depression from them. Rion sometimes rented movies to watch, and the two of us had little pseudo slumber parties in the hospital. He was astounded when I admitted I had never seen *Monty Python and the Holy Grail* and brought it with him the next night. He sat in the chair next to my bed, and we laughed so hard a male nightshift nurse came in and scolded Rion for being there so late. Those few hours were good for me, though. I was able to forget about where I was and why I was there.

chapter
33

I ENDED UP STAYING IN THE HOSPITAL for five days, until the doctor
released me to go home for bedrest. I was relieved when Sam informed
me that since my medical benefits were in full force, they included dis-
ability, so I was covered as far as my job and the mountain of hospital
bills were concerned.

While in the car driving to Sam and April's house, Sam was quiet,
much more than Sam ever was. "Is something wrong?" I asked.

"Mom called," he said. His eyes were fixed on the road and his
knuckles showed white on the steering wheel.

"Doris?"

He nodded. I could see his jaw working as he ground his teeth
together.

"So? What does she want? Money to get her nails done?"

"She wants to come next month. She says she wants to see you."

The thought of her coming was too much. "Well, I don't want to
see her!"

"I told her that. She argued with me. You know how Mom is . . ."

"No!" I shouted. "I don't know how *Mom* is. Doris has never made
one effort to become a 'mom.' Please don't let her come, Sam. Please."

"I told her she couldn't—not until after the baby is born."

217

I relaxed a little. I knew I could count on him for that. When the doctor told him there could be absolutely no stress in my life, I knew he would make certain there wasn't any. I was safe from her, at least for a couple of months longer.

With April's support and encouragement, I called the number for the adoption counselor written on the file. I explained my situation, that I was on strict bedrest, and the woman I talked to was very understanding and sympathetic. We set up an appointment for her to come by my house the next day. Even though the house looked fine, April cleaned like crazy in preparation, and I felt bad I couldn't help.

Sam and April had set me up on the couch in the family room instead of in my bedroom during the day. That way I was closer to the bathroom and kitchen should I need anything.

Rion showed up before April and Sam got home and an hour before the counselor arrived. He knocked, then let himself in. "Hey there, slacker," he grinned.

"I'm not a slacker. I'm bored."

"Oh, c'mon. You've got four or five hundred stations to surf." He sat on the couch by me. "And look at all these magazines to read and—" His grin vanished. "What's this?" He picked up the file for LDS Adoption Services.

I fumbled for words, but when he looked up from the file, my voice failed altogether.

"Is this seriously something you're thinking about?"

"No." My voice was small.

His emotions seemed to be mixed, lost somewhere between relief and pain. "Oh, well . . . not that it's any of my business anyway. I—"

"No. I meant, no, I'm not thinking about it. Because I've already decided."

"And what's that decision?" He was tense again.

"I'm going to give her up for adoption."

He stood, dropping the file back onto the table. "Wow. I mean wow. That's quite a decision to have made." He began to pace, then turned to face me. "Are you sure you're going to be okay with this?"

I stared at the floor instead of meeting his eyes. "When I went to the hospital and almost lost the baby, I had . . . well . . . a strong feeling that I needed to agree to give her away to a *real* family. It's all kinda complicated, but I knew that if she were to live, I needed to make that promise. If I hadn't agreed, He wouldn't have helped me, and she would have died. So I agreed, and now she's okay. What else could I do?"

Rion scratched his head, still caught in limbo between conflicting emotions that I was unable to understand. "Are you sure?"

"Yeah, I am. I could never give her all the things she'll need. I'm convinced. Her future lies with others. That's what I was told."

"Who told you that?"

"I . . . I don't know. It was like a voice in my head. And it was probably just some crazy thinking from my semi-delusional state of mind, but I feel better, now that I've made that choice."

"Let the Holy Spirit guide . . ." he whispered, looking at me with wonder and seemingly lost for words beyond that. "Well, hey, I better go," he said finally. Turning to leave he almost knocked April over who had just come home from work. He mumbled an apology and hurried away.

"What was that?" April asked.

I shrugged. "I have no idea. I told him I was giving the baby up for adoption, and he went all weird on me."

April tilted her head at me, then smiled. "I bet I know what happened." Her eyes glittered, like she had a secret to share. I waited for her to spill whatever she was thinking.

"Before, Rion was only trying to be your friend. It was easy for him to stay just a friend because you were not a Mormon, about to be a single mom, and kind of crabby. No offense but, boy, were you crabby. Anyway, I think he's starting to care about you, but he still has all those barriers to help keep his feelings in check. Telling him about the adoption has taken away one of his reasons not to fall for you."

"April, I don't think—"

"What? Tell me you haven't noticed the way he looks at you."

I had noticed; of course, I had noticed! Every time he looked at me like that, my world reeled, but I thought that was simply because of my feelings. It never occurred to me that it could be because of his. But, then, his reserve toward me was also apparent. His way of making a point of asking out other girls from the office and then letting me know about them was like a huge neon sign saying: "You're a nice kid, but all we are is friends."

I didn't dare think that there might be a chance for Rion and me. It was too unlikely. But there April was—suggesting it might be possible.

"I can't think about this right now. I have enough to deal with without worrying about how Rion feels." I thought about that a moment and then asked, "*Am* I right to make this decision?"

She hesitated. "I can't answer that. Only you know what's right for you." The doorbell rang, and April hurried to get it.

I readjusted blankets and the pillow while I waited for the counselor to come in. She was tall with very dark short hair and a friendly smile. April left us alone, by insisting there was work in the office that needed doing.

"My name is Cyntea. T-E-A," the woman sounded out. "Lot's of people call me Cynthia with a 'th' and not a 't.' Drives me nuts."

I smiled. "My name is Suzanna, but I hate being called Suzanna, and I don't really like Suzie. So most people call me Cue."

"Cue. I like that. Well, now that we have our names straight, tell me about yourself."

"What do you want to know?"

"Anything you want to share."

"Well, I'm twenty-two years old; I work for Utah Workforce Management; and I'm almost seven months pregnant."

She waited for me to continue. When I didn't, she asked, "When is your due date?"

"December seventh."

"Pearl Harbor." She said.

"Yep, isn't that great? Her birthday will be linked to a world war."

Cyntea laughed. "Probably not. Babies are hardly ever born on their due date."

We both fell into a short silence only broken when I asked, "So what do I need to do?"

She handed me a binder, filled with worksheets giving information and also asking information. Cyntea turned to the first page. "First off, you need to be aware of your options. Whatever you do needs to be the best decision for you and this baby."

Cyntea put an arm around my shoulder and gave a squeeze. "My whole purpose today is to make sure you're comfortable. No one's going to twist your arm or make you do anything you don't want to do. We're going to explore all your options and then discover what it is you might need from us."

She was thorough and concerned. She mothered me in a sweet and sincere way, giving me the kind of attention I'd never gotten from anyone, aside from Rion and Sam. We went through the possibilities. Was the father involved in the situation? No. Any significant other or marriage plans? I almost mentioned my feelings for Rion but quickly stamped out the idea of giving way to reckless emotion and answered a resounding no.

After we'd laid bare my soul and concluded I was going through with adoption by my own choice, she handed me a sheet of paper. "Right now I want you to make up a wish list for the perfect family. What is it you want for your daughter?"

"Like what?"

"Like, do you want her to go to a family with other kids, or a family with no children?"

"I don't really care about that. I just want her to have good parents."

"Define good parents."

"You know . . . the socially ideal family. Dad works making a good living. They don't have to be rich, but they need to be able to take care of her. I think the mom should be home instead of working all the time. In fact, I am against the mother of my daughter working outside the home." Suddenly a picture came to mind—an episode from *Leave It to Beaver*: Mom and daughter setting the dinner table; Dad about to arrive home from work. They were talking about school, boys, and life in general. A joke, they both laugh; a secret, they whisper though no one else is there to hear. Later Mom brushes her hair while sitting in front of a dressing table.

Those were the dreams I had for my baby—a life I had never lived. It was worse than pressing my face against a window to a room I would never enter. It was the painful knowledge that in that world, the curtains would be drawn on that window and I would never be allowed to look in at all.

"Cue?" Cyntea looked worried.

"Sorry. Just thinking. I also want the parents to be smart," I continued. "Well-educated, and at least one of them should play an instrument; a piano or flute or harp . . . I don't know . . . something. The type of family that will have water fights and pray together like Sam and April do. People who love a good joke and have a good sense of humor. A mom that won't have a heart attack if her daughter dyes her hair blue just to be different. A dad who will read her stories at bedtime and keep her safe and make her brush her teeth and floss . . . flossing's important." I was crying now.

"And they have to love her, Cyntea, even when she screws up. And forgive her and hug her every day so that she always knows she's important to them."

Cyntea's arm was around me, and my head had found her shoulder. I finished my wish list, and after I had calmed down, Cyntea left.

Cyntea dropped by the next morning before April went to work so I wouldn't have to get up and get the door. I peeked over my round belly to see her.

She looked fresh and upbeat and happy. "I brought you some information about some couples to look at. If you don't like any of them I'll bring some more."

She left me with another binder of letters and photos from various couples looking for a child. There were so many to choose from, and they all seemed to earnestly be pleading for me to pick them. Every time I turned a page to view a new couple, it was as though I could hear their voices crying, "Choose us! Choose us!" There were thirty couples in all.

Each couple's story was unique, and yet they were all the same. They loved each other and wanted to share that love with a child. When they found they couldn't have children on their own, they chose this route in the hope that someone would give them that one thing that would complete their happiness.

I had a hard time reading their stories. The kind of love they described seemed false to me. I'd never seen a home where a child would be a welcomed and cherished gift. Or had I? When I had been in Mary and Ted Stiles's home while Sam blessed her with health, I had felt a love unshakable. Even in Sam and April's home, the peace and security of true love seemed to fill each room. Could I doubt that when she and Sam finally chose to have children of their own, that the same love would continue and grow to include those children?

I went through the book again. Each of the couples had provided many details about their lives: what kind of jobs they held; their church assignments; favorite foods and pastimes. Then there were the details on them as a couple: how they had met; where they wanted to go in life; most described dreams of eternal family progression. There were further details on their extended families: grandparents; aunts; uncles; cousins. Some described holiday traditions, family reunions, favorite vacations. And there were pages of information on their health and financial resources. It was unreal, each of the couples living out one of the fairy tales from Rion's life, except that they needed a child to complete their happiness.

They all described their faith and their love of the Lord and "His Church." Unshakable testimonies were written with firm clarity. I read through them for a week, memorizing every detail, with a growing ache that I had to choose just one.

I cried often while I studied the folder, frequently touched by a sentence or a thought. I found myself going back to one couple in particular. Her name was Anne; his name was Michael.

Anne's humor struck me as likeable. She seemed like someone I would be friends with were we to ever meet. Her blue eyes looked out from her pictures with amusement. I wondered what color my baby's eyes would be. Mine were brown, like Sam's.

Anne had written:

> Hi there, my name is Anne. I am what the Bible refers to as "barren"; and since no holy messengers have come down to tell

me I need to wait until I've got blue hair to have kids, Michael and I have decided to adopt. It's evident that having a child is a gift we cannot give each other. It's a gift only you can give. And so we're pleading with you . . .

I liked her directness and humor and the honest tone of her letter.

There were photos of Anne and Michael rock climbing and scuba diving, and then a larger one of them on the steps of the Salt Lake Temple in wedding attire. In each of the photos they were touching each other affectionately, and in one, the camera caught Michael looking at Anne in a particularly tender way.

I read volumes into that look. His lopsided half-smile showed he was amused by her, but more than that, that he would do anything for her. I could see that he adored her, and I could imagine him hanging the moon for her while she held the ladder. This was a couple whose love was so apparent that all others paled by comparison. After a week of study, it was clear. These people were my daughter's parents.

IT TOOK ME A FEW DAYS TO CALL CYNTEA, not because I was unsure of my decision, but more because I had to gather the courage to voice it. April and Sam were both supportive and agreed that this couple surpassed the others.

I wondered if I should look through other books of other couples; but every time I opened the binder I had and looked into Anne's eyes, I knew there was no need.

Cyntea seemed delighted by the choice I had made. She personally knew the couple, and she raved about them in a downplayed sort of way.

Everything Cyntea did seemed to be aimed at making my life easier or more comfortable. She told me she would take care of things and that I shouldn't worry over any details. She asked me if I wanted to meet the couple and encouraged me to do so. At first I wasn't sure, but the idea of seeing my baby's parents in person and the intrigue of actually speaking to Anne helped me make up my mind.

They would be coming to the house. The home nurse came twice a day to monitor my vital signs and check on me, so we planned the meeting around her visit.

I really missed seeing Rion. I had not heard from him since the day

Cyntea first came, and three weeks without him had made my life miserable. I was at a point where I really needed friends, but I was back down to just Sam and April.

The thought depressed me. One evening, when Sam was updating me on the gossip from work, I stared at him and asked, "Do you think this is what Grandma meant?"

"Grandma?"

"Once, when we were still small, she told us we needed to treat each other better because when we grew up, you and I would be the only friends we had."

Sam laughed. "I forgot she ever said that. But you're right. I don't see my friends much at all anymore. I guess maybe this is what she meant. Good thing I treated you so nice, huh?"

I rolled my eyes and shook my head at him, "Oh, yeah, you're a real angel."

"That's why you call me Halo." He winked.

The truth was he had been an angel to me for most of my life. The only times we had ever really quarreled were when I was being horrible. I was grateful for his friendship now, not that it kept me totally entertained. There were plenty of lulls where I felt it possible to die of boredom.

My only relief from that boredom had become Jan's Book of Mormon. I was almost through Alma and still no one seemed to have taken notice that I was reading it. I kept it under the couch cushion, out of a belief that there was no reason to get Sam's hopes up. I had trouble understanding parts of it but found myself surprised that the story was actually pretty interesting. As to whether it was *true* or not . . . well, I just didn't know, but it was interesting.

April took work off the day of my appointment. The thought of meeting my daughter's parents set off emotions in me I didn't know existed. I was nervous and wanted to make a good impression, so I dressed carefully. After not being allowed to get up and do things for myself, my muscles felt weak and rubbery. I did my makeup, but then cried it all off.

The nurse said I was doing well but reminded me to continue taking it easy. Whenever she came, she would let me use her stethoscope to listen to the baby's heart. The sound always threw me into another fit of tears. Her life had become so precious to me, and I still felt guilty for putting her in danger. I was her mother, after all. I was the only one right now able to take good care of her.

When the nurse was through, I went into the bathroom to try to make myself presentable. My dyed black hair had begun to grow out, exposing a couple of inches of lighter roots. During my crazy years, I had grown used to looking bizarre. In fact, that had been the point. But now, I wished I had done something about my hair—either dyed it black again or at least let it go back to its original color.

I stared into the mirror. "I'm going to meet your mom and dad today," I spoke softly to my belly, something I had found myself doing more and more. I debated redoing my makeup, but with my emotions so close to the surface, I didn't bother. I knew I'd likely end up with mascara running down my face. I patted my belly, feeling a lump where a foot or hand was sticking out. "It's going to be okay." The words were more for my benefit than for hers.

When I came out of the bathroom, April took a look at me. "Are you okay?" She looked worried.

"Fine . . . stellar."

"You look like you're going to throw up."

"I might. I'm worried about my hair. They are going to think I'm some kind of punk with dyed hair like this."

April grinned. "I think that's the first time I've ever heard you say anything that would suggest you care what anybody else thought."

"Yeah, well, I have to care. These are the people who will someday tell her what I was like. I want them to say good things. I don't think I could take it if she thought I was some tweaked-out addict, hopping from rehab to rehab."

"Suzie . . . there is no way they will ever tell her that . . . or even think it. You're giving them something amazing, and they'll love you forever for it."

Cyntea came in first, leaving the couple in their car while she spoke to me. "Are you ready?" she asked.

"No."

"Do you not want to do this?"

"It isn't about me. It's about her now. Let's just get it over with . . . Do I look okay?"

Cyntea gave me one of her comforting smiles. "You're beautiful, Suzie. I'll bring them in now."

I found myself pressing my hands protectively over my belly and biting my lip hard enough I could taste the blood. They were holding hands as they entered, looking nervous until Anne fixed her electric blue eyes on mine. She rushed to me and stopped at the invisible line that marks everyone's personal space. She lifted her hand to wave and then as if thinking better of it, stuck it out for me to shake. As I reached up from the couch to take her hand, she suddenly knelt in front of me and pulled me into a hug. Startled, I held myself stiff in her intense embrace. After an awkward moment, she gave a nervous laugh and pulled away. Her eyes were shining, and she reached for her husband's hand.

"Wow!" she exclaimed, pulling him closer to us. "I haven't been this nervous since my wedding day."

"Me, too," I said, and then cringed. "I mean not since my wedding day. I'm not . . . I mean . . . I'm nervous, too."

Her husband extended his hand. "I'm Michael—" He opened his mouth to say more but closed it again. He had almost slipped and given me his last name. I was glad he hadn't. That was information we agreed not to exchange. At least, not for now. Cyntea had explained that if I had access to their full names, there would be no stopping myself from searching them out after everything was over. He shook my hand, refraining from the hug. "This is Anne. You have no idea how glad we are to meet you." His smile was as quick and warm as hers was.

I sent April a look to sit next to me on the couch. She hurried to obey, seemingly stunned into silence by the situation. She smiled awkwardly.

"My name is Suzanna, and this is my sister-in-law, April." I didn't go into details about my name or nickname; it was simply Suzanna. It occurred to me that Rion never called me anything but Suzanna. I wanted to be the person that I was with Rion to these people. "Cue" suddenly felt like a name I had hidden behind. Suzanna was the person I wanted to be.

They both nodded and said hello to April. After a few awkward moments, I felt my hesitation disappearing. They were the right choice. I could feel it in every part of me, and I couldn't quit crying. Anne was equally emotional, and we both made frequent use of the box of tissues on the coffee table. Michael's eyes shone, but he kept himself in check.

Our meeting was a little like a group session in rehab. We each took a turn telling something about ourselves. Anne said how much they had wanted to have a baby of their own and described the disappointment they had experienced as all their efforts failed. At one point, she suddenly laughed and blurted out, "Can I touch your stomach?"

I blinked in surprise. "Sure. She isn't moving right now, but, yeah, I guess that's okay."

She put her hand tentatively on my belly. It had only been there a moment when the baby turned and kicked out. The sudden movement startled Anne, and her blue eyes brightened and widened in amazement. "That's incredible," she breathed.

"That's your little girl," I whispered back. My voice cracked, and I cleared my throat.

Without taking her hand from my belly, she picked up my hands with her other hand and placed them all together on my stomach. She leaned her forehead against mine and repeated, "That's *our* little girl."

She thanked me. He thanked me. They called me an angel. As they were getting ready to leave, they both hugged me, and by then, I was comfortable enough to return their embrace.

"Wow," April said after they were all gone. "If I had any doubts about you doing this, I don't anymore. Suzie, they're awesome people. Did you feel the Spirit in the room? I swear, I have never felt anything like it."

The Spirit. What did that really mean? I could have asked, but I wasn't sure I wanted to know. I had enough things to think about without adding religion or philosophy to it. I *had* felt something during their visit but couldn't explain it away as the *Spirit* as April had. To me, it felt more like love, though I had experienced precious little of that in my life.

c h a p t e r
36

WHEN SAM GOT HOME, HE WANTED TO hear all about our meeting, and he refused to let me nap until he got the details. I finally pled exhaustion and escaped to my room, where I picked up the phone twice and hung it up each time.

What would I say to Rion? He'd had no contact with me all this time, and it apparently wasn't bothering him. I guess absence actually makes the heart grow forgetful. He had never said he had any feelings for me, I reminded myself. April was the one who had said that.

I ran my fingers over the keypad on my phone, touching them in order of Rion's phone number, but not pressing them. I sighed and scrunched up the paper his number was written on and let it drop to the floor by my bed. How I wished he would be by next week for Thanksgiving.

I sighed again and settled back into the pillows, digging under them to find the hard spine of my Book of Mormon. I pulled out the LDS Services pamphlet marking my place and began reading in hopes of being distracted from thoughts of Rion and adoptions. I was in Alma 32. I began reading without thought or concern, when I sat up straight at verse 17, my heart beating faster.

Yea, there are many who do say: If thou wilt show unto us a sign from heaven, then we shall know of a surety; then we shall believe.

Now I ask, is this faith? Behold, I say unto you, Nay; for if a man knoweth a thing he hath no cause to believe, for he knoweth it.

And now, how much more cursed is he that knoweth the will of God and doeth it not, than he that only believeth, or only hath cause to believe, and falleth into transgression? . . .

And now as I said concerning faith—faith is not to have a perfect knowledge of things; therefore if ye have faith ye hope for things which are not seen, which are true. . . .

. . . if ye will awake and arouse your faculties, even to an experiment upon my words, and exercise a particle of faith, yea, even if ye can no more than desire to believe . . .

A desire to believe . . . did I have a desire? I'd never had a desire to believe in anything. I had, in fact, taken pride in my cynicism, and one of my favorite amusements had been to take potshots at other people's beliefs and insane ideas. But after spending time with Anne and Michael, there was something . . . April had called it the Spirit. I couldn't call it that, but there was *something*. Was it the Spirit?

I eased my legs over the bed and listened. The house was quiet, Sam and April already in their room though it was still early in the evening. It felt late with the early darkening skies of winter. I was starving. Not wanting to bug April for help, I figured it couldn't hurt to get up for a minute to get something to eat. Easing out of bed and waddling down the hall, the question stayed with me. Did I have a desire to believe? Alma seemed to think that just the desire was enough, but did I have even that?

The fridge was tidy; everything organized into little plastic containers and shelved away. Pulling out some leftover chicken salad, I started to waddle my way back to my room and came face to face with the painting of Jesus. He looked so . . . sad. The city of Jerusalem had been a disappointment to Him. Was I a disappointment to Him?

I shook my head. How could I be a disappointment to Him? Did He even exist? If so, was He aware of me? Did I have the desire to believe that? I didn't know. I went back to my room to finish off the chicken salad and the rest of the chapter before flipping off the lights and wondering in the dark, *did I have the desire to believe?* The question bothered me. What had happened at the hospital? What was the voice in my head telling me what I needed to do to save the baby. What was that if not something *spiritual?* What did that mean if it was real? I knew what it meant. It meant that everything I had done in my life was wrong. I had been like Alma's son, off causing havoc and sinning. It meant that I was an evil person. Believing in the gospel seemed to mean I had to believe that too, and that was something I didn't think I could accept. I wasn't *evil.* Not diabolically so anyway. I slept fitfully, wondering if it was my fault that Jesus looked sad in that picture.

C YNTEA CALLED A FEW DAYS LATER TO LET me know that everything was going well and the paperwork was all in place. I was glad to hear it and thanked her for keeping me in the loop.

The day before Thanksgiving, the doorbell rang. Sam went to get it. There was a small commotion at the door where I could hear Sam's voice whispering harshly to someone. And then I heard it: the loud voice of Doris. "Don't be stupid! How could seeing her own mother stress her out?"

And then she was in the house. I couldn't have run away if I tried in the condition I was in. She looked as good as always: trim and shapely, tanned from the fake rays of a tanning salon, her manicured nails filed to the precision of red daggers at the end of her long, moisturized fingers.

"Well, well . . ." I said, feeling as flattened as my voice sounded. "If it isn't the prodigal mother returned."

"Suzanna, I just got here and I have a headache. Don't start."

"Mom!" Sam called, trying to pry her attention away from me. "If you're going to be staying here, we'll have to put you on the pull-out couch in the office. Let's go put your bags away."

Sam took her bags, and she followed him down the hall. After they were gone, April touched my shoulder briefly. "It'll be okay. Take deep breaths. It'll be okay."

Sam came out from down the hall without Doris. "Where is she?" April demanded.

"Bathroom."

"I thought you told her not to come," I said.

"I did, but she apparently didn't listen."

"Well, tell her to get out!"

"I can't do that, Suzie. What do I tell her, 'Sorry, Mom, you're not welcome in my home'?"

"Yes! Exactly like that. We can practice it before she comes out of the bathroom if you want."

Sam rubbed the back of his neck in frustration. "I can't, Suzie. I promised myself a long time ago; I would never stop trying to work a reconciliation there. I can't."

April's eyes went wide. "Sam, Suzie needs to stay relaxed. No one is relaxed around your mother."

"I know. I'll keep her away from Suzie, I just—"

"You have a very nice home," Doris conceded when she'd reemerged from the bathroom.

"Thanks. April's put a lot of work into it," Sam said.

April hurried to come up with a diversion as they all seemed to settle near my couch. "Would you care to join us for dinner? Everything's ready." She led the way to the kitchen and away from me.

"Thank you. That sounds great." Doris started to follow them when she realized I wasn't coming. "Too lazy to even get up for a meal?"

"I'm on bedrest. I'm not supposed to be getting up, Doris."

"It's doctor's orders, Mrs. Quincy," April explained.

"I suppose it's good she follows someone's orders," she remarked, loud enough to be certain I'd heard it as she walked away.

April brought dinner to me, which I ate quickly and then fled to my room, locking the door behind me. Maybe I could hermit my way through her visit. But I knew she wouldn't allow it. It only worked this time because she was tired.

Thanksgiving Day was a different story altogether. Sam planned the meal around me and had set up the table by my couch. They invited Larry, a member of their ward who was alone for the holiday. I hoped Sam had warned the poor guy. Doris was civil through the morning but did suggest April use orange juice to candy the yams next time and made other comments that implied April could have done better. I made a point of complimenting everything, not only because it all really was great but because it annoyed Doris to have me counter any comment she made. Sam kept Larry occupied enough to ease the discomfort Doris brought to the meal.

All in all, things didn't go too badly . . . at least not until pumpkin pie was served. Doris took a bite, swallowed, put down her fork, and said pointedly to me, "It's time for you to come back to Boston." Everyone's forks hung in the air, except Larry's, who didn't understand he should be uncomfortable.

"Excuse me?" I said, dropping my own fork to the bone china plate with a clatter.

"Your father and I have discussed it, and we can turn the upstairs guest room into a nursery. It would be a little work, but we can get it done in time if we focus."

I didn't want to get into an argument with her, but her bossy tone reminded me of all the crap I had taken from her. I could feel a rage rising in me, and I said, "Is your memory failing you? You kicked me out."

"I was upset. I've had time to think about it and since then, I've changed my mind about how I feel."

"How convenient for you, to be able to have such life-altering changes of mind."

Doris waved her hand in agitation. "Oh, Suzanna!"

"Oh, don't you cry for me . . ." Larry sang out before his good senses overcame him, and he blushed and looked down at his pie.

Sam tried giving Larry an awkward smile while April rested her forehead on her palms. I heard her mutter, "Unbelievable."

Doris ignored Larry. "Don't be so melodramatic. I've basically retired from work so I can watch my granddaughter while you work. It will be an ideal situation."

By now, I was ready for a fight. "Ideal for who? Are you totally clueless? You failed in raising Sam and me! Do you really believe I'm going to hand my daughter over so you can ruin her life, too?"

Her face darkened. "How dare you be so ungrateful?"

"Mom, Suzie . . . Now is not the time for this," Sam interjected. Larry had a light-bulb moment and realized something wasn't right in the situation, and he thanked April repeatedly for the lovely meal and bowed out as quickly as his feet would allow.

"Very classy, Doris," I said as soon as the front door had closed behind him. "You just ruined a total stranger's Thanksgiving."

"Listen here, young lady! I came here to bring you home, not to listen to your smart remarks."

"I *am* home. I'm more home here than I ever was living with you."

"Look at you!" she hissed. "Do you really think you could be a mother?"

April was stricken, sitting like stone in her chair. Sam's face was red. "Mother, that is enough!" He got out of his seat and stood between Doris and me, as though to block her attack in some way.

"No, Sam." I tugged on his shirt. "She's right."

The room fell silent. No one believed that such a statement could ever fall from my lips. I couldn't believe I had said it. "I won't be a good mother." I plunged on. "Not now. Not like I am. That's why I'm giving her up for adoption."

Doris couldn't have been more stunned if I had hit her with a club. Her mouth fell open, and she stared at me in disbelief. It was obvious that Sam had not yet told her what I had decided. After a moment, Doris collected herself, narrowed her eyes, and stabbed a red-nailed finger in my direction. "You are not giving my grandbaby away to total strangers. I won't have it! I just won't have it!"

"*You* won't have it? Are you so dense that you think what you want is of the slightest interest to me? Have you forgotten that you kicked me out for not agreeing to kill this baby? The same baby you're so high on keeping now? You lost your right to be involved the day you told me to make the appointment to kill her. You think I would be a terrible mother? Well, look in the mirror, Doris! You've had twenty-four years to work at it, and you still haven't got it right!"

I stood up. I could feel my blood pressure rising with my anger. April jumped to her feet to help me or do anything besides just sitting there. "I'm sorry about messing up your dinner, April. It was really good, despite the rudeness of my mother." I turned to go to my room.

"So that's it?" Doris called after me. "You're just going to give her up . . . just like that?"

I hesitated, not turning to look at her, and replied. "I'm not . . . giving her up. I'm giving her what I can't give. I don't expect you to understand." With a deep breath I made my feet move again, towards my bedroom, away from Doris. I didn't expect her to get it. How could she? It had taken months away from her for me to get it.

I didn't sleep. I lay awake in my bed listening to the muffled but heated arguments from the other room—Sam and Doris battling over our past, our futures, and other things I was glad to not have to hear.

I finally dug out the Walkman with the Simon and Garfunkel tape and turned it on loud enough to drown out their voices. I was much calmer than I imagined I would be. Calm enough that I was certain the baby was still okay and the toxemia hadn't gotten the better of me. I fell asleep to the music with the words *homeward bound* echoing in my dreams.

I didn't leave my room the next morning. April came in to check on me and told me everything was fine and I should come out and have breakfast. I told her I'd come out when Doris was on a plane to Boston. She sighed and left muttering something about wishing she could do the same.

I held out in my room as long as my bladder would allow me. It didn't help that the baby was sitting directly on it and squiggling around. I finally gave up and went into the bathroom.

Once I was up and out, there was no peace to be had. Doris was right there, following me around, telling me things would be different if I would just come home. She told me all the ways she planned to help me so I could keep the baby and talked incessantly of finding me eligible fathers to date and marry.

I rolled my eyes enough during her barrage to make myself dizzy. As though I needed her help to get a date. I wondered what Rion would think of that and then was frustrated that I was thinking of Rion at all. Sam stayed with me while Doris continued, and April gently reminded me I was supposed to be lying down. Sam joked, teased, and cut off Doris's many attacks on my judgment. But she just kept reminding me how stupid I was and what foolish mistakes I had made while I was growing up. It was her opinion that those mistakes were proof of my inability to think, and that the very situation I was in proved I was incapable of making good decisions. I despised every twist of her mouth and blink of her eyes.

Probably so she wouldn't have to deal with Doris, April launched herself into organizing Christmas lights and decorations. When Doris testily suggested April wait until after she had left Utah to decorate, April simply replied that decorating the house the day after Thanksgiving was her own personal tradition dating back to her childhood. I felt so sorry for April.

That Saturday, before Sam drove Doris to the airport, she parted with the words, "You are the most ungrateful, thankless excuse for a daughter one could ever produce." Then she slammed the door.

I smiled at April. "You know, she's wrong about that. I'm *very* grateful . . . that she's gone.

April laughed out loud and agreed completely.

$c \, h \, a \, p \, t \, e \, r$

38

THAT EVENING, THE DOORBELL RANG. Sam answered it and brought the guest to me. It was Jan, my visiting teacher. She had a puzzled look on her face and a letter in her hand. She handed it to me.

"Some very handsome young man gave this to me on the front porch. He looked like he'd been standing there a while, but he left as soon as he'd handed it to me."

I trembled, realizing that the handwriting on the envelope was Rion's. I hurried to stick it between the pages of my Book of Mormon, which was still hidden under the cushions in a haphazard sort of way. Jan noticed the book and smiled as she plucked it from its hiding place. "So you've been reading it, then?"

Both Sam and April gaped at me. My face felt warm as I reached out to take the book back. "Oh, no big deal. It's just something to help pass the time."

Sam continued to look at me with amazement.

"What?" I glowered at him.

He was smiling. "You're reading the Book of Mormon?"

I rolled my eyes. "Don't get all worked up, Halo. I'm not running off to get dunked by your bishop."

He sat next to me. "But you're reading it? What do you think? Do you like it?"

"What's to like? It's just a story."

Jan chuckled. Sam looked frustrated. And I could hear April mumble, "Unbelievable."

Sam tapped my book. "You're treating it like fiction! This isn't Victor Hugo here; it's scripture. Have you prayed about it?"

I thought about how I'd felt when reading about faith. I'd considered praying ever since then, but the one time I got on my knees to do it, I felt so foolish I *couldn't* do it. Who would I be talking to? And what kind of answer would be possible?

"No, I haven't prayed about it. Don't bug me about it."

Sam scowled, but Jan looked amused and quite pleased. She asked if I needed anything and went over a checklist of things I should pack for the hospital. The reminder of my due date only a week away made my stomach pretzel. I'd had many Braxton Hicks contractions that sent me into silent fits of terror. Jan's matter-of-fact way of checking off needs, like a laundry list, took the edge off my fears. April listened, nodded, and agreed to Jan's suggestions while Sam stared with disbelief at my Book of Mormon.

Jan handed me a pink striped gift bag with bows on it. I peeked inside and pulled out a pair of flannel pajamas. "They're for when you're in the hospital. They're from Roberta and me. It's always nice to have your own PJs."

"Thank you. Thank you for everything you've done."

"Oh, Suzie, it's been a pleasure. You just make sure to call me when that baby is born."

"I will."

She left and Sam tried to quiz me further on my reading. When I told him I was in fourth Nephi, he couldn't contain his excitement.

I scoffed at him, debated with him, and finally escaped to my room and Rion's letter.

It took a moment to calm myself down enough to read it.

Dear Suzanna,

I'm sorry. I'm not sure what else to say . . . I know I should have come by more often in this last month but thought it might be best if I gave you some space, especially since you have some big decisions to make, and I didn't want to get in your way. I just wanted you to know that I am glad you are giving the baby up for adoption. It is an awesome demonstration of how much you love her to be willing to let her go to a family that is prepared to have her. I really wanted to tell you that I honestly feel that the family she is going to *NEEDS* her. You are an amazing person and are doing an amazing thing, and even though I haven't been around, I wanted you to know I am your friend and you have my support.

Always,

Rion Evans

I read the letter twice more—taking both joy and pain in it. The last month had been torture without him. The letter proved he was still my friend. Sadly, it also proved nothing further than that. But I appreciated knowing I had his support in the decision I had made. I knew it was the right thing to do, but having him agree was important to me.

December seventh came and left with nothing to mark it as anything more than the anniversary of the bombing of Pearl Harbor. December eighth, ninth, tenth, eleventh, and twelfth also passed with equal tedium, and the thirteenth seemed to dawn as uneventfully as the five previous days.

The anxiety of nothing happening sent me into a full grouch. I snapped at everything, cried with no provocation, and resolutely finished the Book of Mormon just so Sam would stop asking me if I had.

"Are you sure you don't need anything?" April asked once more as she bundled a scarf around her neck. Sam was already in the car waiting for her while it warmed up. It was sweet the way he refused to let her drive herself to work when the weather was bad.

"Positive. Just go already!" I insisted, trying not to growl at her. She had mothered me so much over the previous week I could feel myself tense just from her presence.

"What if you go into labor?"

"Ha! Fat chance. But I'll call in the unlikely event. I think they got my due date wrong. I almost wish they had just taken her out when I went into labor the first time." I put a handful of tortilla chips into my mouth to keep myself from really smarting off and waved good bye.

With a glance at me that showed she was unconvinced I really was fine, she sighed and breezed out the door. A cold blast of air from the snowstorm outside forced me to bundle the blanket around me tighter.

I'd felt a dull ache low in my spine since I'd awakened that morning, and I shifted to take some pressure off it and flipped the channel to the Cartoon Network. *Scooby Doo* reruns. I sighed and looked on the coffee table. April mentioned she'd left some movies she thought I might like. There was a two-disc set of *Pride and Prejudice*. She wasn't serious. She couldn't be. How would anyone think that I would enjoy a movie about women who wore corsets? I flipped through more stations. Nothing was on.

With a grimace I got up and waddled to the TV to put in April's sappy Jane Austin. The movement deepened the ache in my back.

"Must have slept wrong," I grumbled and curled into the fetal position to watch the movie.

When the first disc was over and I had to get up to load the second one, I was amazed by my eagerness to see the rest of the movie and laughed, glad that Chris and Gina couldn't see me now. I was a pregnant basket case who was reading a religious book and watching a Jane Austin movie and actually enjoying both. I had changed and had to concede that I truly liked those changes.

The dull ache now became a throbbing. I rummaged through April's closet to find a heating pad. She had some homeopathic thing that smelled like lavender and had to be heated in the microwave.

The heat helped a little, but only for a short while, as the throbbing ache radiated from my back clear into my front and down my legs. Only by lying flat could I get any relief.

I couldn't concentrate on the movie. The pain was strong enough to fuel tears. This couldn't be normal. What if the pain meant something was wrong with the baby? Sitting up, I cried out involuntarily. A hospital! I had to get to a hospital. Stumbling to the kitchen, I pulled down the phone off the wall and tried to remember April's cell phone number, but it wouldn't come to me. I glanced at the clock. She would have been to work several hours ago, but I had no idea what her number was at her office, either. I dialed Sam at work but only got his voice mail. In agony, I hung up on the electronic voice asking me to leave a message and got a spare key to April's car out of the junk drawer.

My backpack with all my hospital things was waiting for me by the couch. Grabbing it and clutching the keys, I hurried to the car as fast as my aching back and legs would allow. I cursed out loud at the huge flakes sticking to my eyelashes and at the icy wind ripping through my jacket.

I finally crammed myself into the car and turned on the engine. The road was snow-covered now, and every time the wheels slipped, I gasped. "I'm okay," I said out loud every few minutes. "We're okay." I patted my belly for a brief second then tightened my grip on the steering wheel.

chapter

39

By THE TIME I ACTUALLY REACHED THE hospital, I was sobbing so hard due to pain and frustration that I couldn't explain what was really wrong. The emergency people put me in a wheelchair and sent me to the Women's Center.

After they got me undressed and in a bed, one of the nurses examined me. "You're in labor," she said. "You're already at five centimeters. Do you want an epidural?"

I nodded furiously, and she went off to find the guy with the drugs, leaving me to cry alone on my bed in the wood-paneled birthing room.

The nurses hooked me up to the big, now familiar, monitors and IVs, and we waited for the guy with drugs. Another nurse asked me, "Have you taken any Lamaze classes?"

"No."

"Well, here's a crash course for you. Find something to focus on and breathe in deep . . . good, hold the breath a second, now breathe out slowly." She breathed with me and held my hand. "Do you want to call anyone to let them know you're here?"

April. She would be a perfect coach for right now, but I still had no idea what her phone number was. I nodded and the nurse handed me the phone to dial Sam's number. He should've been back in his office by now.

It went to voice mail again. I would have started crying if the contraction hadn't peaked. Instead of following the nurse's advice and breathing evenly, I held my breath, waiting for the contraction to end. Sam's phone hung up on me, forcing me to redial and leave a hasty message explaining he needed to get over to the hospital . . . now!

As the nurse was leaving, I gasped. She wheeled around to see if there was something wrong and rushed to my side when she noticed my eyes getting wider by the second. "What is it? What's wrong?"

"I think my water just broke!"

"That means you'll probably be delivering soon. Don't worry. Everything is fine." The nurse came in often over the next hour to make certain my blood pressure was stable. On her last check in she also took a look at how far I was dilated.

"Looks like you're about to a ten."

"You're kidding! Already?" I gasped.

"Yep. You're ready to start pushing."

"But I don't have drugs yet! Where's the guy with the drugs?"

"It's too late for that now. They wouldn't take effect until after the baby is out anyway."

I grabbed at her smock and screamed. "There has to be something you can do!"

"Just breathe and focus. You can do this!"

"But I don't *want* to do this!"

The nurse chuckled, to which I glowered and held my breath behind clenched teeth. "You have to breathe," she reminded me.

I exhaled with a hiss. "Where's the doctor? What if Sam doesn't get here in time?"

"For first-time moms, it usually takes at least an hour of pushing, sometimes longer. Don't worry. Everyone will be here in time."

I tried to focus on something, but nothing could pull my attention from the agony of each contraction.

Another nurse was there. They had pulled the bed apart and put up the stirrups already. They both shared a look over my large belly.

"You gotta push with the next contraction," one of the nurses insisted. "Take a deep breath . . . now push as hard as you can."

I obeyed. She counted to ten. My eyes were clenched closed, and I was grinding my teeth hard enough that it hurt my jaw.

"You need to breathe," the nurse at the catching end said.

"I can't breathe and push at the same time!" I complained.

She ignored me, watched the monitors, and said, "Okay, here we go again. Push!"

I yelped with the push. Pain beyond comprehension sent flecks of black dots flying through my vision.

The nurse at the catching end looked up and ordered, "Stop pushing!"

She had to be nuts! It wasn't something you could control like a faucet. My body said push, and I was doing whatever was necessary to get this over with.

"What's wrong?" the one holding my hand asked.

"The baby's crowned. You're almost done," the other said.

"Where's the doctor?" I demanded. "Don't I need a doctor? Where is he?"

"I'm paging him again right now." They tried to make me relax, talking soothing and calming words. I wasn't having any of it, though. If that doctor didn't show up and do his job, he was going to learn first-hand about an East Coast temper.

I was in the middle of another contraction when he hurried into the room, shrugging quickly into a scrub top and pulling on a pair of rubber gloves.

"Okay," he said in a singsong voice. "On the next contraction you can push again."

Less than a minute later I pushed and that was when the room filled with ohhs and ahhs and then a tiny cry. My clenched-shut eyes popped open to see her. She was messy and red and blue and as alien-looking as anything I'd ever seen. She was also so beautiful that there was no stopping myself from sharing in her cry.

When they handed her to me after cleaning her up a little and wrapping her in a pink blanket, she seemed to sigh and made a little grunting noise like a puppy.

She was perfect—all her toes and fingers accounted for and her steel-gray eyes blinking dazedly at me. She was alive and a separate person from me.

The nurses and doctor beamed at me while I beamed at her. She was tagged on her too-small-to-be-real ankle as the Quincy baby. When they did the certificate for her footprints, I stopped them to ask them to do a second certificate. Puzzled by the request, they complied.

"Have you chosen a name?" a nurse asked. She had just come on shift, and she received a scowl from the other nurse who knew my situation.

"She isn't mine to name." That reply echoed in my head as my eyes searched her over to memorize every detail of her.

Sam showed up nearly three hours later. He hadn't checked his voice mail. He must have picked up April because she entered the room right behind him.

Sam stopped short upon seeing me. "Are you allowed to hold her?"

"She's mine. Of course I'm allowed."

"But I thought . . ."

"Cyntea said if I wanted to keep her a couple of days and spend time with her I could. We'll be leaving the hospital at the same time, just not together."

I could tell this worried Sam, but I ignored him. April was all emotions. "I asked if you were going to be okay when I left! You should have asked me to stay or at the very least called when you realized there was a problem!" April's anger melted when she realized there was a baby present. She cooed and took the baby from my arms and rocked with her. April giggled. "Look how sweet she is! I can't believe you did this all alone."

"Yeah!" I agreed. "And *without* drugs. Can you believe it? I spent half my life drugged, and the one time I needed it, I couldn't get any at all!"

"Serves you right!" Sam laughed.

"You went natural? Are you insane?" April looked incredulous.

"It wasn't by choice, believe me!"

April handed my girl back to me. "Should you call Cyntea?"

"I already have. I get released from the hospital in two days. So I get two days with her. She said I could take her home for a couple of days longer but . . ." Fat tears, soldiers ready for battle, lined my eyelids. "I don't think I could let her go if I took her home. Cyntea said it would be good for me to give the baby to Anne and Michael myself. That way it would remain my choice to the end."

April and Sam silently nodded, and April bit her lip to keep from crying. Sam's eyes were moist. We had two days.

40

THOSE DAYS PASSED LIKE A BLAZE OVER dried grass. Rion came to visit, but I was in a deep sleep. I only knew of his visit from the card with a daisy tied with a string to it sitting under my digital camera. After a quizzical moment of wondering why my camera was there, I picked it up to see the pictures he had taken of me sleeping and two with him and the baby together.

It would have been nice to see him, but finding his surprises almost equaled the joy I might have taken at talking to him. Besides, what could I have said to him?

I dressed carefully the day Anne and Michael came to get her. The room was packed into two piles: my stuff and her stuff. I had told Sam and April to stay away, but once the reality set in, that I was actually going to have to hand her over and leave the hospital alone, I desperately wished they were there.

I picked her up and she sighed. Together we paced the room. I sat down and read her the book *Oh, the Places You'll Go!* by Dr. Seuss. Sam had read this to me often when we were kids and had given me a copy when I graduated from high school. I asked him to rummage through the stuff in my room to find it and bring it for me. Unable to finish the last page, I started crying at "Kid, you'll move mountains."

I looked down into the tiny alien face and began talking. "You know, little one, I could change my mind right now and keep you, then I could call you something more appropriate than 'little angel,' but I can't do that. I know it stronger than I've known anything. But someday, if someone tells you your mom gave you away because she didn't love you . . . you remember this: I'm giving you to them because I *do* love you. Somewhere in your mind always know that you are loved."

A tear slipped down my cheek and splashed her nose. I kissed it dry. "Please remember me. And be good for your mommy and daddy. Don't talk back to them and stay out late just to spite them. Don't be like me. And stay away from boys! They're all trouble, even the nice ones. But don't forget me. I know I'll never forget you. When you make up imaginary friends, let me be one of them." I looked up at the ceiling. "God, please help me do this!" It was then that I broke down completely. The ache was so deep it tightened and burned the back of my throat.

Cyntea was at my side almost before I was aware of her coming in. She stroked my hair and said, "Are you okay?"

I nodded dumbly.

"You just remember; this is your choice. No one can make you do this if you want to back out."

"No!" I held the baby closer and stood up. "I know this is the right thing. I just didn't know how much it was going to hurt." The last word was swallowed by a sob.

Cyntea kissed my forehead and the baby's forehead. "Michael and Anne are waiting, but you can take as long as you need. This is all about what's best for you."

I swallowed hard. "No it isn't. It's all about what's best for her." I took the Dr. Seuss book and placed it in the bag of her things. I had written on the inside cover the words, "You are loved."

Wiping at my tears with my sleeve, I turned to face Cyntea and said, "I'm ready."

She nodded, took the baby's bags, and led the way. Anne's and Michael's faces were bright with anxiety and excitement. When they saw me coming, Anne straightened Michael's tie as if their new daughter would be concerned about his appearance.

There would be paperwork, but Cyntea promised I could do it later. Anne's lip quivered when her clear blue eyes met mine, red and blotchy from crying. She threw her arms around me and the baby both. *God, help me through this,* I silently pled. Like the nurse had suggested when I was in the birthing room, I focused and made myself breathe. In my mind, I pictured the marble statue of Christ holding the world in the crook of His arm. It was the only image of comfort I could cling to.

Anne asked if she could take pictures of me with the baby. "For her scrapbook," she explained, her lip trembling violently now. "I want her to know how much you loved her."

That was more than I could bear. I broke down again, cuddling the baby to me and unable to breathe between the sobs. "Thank you!" I gulped. "Thank you for wanting her to know that."

They gave me a moment to calm down, and Cyntea handed me some tissues to wipe my face, and I did my best to smile for the picture. I knew I looked horrible. There was still a large bulge of fleshy tummy in my midsection and my eyes were red and swollen from crying. But I was grateful they wanted the image. With that one photograph, there was proof that I existed in her life.

"I should get going; I don't mean to keep you here all day; not when you have your whole lives starting . . ." I kissed her forehead again but stopped as I was about to hand her over to Anne's waiting arms. "What will you name her?" I asked.

"Angellee. She's a reminder that angels exist in the world, not only in her existence, but because of you."

I bit hard into my lips and placed Angellee in her new mother's arms. Anne was smiling through her tears, unable to take her eyes off the baby's face. Michael crowded in close to be a part of their circle. I stepped back.

Michael's head shot up. "Wait! Are you leaving?"

"Yeah, I thought I'd let you guys get acquainted." I pointed to the door.

"Would it be okay if we had a prayer first?"

"A prayer? Sure, yeah, that would be fine."

Everyone knelt like Sam and April did for their nighttime family prayers. As I knelt too, I decided that was what this was—our family prayer. I couldn't remember what was said or how long it took. But I remember feeling joy and peace.

Because of that prayer, I was able to leave strong. Michael hugged me before I exited, again calling me an angel.

Cyntea went with me to the entrance to the hospital and waited while April came to pick me up. We didn't talk, but her shoulder came in handy since I couldn't stop crying.

Twenty-four hours later I signed the papers. The ones that said I surrendered my rights of parenthood to that child. I closed my eyes after, unable to look any longer at my own signature in black ink, finalizing everything.

chapter
41

THE EMPTINESS IN MY STOMACH WAS like a black hole in space. It sucked all life, energy, and light into it. There was no longer movement or rolling like ocean waves. It was simply emptiness. I took on a workout program, anxious to get into shape and lose my tummy.

I had done the right thing, and yet I couldn't help feeling agitated and angry. I was sharp with everyone, including Sam. We argued over something, and I ended up shouting at him, "You don't know what I'm going through! So stop acting like some stupid shrink!" Then I slammed my bedroom door for emphasis. April tried to excuse my behavior as postpartum depression, but whatever it was, I felt miserable and mean.

Christmas came and went without any celebration on my part. Rion sent a card to which I didn't respond.

Winter finally melted into spring and spring warmed into summer. My movements were mechanical. It was necessary to keep them that way. If I put thought or emotion into my daily tasks of getting out of bed, eating, and going to work, I would never have made it through any of them.

At work Rion continued to be my friend, but distantly. He chatted easily in the break room, and twice asked me to go to a movie, but I declined both times. The black hole in my middle had sucked away even my feelings for him. My direct supervisors heaved heavy sighs of relief when they realized I no longer bantered at team meetings. There was a job to do, and keeping it mechanical made it easier to get done.

Relinquishing my child had seemed the noble thing to do at the time. I had been able to console myself that I loved her enough to give her away, but once it was done, the selfish part of me regretted it. I continued to feel I was right in doing it but couldn't stop myself from feeling bitter.

Sam and April worried about me but never pressed anything. At least April didn't, and Sam tried not to. April had started taking me to Young Women activities to keep me away from Sam's unending efforts to help me feel better. He was smothering me, and I couldn't stand it.

I had agreed to take the missionary discussions at Sam's urging. He persuaded me by saying that I needed to understand how my baby would be raised. The sister missionaries were great. I felt calm and strong when they were there teaching. But when they left, I felt as hollow as I had coming home from the hospital. When they asked me to commit to baptism, I hesitated. It seemed like a good enough idea . . . but I couldn't commit.

I had this fear that I was clinging to the idea of God only to help justify the fact that I had given my baby away. I was also afraid. The twelve steps I had learned in rehab helped me to know that temporary highs are never enough to sustain your determination. It occurred to me, what if God is just a temporary high? The missionaries had tried to get me to pray, but I couldn't do it. It wasn't that I didn't have the desire; it was just that the fear of not getting an answer outweighed the desire.

Sam even called my dad to tell him about me and to see if he could help. Sam all but dragged me to the phone to talk to him.

"Hey, Suzie Cue," he said. I could almost feel his smile in his voice.

"Hi, Dad."

"It's been a long time since we've talked. I just wanted to make sure you are okay."

"I'm fine."

"Sam says you're not so fine as you're saying." He said it noncommittally, like he really wanted to pry but was afraid to.

"Yeah, well, what does Sam know?"

"I've been really worried about you—" he started to say when a pause and a beep broke into our conversation. "There's my other line," he said. "Can you hang on for a minute?"

"Sure." I sat down and put my feet up on Sam's desk.

When he beeped back to me, his voice sounded edgy. "Hey, Suzie . . . it's your mother on the other line. Can I call you back later? She really needs to talk to me right now."

The old bitter feelings came back. Nothing had changed. "No problem, Dad. I know how it is. I'll talk to you later." I stared at the phone a long time after we hung up and finally stood up after whispering the words, "I forgive my father."

On the thirteenth of June, a day marking the sixth month anniversary of Angellee's birth, it took every ounce of energy for me to get out of bed. I stared into the mirror only a moment before turning away and picking up the phone. "I'm really sick," I explained to my supervisor. "I can't come in today." He sounded annoyed but agreed, allowing me to go back to bed and burrow into my cave of blankets.

A half hour later, Sam knocked on my bedroom door. "Hey, Suzie! You're going to be late."

"I'm not going! And don't tell me I'm going to get in trouble. I already called in sick."

He opened the door without asking permission and sat on the bed next to me. I burrowed deeper into the blankets as he tried to unbury me. "Suzie," he said, "you can't hide under there forever. You need to stop mourning the thirteenth of every month like that baby died that day!"

April must have been walking by when he said it because I heard her call from the hallway. "Sam! Get out here, now!" The bed sprang up from where he had been sitting, and I could hear them whispering heatedly to each other in the hall, sounding like two teakettles hissing at each other.

"Then you talk to her!" he finally said.

It was now April sitting beside me on the bed. She managed to uncover my head, sending the light slashing into my eyes. When she looked at my face, all red and squishy from crying, she frowned, her own lip trembling. She put her arms around me and held me.

"You know what I think you need to do?" she asked softly. She continued when I only sniffed in response. "I think you need to come to girls camp with me. We leave tomorrow morning. It would do you a world of good."

"Camping is supposed to make me feel better?" I moaned.

"Definitely," she grinned. "Besides, the girls love you. They'll be thrilled to find out you are coming. Will you do it?"

I considered. I had grown to love the girls too. They seemed to breathe life like an elixir, and whenever I was with them, it was like getting to taste of that elixir too.

Besides, going to work was an appalling idea. The very thought of dealing with the corporate bunk that filled that building was enough to drive me over the edge, but camping . . . "Okay. It couldn't be worse than staying alone with Sam for four days." I called into work, asking for more time off, agreeing to work the weekend to make up for it.

chapter
42

THE NEXT MORNING WE WERE UP and packed into vans and trucks heading to a canyon east of Springville. I was surprised when Alison showed up. She made certain to sit next to me for the ride up. Though she had been to all Sunday meetings since the time she had wandered into class almost a year before, she never went to the activities on Tuesday evenings. She seemed to have softened over time. Her makeup wasn't so heavily applied; she had taken the barbell out of the top of her earlobe; and the smell of alcohol had disappeared altogether from her clothing, though the stale tang of cigarette smoke still clung to her.

Alison didn't ever really talk to anyone, not even me, though she always sat next to me and smiled at my jokes in class. Observing her, I realized that this little girl hid a lot of secrets. I wanted to hug her. My despair from the previous day still hung over me, but seeing her there lifted my spirits even if just a little.

When we arrived at the camp and the girls were all busy setting up tents I leaned over to April, "How did you get Alison to come?"

"After you agreed to come, I called her and asked if she wanted to come too."

"She came because of me?"

"She came because she trusts you to accept her. She doesn't really trust anyone else."

"But she still doesn't even talk to me."

April shrugged, "I guess it's enough to know that you're there and not going to judge her. Anyway, for her sake, I'm glad you came."

Camp was like something I'd only seen in movies. There was hiking (five miles), singing, pranks, laughing, teasing, skits, crafts, and more singing. There were campfires, Dutch oven dinners, sandwiches made of roasted marshmallows and melted chocolate mashed between Graham crackers, and more singing. I was invited on a snipe hunt, but I declined. Just because I had never been to girls camp didn't mean I didn't know about snipe hunts. My friends and I had done drunken versions of that on the beaches of Martha's Vineyard, and the results were never pretty.

I had just settled into my canvas armchair by the fire when I noticed the girls had tied a bandanna around Alison's eyes and were leading her off into the forest. I panicked. What could they mean by that? It was one thing to mess around and tease your friends, but absolute cruelty to do it to a girl who struggled to be in the same room with you. I stood up to go after them, but April pulled me back down.

"Let them go," she whispered.

"But she—"

"—needs to be a part of them. They all go through this. It's a rite of passage for first years."

"What if they're mean to her? What if they hurt her feelings?"

April smiled. "Trust them, Suzie. These girls aren't sorority sisters trying to break her will. They *want* Alison to be a part of them. They'll do the right thing."

"Just because people are Mormons doesn't mean they're always going to do the right thing," I argued.

"I know. But I really believe that they will and that it'll be okay. If you bring her back, you'll have marked her as different from them. The last thing she needs is some wedge to keep her separated from the others. She'll be fine."

I huffed a moment before conceding, and my fingernails were all chewed away before they came back laughing and singing "Father Abraham." My eyes frantically picked through them until they fell on Alison, laughing and trying to get the words right to a song she had just learned.

April nodded at me with an I-told-you-so smile. Whatever had gone on out there had succeeded in making Alison part of the group. The girls had done the right thing, and no one had told them to.

The next two days were more of the same. I became adept at singing "Father Abraham" and finally got the hang of toasting marshmallows without setting them on fire.

On the final night, we gathered around the fire and instead of singing, jokes, and pranks, everyone was quiet and subdued. I thought maybe it was because we were all so tired from staying up late and being constantly on the go. But it was more than that.

After everyone was there, the Young Women president got up and began to speak. She expressed her love for the girls and their leaders and bore her testimony that the Mormon church was true. She got pretty emotional, and when she sat down, I realized that my cheeks were wet, though I didn't remember crying. Then one of the girls stood. "I'd like to bear my testimony . . ."

It was unlike anything I had ever experienced. One by one the girls stood, even the youngest ones, to express their love for each other, for their families, and for their leaders. Many of them said they knew the Church was true. One of the most amazing things was that they didn't ridicule or make fun of each other. In fact, some of them apologized for something they had said or done to hurt one of the others. Almost all of them ended up crying.

I almost gasped out loud when Alison stood. For a long moment she didn't say anything but just stood there next to the fire, shifting her weight from foot to foot. It seemed even the forest was holding its breath, waiting for what Alison would say.

"I wasn't going to come up here," she finally squeaked out. "I was afraid to be with you guys when I wasn't really like you guys." Her voice gained strength with every word. Her eyes rested on me briefly and she smiled. "But I've never felt so much like I belong in my whole life. I know I've done a lot of bad things; I know I haven't lived like I should. I've made my parents cry a lot. But I'm so grateful for the Atonement. I am so grateful that the Savior loved me enough to sacrifice everything for me. I'm really going to try harder. I want to be better. I want to be able to go to heaven when I die, and when I walk through the front door, I want to yell, 'Mom, Dad, I'm home!' and I want my older Brother to come out to greet me too, and I want to hug Him and tell Him thanks for thinking I was worth dying for. I want to . . ." She gnawed at her lower lip. ". . . I guess I just want you to know that even with everything, I do know the Church is true, that God is real. I know my Savior suffered for me, and I want to be better. Help me be better." The last came out as a plea, and she sat down after closing in the name of Jesus Christ.

My chest felt like it was on fire. *God is real.* The words echoed in my head. *God is real.* I wanted to start laughing. I understood! I finally got it! I *knew* she was right, and that fact filled me with joy. If God was real, then it really was Him who had led me to choose Anne and Michael to be Angellee's parents. If He was real, then I had truly done the right thing. She was made for that family. I was led to give them the one thing they could not give themselves. It made me happy that she would grow up in a good home where she would be loved, that she would be like the girls I was sitting with. The thing that made me mourn the day of her birth was that I doubted He was real. *Mom, Dad, I'm home!* I was on my feet before I thought to stop myself.

"I just want to say that I also know that God is real," I said. April was sitting next to me, looking down at the fire, and I couldn't see her face, but I knew she would be in shock.

I shrugged. "I do," I insisted. "I really do. You guys would never believe what I've been through. I'm serious; you have no idea how horrible I've been, but when I was at rock bottom with nowhere left to go, God was leading me here to Sam and April and to all of you. You all know that I had a baby and that I gave her away. I gave her away because I truly felt like that was what I needed to do, and I know now that it was the right thing to do."

I reached down and put my hand on April's shoulder. "I don't have to mourn anymore, April!" I exclaimed, nearly laughing through my tears. "God is real, and I know giving up my baby was the right thing to do. I finally get it! Thank you so much for taking me in and putting up with my attitude. I owe you and Sam everything. I—"

It was then that reality hit me. There I was, standing in front of a group of teenagers and their leaders, bawling and spilling my guts about the most personal things in my life. I should have been embarrassed, but I wasn't. Instead, I smiled and licked at the salty tears on my lips. "God is real. He really is . . . I say this in the name of Jesus Christ . . . Amen."

My legs were like Jell-O that had sat out too long and was going watery. They finally went out on me, and I collapsed into my chair. The light from the fire danced and flickered, illuminating the faces of the girls that my daughter would one day grow to be like. The silence was broken only by the hissing and popping of the fire and the sniffling— my own mingling with those of the girls and other leaders. *God is real.*

chapter
43

LATER THAT NIGHT, AFTER APRIL had slipped into the shallow snoring of a good sleep, I got out of my sleeping bag and settled on my knees.

"God?" It was a lame, roll-your-eyes kind of beginning, but was the best I could manage with my limited experience in praying. "I'm sorry." In my mind I was picturing the statue in the visitors' center. But that image dissolved into the soft gentle features of a man of flesh, the one from April's picture in the main hall. She and Sam had told me that the Savior was made in the exact image of His Father. I hoped so, since that was what I pictured as I prayed.

There were more tears, but they were not from despair. Hope and joy and a lifetime of images flashed before me all in the same second, and the words *I know what you're going through* sent me into shaking, silent sobs.

Doubt not, for I know what you're going through. I stayed on my knees until they ached, pouring out all my heartache, anger, and failure until it was drained from me and replaced with peace. There was no thunder or earthquake; it was so much more than that. It was someone finally understanding everything in my heart and all I had been through.

When I finally stood, my knees burned and my feet had gone to sleep, and yet I felt like I was floating. He understood. He had only been waiting for *me* to understand. All those years with His hand out-stretched simply waiting for me to step across the gap and take it. *I'm taking it now,* I thought as I drifted off to sleep. *I'm taking it now.*

A few nights later, while eating dinner at home with Sam and April, I made an announcement. "I've saved enough money that I think I can afford a place of my own."

Sam formed a unibrow frown and leaned in. "Do you really think you're ready to do that?"

"Oh, c'mon, Sam-Halo, I would've thought you'd do a back flip over me leaving."

"You've always been welcome here," he countered.

"I know, but it's time for all of us to move on. I'm gonna be okay . . . really I am. I want you to know I appreciate all you've done, Sam."

"I haven't done much."

I shook my head. "You've done everything." I took a sip of my water, then casually added, "I'd like you to baptize me, too, if you'd be willing. I swear it's the last big favor I'll ever ask of you."

The effect on him was perfect. He looked like one of those cartoon characters whose eyes bug out of their heads when they're shocked. It was gratifying. April choked on her mouthful of food as Sam belted out, "Are you serious?"

"What? Bad idea?"

Sam jumped up and yanked me out of my chair. He whirled me around like I was a doll or something until I forced him to put me down. I'd had the discussions already so the plans were easy enough to make. I would have to go through an interview, get wet, and start over.

I decided to start apartment hunting the next day, since it was Saturday and I had the day off. Sam and April wanted to go with me but had plans already to go and do couples stuff with some college friends who had just gotten married.

I started out early in the morning and went to a dozen apartment complexes. Nothing struck me as right until I found one that featured a pond with a waterfall and a little stream running through the grounds. The complex was older and therefore not nearly as expensive as some of the others that I'd seen. I was excited to go home and tell them I'd already found a place, though there would be a wait of a little over a month before I could move in. I made dinner while waiting for Sam and April to come home—a first for me. I even set the table.

"Who do you want to come to your baptism?" Sam asked after blessing the food.

"People go to those things?"

He grinned. "Yeah, people do."

"I dunno. How about Doris and Dad?"

April could never tell when I was joking, and she started to wonder if that was a good idea.

Sam laughed. "Seriously, do you want to invite anyone?"

"Not really. It'll be just us."

"What about the visiting teachers?" April suggested.

"Oh . . . yeah, they can come."

"And all the girls from Young Women will want to be there. They'll come whether you invite them or not, so you better just invite them. Do you have any friends at work?"

I considered it before shaking my head no.

"What about Rion?"

"No. I've hardly even talked to him in the last six months."

"He'll want to be there," Sam said.

"Yeah, right. I can tell he's just so interested in what's going on in my life."

April rolled her eyes. "It's not like you've made it easy for anyone to get close to you the last few months. . . . I'm sure he still cares."

The way my heart jumped made me realize I hadn't entirely gotten over him. But I didn't want to admit it. "I doubt that, but I'll invite him if you want me to."

Sam said he would get in touch with the sister missionaries and set things up. While we were cleaning up after dinner, I tried not to dwell on anything to do with Rion, and as soon as we were finished, I escaped to my room to write a letter.

Dear Anne and Michael,

This has been a very difficult six months for me. I am sure you can imagine. Though I knew at the time giving Angellee to you was the right thing to do, as more distance between me and that decision grew, the doubts were eating me alive. I finally faced this doubt with prayer. I received an answer that I did do the right thing. She was meant for your family. I hope all is well with you and her.

I am getting baptized soon and was reminded that a very special friend of mine bought Angellee a present the day we found out she was a girl. He had said we could use the dress for her blessing. I don't know if you've had her blessed already or not, but hoped, if you don't mind, that you would send me pictures every now and again of special events like that. I promise never to go searching for her or to stalk you guys in any way. I just want to be a silent witness to her growing up. If you choose not to, I understand. Kiss her for me.

Love Always,

Suzanna

I enclosed the letter with one to Cyntea, telling her about my baptism and asking her to forward my note to Anne and Michael. Then I slipped out of the house to go to the post office. I had recently bought a used car. It hadn't been too expensive, but seemed reliable enough. At least it didn't have a starter problem.

It felt good to drive, to just be out and doing something and to feel like I was moving on with my life. The air was cool walking back to my car from the postbox. I glanced up for a second and then back up to stare. The stars were brilliant, clear and perfect. And standing out in glory among them was the Orion constellation. O-Rion.

I did want him at my baptism. Even if he wasn't interested in me romantically, I wanted to have his friendship. Could I tell him that? I sighed deep enough to sound like a groan. I wasn't sure I could.

44

B<small>EFORE</small> I <small>COULD BE BAPTIZED</small>, I had to have an interview with one of the elders who was over the ward district I was in. I didn't realize how deeply he would go into things until we were well into it. He asked me very pointed, very personal questions about my past transgressions. Sin. The hammer of guilt pounded unmercifully into me.

"Have you had a problem with the Word of Wisdom?" he wanted to know. Have you . . . Have you . . . question after question left me reeling.

Yes . . . I did . . . yes! I had done anything and everything just short of murder, and I had come within a hair's width of doing that too!

Elder Christensen was about my age, and even though he had a boyish look about him, he seemed very responsible and capable. To his credit, he handled everything I told him without flinching, even though I'm sure he was shocked by the things I had done. He did get a little flustered at one point, when I told him about my going to the abortion clinic, and excused himself to make a phone call.

It was strange, but as I talked about my transgressions, it began to feel as though I was describing things that someone else had done; and I realized how much I had changed over the past year. Still, I wondered if I was worthy to go ahead, and I asked Elder Christensen for his opinion.

"Is there anything else you need to tell me?" he responded.

I thought for a moment. "No. That's everything I can think of. But can the Lord really forgive someone like me—I mean, someone who has done all the things I've done?"

He opened his Bible to the book of Isaiah and asked me to read verse 18 in chapter 1.

"Come now, and let us reason together, saith the Lord: though your sins be as scarlet, they shall be as white as snow; though they be red like crimson, they shall be as wool."

It seemed too good to be true. "Even with everything . . . Do you really think I'm worthy?"

"That isn't the question here. The question is one I've already asked you. Do *you* think that, at this moment, you are worthy?"

"But all the things I've done—"

"Are in the past. I didn't ask if you were worthy a year ago. I'm only interested in today and in your future. How do you answer that question?"

I thought about Rion's analogy of the patchwork quilt and some of the things I used to struggle with—like drinking and smoking. They were hardly even a temptation anymore. They were just part of the quilt . . . patches and colors. Today's patch brighter, and tomorrow's brighter still. If God and Christ were willing to forgive me, then, yes, I felt worthy, and I told Elder Christensen so.

He smiled then he signed the recommend that authorized my baptism.

He shook my hand. "It's been a long trail for you, but you still managed to find the right destination."

"That's it, then?"

"That's it. Congratulations, Sister Quincy."

When I got home, April agreed with the elder about my worthiness. "A broken heart and contrite spirit are all He is asking for. Believe me, Suzie. I'm a convert, too. I know what you're going through, but you have got to believe me when I say, God wants you to be happy. He wants to forgive you, but you have to forgive yourself as well."

I thought that was the end of the conversation, but she had another lecture for me.

"Have you invited Rion yet?"

"No, I figured I'd let Sam tell him and then if he wants to come he will."

"Oh, that is so cowardly. You don't need Sam to do your dirty work."

"What should I do?"

"Duh! Call him!"

Call him? Could it be as easy as that? Maybe. Maybe I should call. I missed him. Maybe all that friendship could return with a phone call. April dropped the cordless phone in my lap along with a slip of paper with his phone number and left to go help Sam with dinner.

It's just a phone call, I said to myself. *Anyone can make a phone call.* I dialed the number, let it ring once, and hung up. "He's not home!" I shouted to April, without letting go of the phone and then jumped when it rang in my hands. Startled, I dropped it, fumbled a moment, and then answered it.

"Hello?"

"I have caller I.D., you know."

A twinge of elation fluttered in my stomach.

"Well aren't you smart? So, hey, O-Constellation, I'm calling with good news."

"Oh, yeah? What's that?"

"Guess."

"You got new shoes?"

"No." I laughed, feeling the warmth of his smile in his voice.

"You decided I am a hot guy and want me to run away with you and serve a humanitarian mission with the Peace Corps in Zimbabwe?"

I grinned. "Who told?"

"I'm just brilliant."

"Goes without saying, but, actually, I . . . uh . . . I've decided to be baptized . . . and I was wondering if you would like to be there." I held my breath, waiting for his response.

"Suzie, that is such good news." Then he laughed.

"Do you think it's a joke?"

"No, I think it's great. The thing is, Sam already told me about your decision. I was going to act like it was a surprise, but then I couldn't do it."

"Sam already told you?"

"Yeah. He was so excited, he couldn't help it."

I hesitated, then asked, "So what do you think?"

"What do I think? I think that is one of the best things I've ever heard. Congratulations."

"You gonna come?"

"I wouldn't miss it."

His response was such a relief, like a last puzzle piece that had been missing for months had finally been found and snapped into place. I hesitated a moment, then asked, "Would you mind if I stopped by to see you?" I closed my eyes, sick that I had said that out loud and fearing his reply.

"You mean now?"

"Yeah, . . . if it's not okay, don't worry—"

"No. Come on over. Do you know where I live?"

He gave me his address, and I hung up. I got up from the couch and bounded up the stairs to my room, scrambling to find my keys, pulling on shoes and trying to stomp my feet into them because I was too hurried to untie and retie the laces.

As I hurried through the kitchen, Sam looked up. "Where're you going?" he asked.

"Rion's," I called over my shoulder and closed the door on April's triumphant grin.

It took me about fifteen minutes to find the address in Orem, and a guy I'd never met answered the door.

"Well, hello there! Come on in!" he said.

Rion also came to the door. He shouldered his roommate out of the way and grabbed my hand. "Sorry, Tony, she's mine."

Tony smiled good-naturedly and shrugged. "Well, when you discover how useless he is, you know where I live."

I ran a hand through my now brown hair. I had dyed it back to my natural color after the baby was born. With my rigorous exercise routine, there was very little baby fat left on me, and I felt good about how I looked. But I hadn't received any male attention since before I found out I was pregnant, and their banter felt nice in a strange and fluttery sort of way. It felt really nice to hear Rion claim me as his.

Tony left us alone, and we sat down on the couch. We made small talk for a few minutes, then Rion asked me, "So what happened? What made you decide to get baptized?"

I shrugged. "The worst thing that can happen to an agnostic in a situation like mine."

"What's that?"

"I made the mistake of praying."

Rion grinned. "That is just awesome!"

I bit my lip and asked, "When did you discover the gospel is true? Where were you and what were you doing the moment you knew?"

He thought a minute. "I was in ninth grade and had just started seminary and was reading the Book of Mormon for the first time on my own. I was in my room on my bed and hadn't even gotten through the first page when this incredible feeling came over me, and I just knew. From then on, I never doubted that the Church was true."

"So young. My life would have been so different if I'd had that in ninth grade."

"Maybe you needed to go through all you've been through so you could help others in similar situations."

"Maybe . . ." I concurred. "Are you mad at me?"

"Mad at you? Why, what did you do?"

"I don't know. Whenever you asked me to hang out with you or to do something during the past few months, I always said no. I've been kind of a hag lately."

He laughed. "What do you mean *lately?* You've been a hag since the first time I met you!"

Heat crept up my neck to my face. "I'm so sorry."

"Don't be. I liked you that way."

"Well, I'm a kinder, gentler hag now."

He raised his hands in a plea of innocence. "Hey, you said it; I didn't." He was silent for a moment, just looking at me. Then he said, "Do you know what I've missed about you?"

"Not a clue."

"I like that you were the reason half the supervisors at work took antacid before meetings."

I laughed at that. As we talked, I wondered if he was going to kiss me. He never did. I was there another hour, and he never even tried. Part of me was elated by the show of simple friendship; part of me was annoyed there wasn't more.

THE NEXT DAY RION CALLED ME AT MY desk and asked me to go hiking with him after work. I agreed readily, and early that evening we were on the trail, headed up to Timpanogos Cave. I had never even heard of the cave, but Rion promised me seeing it would be worth the short hike.

The sky was clouded over, and the air was thick with humidity in the late June heat. Halfway up the trail, rain started to fall. It was warm and wonderful to be with Rion like that: laughing, running, and slipping to get to the top faster and into the cave to shelter from the storm.

Inside it was cool and our clothes, soaked from the rain, added to the cold. I was shivering, and when the ranger turned off all the lights to demonstrate how dark it was in the cave, Rion put his arms around me and held me close to keep my teeth from chattering. I was still shivering, but now for entirely different reasons.

On the way down to the trailhead, Rion tripped and I helped him up. He didn't let me go once he was back on his feet and nose to nose with me. I stared hard at him, wanting to ask why my heart was racing; wanting to beg him to tell me what he could possibly see in me; and wondering why I wanted him to see something enough in me to stay around. It was during all of the wondering and wanting to know that he leaned in abruptly, his lips finding their way to mine.

That kiss was soft, brief, and yet fervent. And it wasn't like I'd never been kissed before. I had kissed more guys than I could count. But that kiss was like a cold shock of water drenching me out of a deep sleep. Shock made it impossible for me to reciprocate the kiss.

"Why did you do that?" I asked.

"'Cause I like you so much." He shrugged, taking my hand and not letting it go until we were back at the car.

Once home, with Rion gone, I told April what had happened. She couldn't stop grinning. "See! I knew it! He loves you!"

"Maybe he shouldn't though. What if he finds out who I am?"

"He knows who you are, Suzie."

"No. You're wrong. He *thinks* he knows who I am, but what he sees now as me and what he will see later as me are not the same thing. Time changes perception. What is love in one light is simply heroic valor in another and in time will be nothing more than an ardent desire to run away."

"Why are you so sure he'll change his mind?"

"Because of who I am, who I was. I was a drunk, an addict, a skank, a thief—you name it and I've done it. And my parents? What great in-laws he'd have! The sarcasm that he finds so adorable now will be an annoyance to him later. He says he thinks it's so cute that I'm the reason the heads of our company take antacid, but he can't think it's cute when it's *him* taking antacid!"

April bit her lip trying to come up with an argument against that. I continued, "He doesn't really understand how totally unprepared I am for a real relationship."

"It's not entirely your fault, you know. You've had a pretty ruptured past. Maybe if you get things resolved, you'll have room in your life for someone else."

"How do I resolve my past? How does a person resolve a nightmare?"

"Stop living in it." April's voice was soft, but her words were like shouts.

"I don't know if I can. What if it doesn't all wash away when I'm baptized?"

"Do you believe the gospel is true, Suzie?"

"I wouldn't be doing this if I didn't."

"Then you need to believe the Atonement is as real for you as it is for everyone else. If you're going to believe, you have to believe all of it, not just certain parts. You need to let the past go."

I went to sleep that night thinking the words *let the past go*. I wanted to, but the memories came unbidden to my mind, and sometimes the desires did too. *Let the past go*. It was frustrating that even as I said the words to myself, memories I wanted desperately to forget, forced their way to the front of my thoughts.

Rion took me out a few times over the next two weeks. Each time I was with him, I felt like my heart was going to pound out of my chest. And it drove me insane, wondering what he was thinking of me.

He did seem more attentive and stopped by my desk whenever he was in the office. So I shouldn't have been surprised when his voice jolted me out of my thoughts of him while I was working. My fingers stumbled on the keyboard, making me frown and hit the delete button to back up several words. Rion leaned on my computer monitor and grinned. "I'm heading out from work early today, but I was hoping to meet up with you after you get off. Is that possible?"

"Sure," I answered, shaking my head at his grin. He grinned wider and strutted away. Why did I let him get to me like that? How was it that the sound of his voice made me so fluttery?

He took me to dinner at the Italian restaurant again, and if it was possible he was grinning even wider now than he had been when he left my desk. "What?" I asked, finally, suspicious of his good mood.

"What do you mean, 'what'?"

"You're grinning like an idiot."

"Well . . . I went to the temple today."

I smiled. "So?"

His grin faltered as though he were thinking. "Let me ask you something. How important will the Church be in your life after you're baptized?"

"You're kidding, right? Honestly, it is the most important thing in my life, and I don't expect that to change. Why?"

His smile grew a little wider, deepening those crinkles a little further. The answer apparently was satisfactory. "Aren't you going to ask me what I went to the temple for?"

"I wasn't aware people went to the temple for anything in particular. I figured you just go to commune with angels or whatever."

He chuckled. "So ask me."

I rolled my eyes. "Fine. Why did you go to the temple?"

He took my hand in his. "I went to ask one of the most important questions a man will ever ask."

"How to get rid of nose hairs and prevent male pattern baldness?"

"No! You goon! I went to ask about the woman I want to marry." He waited.

I stiffened, my attention directed toward the basket of apples behind him and away from those hypnotic eyes.

"Hey?" He put his face directly in front of mine, forcing me to look at him. "I'm trying to tell you that I love you."

"You love me?" The words were flat and filled with cynicism. The memories from my past that I'd been trying to clear out of my head came crashing in. I waved my hand in front of my face to try to wave them away, almost knocking Rion's square jaw in the process.

"Yeah, I love you. Is that so hard to believe?"

"Truthfully . . . that's the most unbelievable thing anyone could say to me."

His brows squished together as he rubbed the back of his neck. "How can you say that? I love everything about you. It's like I've been sleeping my whole life and didn't wake up to live until the moment I met you. After what happened with you and the baby, I've never had such a powerful experience in my whole life. And then when I prayed and felt so certain that you were right to give her to that family, I don't know. And today I fasted and I got my answer about *us* being right. I swear, anytime I pray about you, it's like God is sitting right there waiting to tell me anything as long as it concerns you. I've never had such success with prayer before. You told me once I lived in a fairy tale; truthfully, I don't." He shook his head in frustration. "I want to, though; and with you . . . it is a fairy tale, exactly the story I've wanted."

I bit my lip and frowned at him. "What happens when you find out you fell for the witch in the story?"

He blew out a deep breath and rolled his eyes. "What happens when you find out you aren't the witch at all, but a princess placed under an evil spell?"

"There isn't a spell evil enough to create the person you're looking at right now."

"Sure there is."

"Oh, yeah? What? Snake spit and hair from a black cat?"

"Try peer pressure, loneliness, and disinterested parents. Mix it all together with recreational drug use and a daiquiri umbrella and voila! You have the spell for cynicism."

It hurt that he had hit so close to the truth. Yet he said he loved me. How could that be? It was something I had wanted to hear him say for months. It was something I knew I felt for him, and yet I could not get the memories of endless parties and the images of other men out of my head. I wondered, if he could see my life like a movie played before him, would he still be able to say that? I looked away from him despite the fact that he was in my face and changed the subject. "I never drank daiquiris. Only wimps and cheerleaders drink that."

He closed his eyes in disbelief and pursed his lips. "Okay, do share. What was your poison?"

"Corona with a lime."

He took my hand and traced over the lines in my palm. "Some fairy tales have apples; others have limes." He shrugged.

I snorted. "Oh, for crying out loud, forget the fairy tale, would you? Just let it go."

His face moved closer to mine. "Not a chance, Suzanna."

He was close enough that I would only have had to tilt my chin to kiss him. I leaned back, silent with the shock of his declaration.

He took my silence in stride. "Anyway, I just wanted you to know," he said. "It . . . isn't like I expect you to feel the same right now. There's time. We have plenty of time."

Time heals all wounds, I thought and was grateful I'd had the sense to not say it aloud. He loved me. Was he insane? I had told him everything about me, and the things I didn't tell him, he had been a witness to, and yet he went to the temple to pray about me. He loved me . . . was *I* insane?

April and Sam were home and playing double Solitaire in the kitchen. "What's wrong?" April asked when I sank onto a barstool and dropped my forehead on the counter hard enough to solicit a verbal "ow" from me. "He lives in a fairy tale," I responded and started crying.

After I'd related the entire moment to her, she patted my shoulder. "The thing is," I went on, "I love him, too. Isn't that ridiculous?"

"Not at all. He's nice, stable, and cute. Almost a perfect guy."

"Almost?"

She smiled. "He'd have to be Sam to be perfect."

Sam's face lit up. "Thanks, honey!"

"Sam's not perfect; he's—" I stopped myself, so depressed that even slamming Sam was an activity I could find no joy in. The only man to ever evoke that deep kind of emotion from me had told me he loved me, and I hadn't done anything but stare at him. A tree would have shown more emotion from such a declaration. I was a fool.

c h a p t e r
47

I T WAS TWO DAYS UNTIL SATURDAY. I had two days to worry about being baptized, but I spent most of it worrying about loving Rion but not being good enough for him. What would happen when he knew all my dark secrets intimately? Would all of that really wash away when I was laid back into the water?

I was surprised at the large number of people at my baptismal service. There were a few people from the ward who I recognized but didn't really know. One played the piano, the other led the music. All of the young women in April's class showed up, including Alison, who had started to really blend with the other girls. The bishopric was there, as well as Jan, Roberta, and even Cyntea. Rion had asked Cassie to come, too, and she was grinning as wide and as much as Rion had been the few days previous. Rion would be a witness for the baptism and would stand in the circle for the confirmation.

Sam performed the baptism, and I broke down and bawled after coming up out of the water. The warm water wrapped around me like an embrace, and I felt an elation and sense of peace I had never felt before.

Later, in the dressing room, I looked at myself in the mirror. It was good to see my hair its natural brown color again. I wrapped my arms around myself. *It's true,* I thought. *I'm clean. I am washed and clean.* Every part of me felt clean, from the tips of my hair where water dripped into my eyes to the tips of my toes that stood cold in water that had puddled from my soaked white jumpsuit. I was clean! I truly felt it. I didn't just *believe* I had been washed clean, I *knew* it.

After dressing, as I settled onto the chair to be confirmed, I caught Rion's eye. A warm smile spread over his face. He saw it, too. He knew just as I did. And when Sam said to me, "Receive the Holy Ghost!" I experienced a chill. It was a tingling that spread to every part of me to fill me with warmth. *I'm clean.*

Hugging was the thing. I hugged everyone, but hugged Rion a little tighter and longer than the others. Jan was there, grinning and sobbing like a baby. As we held each other, I said to her, "I finally figured out what I am."

"What do you mean?"

"When I was in the hospital, you told me that women are either daisies or roses and that I needed to find out who I was and be that person."

"So which are you?"

"Neither. I'm a dandelion." When her face crumpled in concern, I laughed. "No, no, nothing like that. This is a good thing. Dandelions grow and thrive even when they're not wanted. They're still pretty, offer joy to small children, and add color and variety to the world. That is who I am and who I want to be. I couldn't live with myself as a rose or a daisy, but I make a dandy dandelion."

She laughed and pulled me into another hug. "Oh, honey, I think you're wonderful!"

Rion came to claim me at that moment, bringing Cassie with him. As we hugged, she congratulated me and whispered in my ear, "Welcome to the family," which made me blush.

Rion and I went on a double date with Sam and April to dinner to celebrate and then back to their house for dessert.

When it was time for Rion to leave, I walked him to the door. He leaned against it and grinned at me. "So, you're one of us now."

"I guess I am."

"How does it feel?"

I shrugged and picked a speck of lint off his suit jacket. "It feels like . . . like I belong somewhere; that I'm not alone and there's a purpose for my existence." I felt myself getting emotional again, and didn't even try to resist the tears that spilled from my eyes.

Rion reached to touch my cheek with his fingertips.

"What a mess I am. I swear I thought I was all done crying. Who knew I was such a baby."

"I like you this way," Rion whispered, before leaning in and kissing me. I kissed him back this time and realized it was the first real chaste kiss I had ever shared with a man, and it was by far the most perfect. He didn't kiss me because I was some new quest to conquer or because he was drunk and was surrendering to carnal instinct. He kissed me because he loved me.

When he broke away, he asked, "So do you believe me now about loving you?"

I smiled and nodded. "I think so. But let's just take our time and see where it takes us?"

He agreed to that, hugged me, welcomed me again to the gospel, and then left. April and Sam soon said good night and went to bed, leaving me to myself. I got a chair and planted it in front of the portrait of Christ in the hall just to stare at it. It seemed different to me now. The caption "O Jerusalem" seemed less sad. There was hope there. Perhaps the Savior looked to the city with hope that one day the people would come around, see the light, and desire that light to shine on them. Hope, like the hope there was for me.

My life would have moments of anguish in the future. There would be trials, pain, frustration, and failure, but I wouldn't be alone. My Heavenly Father and His Son, my Savior, would be there for me.

I wondered what it would be like to meet Him. If I looked Him in the eyes, would I see every bruise, scratch, and crack in my own heart? I felt certain I would. April had taught me that when He suffered, it wasn't just for our sins. It was for every part of agony that enters the human soul. For all the times we suffer from lost love or lack of love, for all the times we came in second or didn't place at all. He suffered it all that we might not have to go through anything alone.

I felt an overwhelming sense of gratitude to know that when I do meet Him, He will really understand me. And instead of crying out the words "You don't know what I went through!" I will fall to the floor, kiss His feet, and through my tears say, "Thanks for being there."

I took a deep breath. I was a daughter of God, and my Brother was a champion. Maybe my life was like a fairy tale after all.

I<small>T WAS ONLY A FEW DAYS AFTER THAT</small> when I received a letter and some photos from Anne through LDS Family Services. She sent a picture of Angellee, wearing the white dress and a huge toothless smile. The innocent happiness reflected in her face confirmed again how right my decision had been.

Dearest Suzanna,

I worried over the first part of your letter and was rejoicing by the end to hear of your baptism! It sounds as though you've grown a lot over these few months.

Angellee is an incredible baby. She started sleeping through the night just two weeks after getting her home. Michael gets up with her in the morning (she gets up at five A.M.!) One morning I went out just to see what he did with her during this time. He was sitting on the couch balancing her, the bottle, and the book you gave us and was reading to her. It was such a tender scene, it brought me to tears. I cannot begin to tell you of the joy she has brought to us.

You need to know that you are always in our prayers and hearts. There is no way to adequately thank you for your gift to us. We feel so blessed.

We weren't able to use the dress for her blessing as we had to wait until six months had passed, and by then she had outgrown it. But she wore it to church nearly every week for a while there. It was perfect. She was blessed on July 13th. Neither Michael nor I have ever felt such an amazing spirit as we did that day. Thank you again, though thanks will never be enough, for bringing her to us.

We love you!

Anne, Michael, and Angellee

She had been blessed the day after I was baptized! Just when it seemed there were no more tears left in me, I was crying again. The difference was . . . there was no more mourning the loss of her. The gospel gave me the ability to simply celebrate her life and be happy that she was safe and loved by wonderful parents.

Once I moved into my new apartment, Rion and I found it necessary to double date a lot with Sam and April or with Cassie and whoever she was dating at the time. Rion also always dropped me off first. That way we never found ourselves alone. It was different to have someone love me enough to want the best for me. Every other guy I had known in my past had looked at me, wanting something from me and not caring about the person I was.

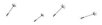

The closer we got to the one-year anniversary of my baptism, the more careful Rion and I became. Once I had been baptized, the urgency to be good overwhelmed me. I took April's advice on getting over my past by not rehashing it, but it took a long time before I felt like I could really move on. It took a long time to say the words, "I forgive my mother." I held Rion at bay with his proposals and plans for the future until the day I could say, "I forgive Doris" and mean it.

Rion insisted he knew we were to be married and brought the subject up every chance he got. When I would tell him I wasn't sure or needed more time to make certain we weren't rushing into anything, he would throw his hands up and tell me, "That's because you refuse to pray about it!"

He was right. I hadn't. It could have been because I feared the answer or because I wasn't ready, but I had to concede he was right.

So I went to the mountains one night, to clear my mind, and to pray. I stared at the nighttime sky out the sunroof, then got out and knelt by my car. The question came readily to my mind, but I avoided asking it by going over all my blessings. Once that vein of thought had been exhausted, the question, refusing to be ignored any longer, pushed back to the front of my mind. So I asked.

"Heavenly Father, Rion wants to marry me. I guess I've decided to do so. What I need is some confirmation that I have made the right decision."

I would have said more, but I had a sudden explosion of warmth that started in my chest and tingled out through my extremities. It was so powerful that I couldn't mistake the answer. And when I opened my eyes and looked up at the dark sky, I saw the constellation Orion the hunter above me. If I needed any additional convincing, that did it. I knew what I needed to do.

"Are you nervous?" Rion asked. We were standing outside the doors to the Salt Lake Temple. Sam and April had already gone in with our wedding attire. Rion's brother, Ammon, who was the best man, hesitated at the door to wait for us until he realized we needed a moment alone.

Rion's entire family had welcomed me into the family like I was a long-lost daughter, especially Cassie. And they had all traveled to be to the wedding. Doris and Dad had come too, but Doris was still upset that I would get married in a place where she could not be and was furious that I refused to let her give me an open house in Boston so her friends could see I married well.

Ever since she arrived, I had been saying to myself, *I forgive my mother.* It was something I really wanted to do, but it was hard, enduring her continuing sarcasm and insults.

"I'm a little nervous." I admitted.

"Why?"

"Because everyone in that temple is from your side of the family. I have Sam and April. You've got Mom, Dad, brothers, sisters, aunts, uncles, cousins—everyone!"

He kissed my knuckles. "They love you. Don't be nervous."

"Are you nervous?" I asked him.

"Not a bit."

"Why not?"

He grinned. "Because everyone here is from my side. If you decide to change your mind and bolt, they've been instructed to tackle you."

I slugged his arm.

"Ow! Domestic violence already?"

"Gives us something to make up over for later."

He laughed. "Let's go, Suzanna. We've put eternity on hold long enough." He brushed a quick kiss over my lips and with my rapidly beating heart, we entered our Father in Heaven's house together.

Author's Note

Writing this book was painful for me. From the moment my aunt phoned to ask me to make Suzie someone she could love, I knew I had taken on a challenge. Throughout the writing process, I asked myself many times, *Could I give up a baby for adoption if I were in this situation?* The answer? Yes. After all the research and all the writing and all the thinking about it, I know that I could. In essence . . . I did. Handing Suzie's baby over to Anne and Michael was almost as though I had handed over one of my own children. It was hard. It hurt, but it was the right thing to do.

"When deciding to place the baby for adoption, the best interests of the child should be the paramount consideration. Such a decision enables the unwed parent to do what is best for the child and enhances the prospect for blessings of the gospel in the lives of all concerned" (First Presidency letter, 1 February 1994).

It is for that reason I found myself supporting my character as she gave her baby to parents who were ready to be parents.

Unwed pregnancies are becoming more common with each passing year. Not teenage pregnancies, which are actually on a slight decline, but *unwed* pregnancies. Even though the United States is among those countries with a falling teen pregnancy rate, it still has by far the highest rate of teen pregnancy throughout the western industrialized world and the highest rate of unwed pregnancy.

The absolute best plan is to abstain from sexual intimacy until you are married. The bonding of a man and woman committed to one another prepares them far better for child rearing than two people living separate lives and going different directions. If you or someone you love is pregnant and unmarried, please know that there are options. Each option should be prayerfully and seriously considered. Though it is easy to be selfish and think only of how the future affects you, this is a time to think about how the future will affect your child.

Here are some Web sites that will provide information and help you make an informed decision:

http://www.adoption.com/
http://www.adoption.org/adopt/lds-adoption-utah.php
http://www.providentliving.org/familyservices/strength

Whatever decision you make, know that if you stay close to the Lord, you will find the direction you seek and find yourself better prepared to do what will bring the greatest happiness to you and your child.